MW01128278

IN TOO DEEP

a novel

JENNIFER K. CLARK

Quill Fire Publishing

Cover image
Copyright: <a href='https://www.123rf.com/profile_123roman'>123roman / 123RF Stock Photo</a>
Copyright: <a href='https://www.123rf.com/profile_eugenesergeev'>eugenesergeev / 123RF Stock Photo</a>
Copyright: <a href='https://www.123rf.com/profile_poznyakov'>poznyakov / 123RF Stock Photo</a>

ISBN-13:978-1547213733
ISBN-10:1547213736

OTHER BOOKS BY JENNIFER K. CLARK

Mark of Royalty

Bonds of Loyalty

Knight of Redmond

IN TOO DEEP

CHAPTER 1

The sound of discarded love being pureed to a pulp was not much different than that of blending a morning shake. There was nothing unusual about the grinding noise. Nothing ominous or spiteful. Not even happy or blissful. Haley tipped her head, listening as the blender churned, whipping its contents around in a cyclone of red liquid. It could've been anything. Strawberries. Apples. Cherries.

Haley turned the speed dial up again and again to finish the job. It was as easy as taking out the trash or washing the dishes. Nothing to it. Oddly, she didn't feel very excited. Not like Caleb who bounced up and down from sheer pleasure.

He wiped his wet fingers on his Spiderman shirt and gave her a thumbs up. "At least Liam will think twice before he sends you flowers again."

She turned the blender off and the liquefied roses swirled to a halt—a puddle of red regrets.

"Best science project ever!" Caleb pumped his fist in the air.

"Nice try." Haley tousled his blond hair. His long shags aged him closer to ten rather than the twelve he'd be turning in a couple of weeks. "Destroying the nonsensical symbol of love doesn't count. Your grandma asked me to help with your science worksheet." Haley looked at the paper on the table. "Acids and bases."

"Okay, okay." Caleb frowned as he silently read the first task. "I need to describe the taste of something acid."

Haley motioned to the blender. "My relationship with Liam was acidic. Do you want to try the rose mixture?"

"Ugh. No way. I'll grab the lemon juice from the fridge."

Despite Caleb's bored attitude, Haley noted the eager tone in his voice. Sadly, it had nothing to do with his assignment and everything to do with looking through the fridge. His grandma did the best she could to provide, but Caleb had practically worn a path down the hallway between their apartments asking for afterschool snacks, so Haley didn't mind letting him peruse a little while he looked for the lemon juice.

While she waited, she picked up her tablet and scanned through the job application on the screen. Everything was filled out. All she needed to do was press *submit*. The deadline expired in less than twenty minutes, but she still hesitated. *Better pay*, she reminded herself. This job would be a step up. But upgrading often came with its own set of problems. Proof—Her bogged down, bug-infested laptop with the newest version of Windows.

The clock ticked down the minutes—seventeen. She held her finger above the *submit* button. The job would be risky, but she could handle it. Maybe. She sat the tablet down next to the mail pile on the counter. As hard as she tried not to look, a gray envelope caught her eye. The health insurance logo grabbed at her like an icy finger jabbing her in the chest. She shoved the letter to the bottom of the stack as though that would keep its prying tendrils from reaching her. How much did they want now? She calculated what was left of her paycheck and felt the emotional weight hanging over her.

"Lunch meat!" Caleb called. Haley sucked back her anxiety as Caleb pulled out a package of Black-Forest ham and licked his lips. "Can I have some? Gran's going shopping today, but she won't get off work till late, and I'll starve by then."

Out of everything in the fridge he had to pick one of the forbidden items. "There's bologna there." She didn't want to disappoint him, but the high-dollar deli meat belonged to her roommate, and Kim wasn't good at sharing. She liked total ownership. In fact, practically everything in the apartment belonged to Kim: the IKEA zebra print furniture, the fake designer throw rug, even the metal wall decoration with the crystal accents. Kim owned it all—except for the repurposed cereal boxes that sat under the kitchen sink with tools in them—those were Haley's. And the bologna.

Caleb's expression tightened as if insulted by the inferior offer. "Does the ham belong to Godzilla?"

"I told you not to call her that. Kim's not that mean." Granted, Haley's roommate had grown snappier over the last year, but that was still tolerable compared to having to find another roommate.

Caleb waved the package in the air. "I bet she won't even notice."

"Fine. Eat it." It was the neighborly thing to do. But then again, Haley would have to take the blame. "You better only take a couple of slices. And make sure you don't tell—" The front door creaked open. "Kim! You're home from work early."

Her roommate walked in and tossed her Louis Vuitton knockoff handbag on the zebra chair. "No, I just fit eight hours of work into seven. I've been doing research on my new tourist brochure. Someday, I'll have it signed, sealed, and delivered."

Haley inched her way over to Caleb, grabbed the forbidden contraband from him, gave him three slices, and then tossed the package back in the fridge. He promptly stuffed the whole wad into his mouth.

"Don't choke," she whispered before sauntering back to the counter where Kim insisted on fingering through the pile of mail. Hopefully, she'd stop before she reached the demon letter at the bottom. "I can't believe you're running with that tourist brochure idea."

"This will be the first time we use our natural resources to draw people in. It's brilliant."

Caleb swallowed the last of the meat. "What natural resources?"

Kim's shifted to look at him. "Coal, of course. Carbon County is bursting at the seams with it, and it can be tapped for so much more than an energy source."

Haley struggled to contain her eye roll. "Being Director of Tourism has finally gone to your head, Kim. Coal mining and tourism don't belong in the same sentence. Believe me—there is nothing about that industry to attract sightseers." Caleb nodded in agreement and gave Haley a knowing look, expecting her to say more. But she couldn't. Her expertise was limited. Currently, she worked on the surface of a mine, in the warehouse. She wasn't an actual miner—yet. She glanced at her tablet. Twelve minutes.

She gave a small, almost imperceptible, shake of her head, warning Caleb to stay quiet. He took the hint and turned back to the fridge.

"I admit, it's a hard angle to work." Kim pulled the newspaper out from under her designer purse and pointed to the article on the front page. "Especially when the mines are getting bad publicity like this."

Haley read the headline. "'Safety Inspectors Wage War Against Price Canyon Mine.'" The blood drained from her face, and the hair on the back of her neck stood up. Out of all the mines in Carbon County, P.C. had to be the one being attacked on the front page.

Kim didn't seem to care. She put the paper down and drew in a long, deep breath. "What's that smell?"

Haley darted a glance at Caleb—the source of the distinctive ham odor. He must've grabbed another piece of meat from the fridge because he was trying to force down another mouthful.

Kim walked around the counter, her petite nose sniffing. Haley stepped in front of her, but she pushed past. "I don't believe it." She rounded on Haley. "I smell . . . roses."

"Oh, that." Haley sighed. "It's nothing. Liam sent me a dozen."

"He's trying to make up with you—" Kim froze as her eyes fell upon the long green stems. She picked one up. "Where are the buds?"

"Um . . . I kind of—" Haley broke off and pointed to the blender full of fragrant, red liquid.

"You didn't!"

"It was a science experiment," Caleb cut in.

"Do your homework." Haley grabbed a box of baking soda and set it next to his science worksheet. No one paid her to help Caleb, but she liked him and related to his dysfunctional family life which had left him being raised by his grandma. Likable or not, she didn't need Caleb rationalizing her pulpified perennials.

"Science experiment?" Kim pointed a slender, ring-clad finger at Haley. "It was an insignificant argument in the Walmart parking lot, and you turned Liam's apology into a smoothie. Why do you hate men so much?"

"I don't." Considering who Haley's father was, it would've been perfectly normal for her to hate men, but she didn't—not really. She just hadn't found one she could have a serious relationship with.

"You're twenty-four and you've dated one guy in your whole life. One." Kim looked Haley up and down as if she were appraising her. She didn't frown, so Haley's slender frame and light brown hair must've been passable. "I don't know what it is about you." Kim's voice rose in pitch. "But as far as being normal goes—socially—you're broken."

Haley groaned. "Not dating doesn't mean I'm broken. It means I'm modern."

"She doesn't hate men," Caleb said. "She likes me."

"No offense, but you're not a man." Kim gestured toward him, her silver bracelet jangling down her wrist. "What are you . . . ten?"

"Almost twelve," Haley and Caleb answered in unison.

"Whatever." Kim leveled her gaze on Haley. "I understand why you've avoided the dating scene, considering how you were raised, but you've come so far. You should think twice before breaking it off with Liam."

"I did think twice. That's why this is my *second* attempt at breaking up with him." Haley wasn't good with relationships, but apparently, she was even worse at ending them.

Caleb nodded as if he were sympathizing. "If the breakup doesn't work this time, third time's the charm. Right?"

Kim put her hands on her hips, turning her petite 5'1" frame into something more intimidating. If she could add eight more inches to her height, she would reach model status. Her meticulously plucked eyebrows drew together to a point, and her dark eyes flared. "You shouldn't take dating advice from a ten-year-old."

"Almost twelve." Haley stacked the rose stems into a neat pile. "And the text message I sent to Liam was civil. I didn't even accuse him of being pushy—which he is."

Kim looked up from the decapitated flowers. "I'm pushy and we get along just fine."

True. They had grown up as next-door neighbors, which morphed into rooming together after graduating high school, and it seemed to work despite their differences. Haley—whose only goal consisted of moving beyond her past and earning an adequate living—had selected their cheap rental in the apartment building near the tracks, and Kim tolerated it. But not very well. Price, Utah, was too rural for her.

"I know Liam has a few quirks," Kim continued as she thumbed through the mail pile. "His environmentalist views are a bit liberal for this area, but he's nice."

"I think he's a jerk," Caleb said. His mouth puckered as he squirted a stream of lemon juice into his mouth.

Haley nodded. "Trust me, I know from experience what an unhealthy relationship looks like." It was enough said. Her parents were like *Beauty and the Beast* without the fairytale ending. Her dad's domestic affairs were the kind that ended up on the evening news, and with that background, she didn't have high hopes for herself. But being single wasn't that bad.

Kim appeared to have given up on the argument. She turned her attention to the envelope at the bottom of the pile and handed it to Haley. "Another claim denial?"

Haley took the letter, its icy logo leering at her. "Probably. My mom used up her allotted therapy sessions for the year, and the insurance won't pay for more."

"But they were helping, weren't they?"

"Yes. I'll just pay for them out of pocket now."

Kim's brow pinched together as if she didn't believe Haley could do it.

"I'll handle it." Haley opened the letter, pretending like the paper didn't sting her fingers, like the dollar signs didn't burn her eyes.

That much? She looked at the total again. "It's not that bad," she lied. "Besides, I'm thinking of applying for a better job at the mine, so I'll be getting a pay raise."

"What do you mean—a *better* job?"

Haley touched her tablet. Five minutes. She didn't want to explain. Her career choice wasn't exactly mainstream, and Kim would see it as more evidence of being socially broken. Unfortunately, Caleb was quick to sell her out.

"She's going to be a real coal miner."

Kim's eyes widened and her mouth went slack. "It's OK to get a job around men, in fact, it might help acclimate you. But get a job in an office building, not a coal mine."

"I'm not cut out for a desk job." Haley tossed her hands in the air. "I want something I can move around in—something active. There are four openings on the belt line, and the pay is double what I get in the warehouse."

Kim made a disgusted face. "I never did like you handing out tools all day to dirty coal miners, but that's preferable compared to going underground. Mining is dangerous, especially at P.C. That place is prone to roof falls." She pointed to the ominous headline on the newspaper again. *Safety Inspectors Wage War Against Price Canyon Mine.*

Admittedly, P.C. had the worst safety record of all the mines, but Haley worked there, and if nothing else, forty hours a week for two years had at least earned some of her loyalty. "Statistically, the risk isn't that bad." She turned the newspaper face down.

"Don't try to hide it. Besides, I heard that—" Kim paused and took a deep breath. "P.C. Mine might be closing down. They're thinking about selling out."

Haley leaned against the table, spilling the baking soda. "Closing? Are you sure?" Coming up with money to pay for her mother's therapy was one thing, but if she lost her job, she would have to forget the therapy altogether. In fact, she'd probably have to move her mother to a cheaper facility.

Kim's face softened and she stepped closer to Haley. "It's true."

Haley touched the screen on her tablet, waking it up. The job application appeared before her. The *submit* button lit up, bright and green. Two minutes. Apart from the safety issue, and the awkward fact that she'd be the only woman on the crew, Haley actually liked the idea of mining. "I could do it," she said. "It would be exciting—like an adventure."

"Um, no." Kim brought a finger down on the counter to make her point. "There's a reason women don't take those jobs. In fact, only about one percent of miners are women. I'm pretty sure it's even less here in Carbon County."

True, there weren't a lot of female miners, but they did exist. "Lila Canyon Mine has a lady working underground, and I hear she does just fine."

"And you're at a completely different mine. You'll be alone, and you hate men." Kim pointed at the liquid rose mixture in the blender. "Liam's the only guy you've ever given the time of day to, and you can't even stand to be around him. Now you want to get a job where you'll be suffocated by testosterone?" Her eyes narrowed. "Think back to when I had a crush on Derik in high school, and we followed him to the locker room after his wrestling match. Do you remember the things we overheard?"

Haley darted a glance in Caleb's direction reminding Kim of the young ears listening. Caleb dropped his eyes to his worksheet, but leaned forward, eager for more.

Kim lowered her voice. "It was . . . *eww*." She shivered. "I can't even repeat it. And working in a coal mine would be like working in a men's locker room. It's a horrible environment. One you don't want to be in, especially if they're going to close down."

Haley took the gray envelope with its fateful logo and crumpled it in her hand. "That's exactly why I have to do it. A month or two of underground pay would be better than nothing. It would at least cover a few therapy sessions." She let out a long breath. "And a few more sessions might be enough for my mom to regain her memory." Haley leaned over her tablet. With less than one minute left, she brought her finger down on the *submit* button. "There. It's done. I should know in a day or two if I get the job."

Kim dropped her head back. "Fine. You want to be socially broken—go right ahead." She walked out of the kitchen and headed to her room.

Haley sagged against the counter. "Don't worry," Caleb said. He licked the baking soda off his finger and made a bitter face. "If you're broke, that means you can be fixed."

"There's an idea." Haley ruffled his hair. "Who should I call? A plumber? No. I think it's more of an electrical problem. I'm just wired wrong. A supposed man-hater going to work in a coal mine— I'm going to need a lot of fix-her-up tools."

CHAPTER 2

"It's dark in here, Brooke. Are you going to turn the lights on?"

Haley shifted in her seat, ignoring the fact that her mother called her the wrong name. "The lights *are* on, Mother." She blanketed her voice with a calm, soothing tone as though it could mask the care center's environment. Her mother, only forty-eight, was too young for hospital beds, plastic tiled floors, and roll-away serving carts.

"Are you sure?" Her mother squinted. "It seems so dark."

Haley looked up at the bright fluorescent bulbs. The doctor had reassured her that her mother's sight was near perfect, so it unnerved her whenever her mother talked about the encroaching darkness.

"Come along, be a good girl, Brooke, and turn on the lights."

"It's me, Mother. Haley. Brooke's not here, she's in Houston." Haley looked into confused, dull eyes, hoping for some recognition. Please. She had to be somewhere in there—tucked away in that infected mind.

Nothing.

Haley sighed and moved to the window, parting the curtains to allow more light into the small room. The worry lines on her mother's face dissolved, calm and placid.

"I've got to go to work, Mom. I'll see you tomorrow." Haley embraced her, but her mother sat unmoving in the pink vinyl chair. *Six years and seven months*, she calculated the passage of time, yet refused to let the images of that horrific day creep from the recesses of her memory. She kept those thoughts locked away, but the nightmare was never far, especially when her daily visits were a blinding reminder of the past horrors.

Haley had reached the front foyer of Parkdale Care Center when Mrs. Sandra Frackle walked into the building.

The woman waved, her hand flapping like a flag in the wind. "Miss Haley Carter—just the person I wanted to see!" She fumbled through a stack of documents in a file folder. Three loose papers floated to the floor before she came up with the one she wanted. "We achieved a milestone with your mother during our last session." Mrs. Frackle leaned forward, a glint of excitement in her eyes. "Your mother actually discussed Christmas." She looked down, scanning her hand-scrawled notes. "Christmas of . . . well . . . we didn't actually get a date, but it was definitely before the accident." A triumphant smile spread across her face.

Haley liked how everyone referred to it as an accident. She did too—sometimes. She hoped it had been an accident—that her father hadn't meant to do it. "Are you sure it was a Christmas *before* the accident? Did she mention me?"

"Well, not you specifically. But she mentioned your sister, Brooke, and your brother, Noah." She shook her head as if dismissing that part. "Your mother is suppressing memories of that night, and since you were the only one who witnessed it . . . she's blocking you out along with it." She lowered her voice. "I hate to bring this up, but we've used up our allotted sessions for the year. What would you like to do?"

"We're going to continue. Whatever you're doing is working, at least mom is talking more. We can't quit. I know you require payment at the time of service, so I'll call your office and make the arrangements."

Mrs. Frackle nodded, her expression still glum. Maybe she suspected Haley didn't have the money. But that would change soon. It had to.

They grew silent as an elderly gentleman shuffled past in worn-out, mismatched slippers. He made his way to the door, leaned against it to push it open, and walked outside. Haley worried about the man going out by himself, but Mrs. Frackle drew her attention back. "I apologize, but our billing department notified me that your mother's insurance won't pay for the new medication either. And I know you've had a hard time getting her to qualify for Medicaid, but we'll help where we can. How about a payment schedule—"

"I'll handle it."

Despite Mrs. Frackle's nod of the head, a shadow of disbelief crossed her face. She regrouped her papers without another word and walked away.

Haley calculated the upcoming expenses as she walked outside. The bills were piling up, and she needed money. She *needed* the underground job at the mine.

"Haley!"

Cindy, one of the nurses, ran toward her. They'd become friends since her mother moved to the care center. Kim would've labeled it as an acquaintance, and if Haley started gauging her relationships by the depth of her interactions, it might fall into that classification. The *accident* had done that—kept her from getting too close to people.

"Did you see Mr. Pruitt come out here?"

"Mismatched slippers?" Haley asked.

"That'd be him."

"He walked outside a minute before I did." Haley looked around. "But I don't know where he went."

Cindy stuffed her hands into the pockets of her hot pink smock. Her outfit matched the fluorescent stripe in her hair perfectly. "He takes a daily stroll around the building," she said. "I'm sure he'll turn up in a minute. He always does." She nodded toward Haley's car, a yellow rusted Bug in the nearest parking slot. "I saw you drive up in that thing. What happened to your Ford?"

"Sold it. I needed something more . . . um . . . economical." Translation: She couldn't afford a truck payment.

Cindy frowned. "I overheard your conversation with Mrs. Frackle. It's too bad the insurance won't cover more therapy sessions."

"Well, I applied for another job, and it will cover the cost."

"That's great." Cindy bounced her words like a peppy cheerleader.

"I bet you're excited to get out of that mine warehouse."

Haley's muscles tightened. Why did everyone assume she didn't like working at the mine? She wanted to wear a sign that said *All women aren't the same.* "I actually like where I'm at, but other positions pay better. I'm looking forward to a miner's paycheck."

Cindy's gaze slipped out of focus. "You mean you applied for a job underground? Like a coal miner?"

"Yeah. I'm working my way up from a basic laborer position."

Cindy's voice lacked enthusiasm, a dreary, monotone preacher replacing the cheerleader. "Are you sure you want to do that? A woman in the mine could cause problems. I know from experience."

"You worked underground?" Haley tried not to sound too surprised.

"Before I went into nursing, I worked with an engineering crew in college, and we did a job in one of the mines. Those men harassed me every day until I quit. You have no idea how awful and obscene they are. It's a good ol' boys network down there, and they don't like girls coming into their club."

Haley understood. Maybe she didn't see so much of it on the surface, but she still knew. Men became more abrasive in the rough, secluded work environment. It was probably no different than the man-camps in the oil fields or in other extreme occupations like logging. "I know how they get," she said. "And I've thought about it—a lot—but I need the money, and I can handle it."

Cindy opened her mouth, ready to launch into another argument, but the mismatched-slipper gentleman came shuffling across the lawn. "Mr. Pruitt! You need to take your medication." Cindy put a hand on Haley's arm. "If you go underground, I want you to be careful. It could be trouble."

Haley almost said something but then froze. Speaking of trouble—across the parking lot, Jake Hunt climbed out of his red Tacoma truck and headed directly toward them. Haley turned around, hoping he would walk by without notice.

Cindy caught the evading movement. "You know Jake?"

"He works at the mine."

Haley didn't mention they'd attended high school together, or that, besides Liam, he was the only guy she had considered dating. Not that Jake would ask her out. Not after she had turned him down flat in high school. It was silly to avoid him now; she saw him every day at the mine, even waited on him countless times in the warehouse, but seeing him outside of work was different—more personal.

She looked over her shoulder. Jake was closer now, his narrow figure moving quickly, his dark hair tossed like the wind had caught it, only there wasn't even a breeze. He looked like a mad scientist, which fit perfectly with his techy side. But tragically, he didn't smile. She really couldn't call that particular expression a smile. For Jake, it was more like a nuclear reaction.

Haley wiped the palms of her hands on her pants like a timid school girl. She'd seen Jake in public before and it hadn't made her this uncomfortable. A couple of weeks ago they crossed paths in the grocery store. Technically it was a glance across the canned food aisle, but it still counted. They never spoke beyond the obligatory greeting, so why was she so nervous?

Because her mother was here, and this part of her life was *too* private. She didn't want anyone to remember what happened to her family. She could share it with strangers—Mrs. Frackle, Cindy, the other nurses. They viewed it as simply business. They didn't know what her family was like before the accident. They hadn't watched her go through that terrible time. But Jake—he knew her, and she knew him—the computer nerd who warmed the benches during every basketball game but excelled at winning academic awards and received a scholarship for his science fair project. He was smart. So smart he had earned the nickname Einstein at the mine.

"Hey, Cindy." Jake's baritone voice sounded right behind them. Cindy greeted him, then excused herself and walked across the lawn to Mr. Pruitt, oblivious to the mental spit wads Haley was shooting at her for leaving her alone.

Haley turned and smiled. She couldn't be completely rude, after all. "Hi, Jake." She stumbled over her words, looked into his dark-lashed eyes, then waited for the standard response.

"You here to see your mom?"

She clamped her teeth together. What happened to the normal one-word greeting? This was the reason she had distanced herself from all of her high school classmates except for Kim, her one and only support. Haley didn't need anyone else. She kept her answer short. "Yes."

He nodded toward the brick building, his dark hair even more tousled by the movement. "My grandma's here, recovering from surgery."

Haley didn't know how to respond, so she didn't.

The look in Jake's dark eyes intensified as if he were unwilling to give up on the conversation so easily. "I don't think you've ever met my Grandma Hunt."

"I don't think so. Is she all right?"

"She's doing pretty well. She should be home in a week or two."

Haley studied his face. He didn't appear optimistic. Not that he had indicated anything to the contrary, but the grin that often played on the corner of his lips was still M.I.A.

"I hope she gets better soon." She almost turned to go then stopped herself. "Jake, have you heard any rumors about P.C. Mine closing down?" She thought about telling him that she had applied for an underground position, but that pushed beyond her comfort zone. Maybe Kim was right about her being socially broken.

Jake's brow lowered in a thoughtful expression. "No. Have *you* heard something?"

She shook her head. She didn't want him to worry about something hearsay. "Rumors. You know how they are."

"Yeah, there's always talk floating around, but I'll keep my ears open." He motioned to the care center again. "I've got to get going. I guess I'll see you at work."

Cindy directed Mr. Pruitt onto the sidewalk as Jake disappeared through the door. "Something seems different about Jake today. Like he's a little off."

"It's the smile," Haley said. "He didn't smile."

"Maybe." Cindy shrugged. "Too bad he's a miner. Ever since I did that job in college, it's ruined my good opinion of people in that profession." She gave Haley a sympathetic look. "I'd reconsider that job choice if I were you."

Haley's jaw tightened. The warning only made her more determined to go through with it. And she could. At least she hoped so.

CHAPTER 3

Haley walked out of her bedroom and tossed her purse—not a designer knockoff—onto the zebra-striped chair. She didn't match her accessories with her work outfit like Kim did. She wore an old pair of Levi's, her steel-toed boots, and a company-issued long-sleeved shirt with the P.C. Mine logo over the breast pocket—all standard wear for someone working in the warehouse. She sat her hard hat on the counter, which was the only place Kim allowed it. Anything dirty was exiled to a certain section of the counter.

"Before you go"—Kim walked into the room and eyed the hat—"I'm going to add Mitch's number to your contacts." She picked up Haley's purse and sat down in the zebra chair.

"Mitch? You mean the bum in the apartment at the end of the hallway?"

"He's not a bum. He drinks a little, but he's always around and always answers his phone. Which is why I'm putting him in as your emergency contact." She pressed a few buttons without looking up. "Everyone should have someone listed under *emergency*. Especially someone trying to get an underground job."

Giving Kim the passcode to her phone had been a bad idea. But on the other hand, Haley knew all of Kim's passwords. It wasn't hard—she used the same one for all of her accounts. *#1SignedSealed&Delivered*.

"Fine. I get it," Haley said. "But if you insist on listing someone under *emergency*, then it should be *your* number, not Mitch's."

Kim raised a perfectly manicured eyebrow. "My number is the

only one listed in your *favorites*, so they'll try me first. But I don't always answer, so this is the backup plan."

"But there's got to be someone besides Mitch."

"Who? I told you, you have social problems, the lack of friends being one of them."

"I have friends. A hundred and eighty-four of them—"

"Don't ever mention the number of social media friends you have. It's sad. Very, very sad. Besides, spending an hour looking through other people's posts doesn't qualify them as a friend. Name someone that you actually have a conversation with on a regular basis."

"There's Caleb," Haley said.

"Ten-year-olds don't count."

"Almost twelve." Haley dropped her head back and gave an exasperated glare at the ceiling. Great. If Kim was on one of her emergency preparedness kicks, this argument wasn't going anywhere. "Fine, but Mitch? I can't imagine the gutter king, who can't even stay on the sober wagon, as emergency contact material. Besides, we barely know him."

"I know him pretty well. I even gave him a spare key to our apartment . . . just in case."

Haley smacked her hand to her forehead. "Just in case what? He needs an easy way to break in? Why didn't you give the key to Caleb's grandma or that nice lady that lives in the corner apartment downstairs?"

"Caleb's grandma is never home. And Tammy—in the corner apartment—would lose the key. Remember when she lost her daughter last month? The cops found the girl wandering along Main Street with nothing but her diaper on."

"And you think Mitch is any better?"

Kim crossed her legs and smiled. "Of course. He never wanders Main Street in a diaper."

"Ha, ha," Haley said flatly. "But I can't have the neighborhood drunk as my backup emergency contact."

Kim straightened her posture. "Look. It was either Mitch or your brother. He's still listed in your phone contacts."

Haley groaned. "It definitely can't be my Noah. He's . . . well, you know . . . he's Noah, so we can't."

Kim nodded. "That's what I thought. And you haven't talked to your sister in over a year, so that's out too. I can put Liam in—"

"No way!" Haley's stomach began to tighten.

"It's not like you have other options. Besides, I've put a lot of thought into this. Who—over the age of ten—knows where you live without having to look up your address?"

That was a valid point. Since they moved into the apartment, Haley had kept to herself.

"Mitch is a good neighbor," Kim went on. "And he at least knows the basics about you—where you live, that your mom's in Parkdale, and that your brother lives upstate. He knows you better than anyone else, next to me and Liam."

Kim's comment hit home. Haley hadn't realized it until now, but she really didn't have anyone close. There was Mrs. Frackle, Nurse Cindy, and Kayla who worked with Haley in the warehouse, but she would feel just as uncomfortable calling them as she would Mitch. Kim didn't have that problem. She had friends. Mostly guys and coworkers, but they hung out. She went on dates with the most eligible bachelors and even had girls' nights with other women.

Haley was the opposite. Maybe she had let it go too far. Maybe she did need to reach out to people. But how would she go about that at her age? How did someone make friends? Was there a specific formula she could apply? She thought of Cindy at the care center and how they might hang out sometime or grab dinner together. Haley's chest tightened. It all seemed too awkward, and Kim's description of her being *broken* loomed larger in her mind.

"Is something wrong?" Kim asked. "Did Liam send you flowers again?"

"Nothing so devastating." Haley grabbed her phone from Kim and looked at the new entry. It felt like a slap in the face.

Kim stood and smoothed her pencil skirt over her black nylons. "When will you find out if you get the underground job?"

"Hopefully today, but it might be weeks before I start."

"And what if I talk you out of it by then?"

Haley pressed her lips together in a tight line. "I want the job, Kim, and not just for the money. I think I might actually like that kind of work. You don't think I can do it?"

"It's not that. Of course I think you'll be able to handle it. You were always the toughest girl in school. Remember how you ruled the playground, keeping all the bullies in line? Miners should be easy."

It was the physical abuse Haley witnessed at home that made her so tough at school. It was a good quality that might help her now. Any woman working underground needed to be tough.

Kim walked over and picked up Haley's hard hat and handed it to her. "I just don't like the idea of you working underground at P.C. and dealing with their plethora of problems. It's no wonder they'll be closing soon."

"You don't know that for sure. It could be just a rumor." Haley would know soon enough. The warehouse was like Grand Central Station for mine gossip, but apparently, Kim's office was too, and no wonder since a couple of miner's wives worked with Kim.

"Just last week," Kim went on, "someone drove a nail through a cable and when they reenergized it, it ruptured and nearly killed someone."

"No one was hurt," Haley said. It was a miracle though. She talked to the miner in the warehouse after his shift. The funny thing was, he swore up and down that he didn't do it. He didn't even have nails with him in the section. It could've been an accident though. Even a small nick in the shielding of a cable could cause it to arc.

Kim shook her head. "I don't know why I should even worry; statistically speaking, the odds are against you even getting the job."

"What do you mean? They have four positions to fill, and when I talked to Sherry in the mine office, she said there were only a few applicants. Plus I've been at the mine for two years, and I've already taken the safety training. I own that job."

"Maybe." Kim tapped her fingernail on the counter. "Maybe

they'll give it to you *because* you're a woman."

Haley's stomach churned like she had swallowed a cup of sour milk. "I'm not looking for feminist favoritism."

Kim shrugged. "Good. Because in a man's industry like coal mining, I suspect they keep the glass ceiling pretty low. I know all about pushing against that barrier. Maybe the only way they'll give you the position is if you play the gender discrimination card."

Haley slung her purse over her shoulder. "It won't come to that. And whatever happens, I'll be okay with it." It was a lie.

As she walked out, she said a silent prayer that she'd get the job. It wouldn't be an easy road to walk. Secluding herself to a man's crew would mean that any chances of creating close friendships would go from slight to nonexistent.

A memory of her father flashed in her mind. She pushed it away, but not before she wondered if any of the miners would be like him. Maybe this job would keep her *broken*. Not just socially, but emotionally as well.

Haley stopped at the bottom of the stairwell to check the mailbox. She didn't expect to receive her notice of hire there. It would be in her mail slot at work, but her fingers still tensed as she turned the key and opened the tiny door. There were two envelopes. The phone bill and another insurance statement. She crushed the envelopes as she removed them from the box. At least the monthly bill from the Parkdale Care Center hadn't arrived yet.

"Please," she said, shoving the letters into her purse. "Let me get that job."

CHAPTER 4

Haley pulled the steering wheel to the left and smashed her foot on the accelerator, passing the double-trailer coal truck. The blue Savage label on its side blurred as she flew by. She moved back into the right lane just before another oncoming coal truck breezed by. The semi drivers were paid per trip so they didn't waste any time on the mine road. Haley didn't either. She was a good driver and didn't think anything about maneuvering between the large trucks on the winding road.

It was only sixteen miles up Price Canyon before she drove through the large gate and past the *No Trespassing* signs marking the perimeter of P.C. Mine. She looked toward the tipple. The silo-type building was used to load the coal trucks, and today the coal piles were mounded high around it. The belt line running from the mountain was feeding the ever-growing piles. A Savage truck was being loaded, and another one was waiting its turn which meant that the mine was running good coal today.

Haley pulled into the parking lot, which was situated next to several boxy trailers used as offices. Across the lot were the larger shop buildings and several equipment sheds. It always looked like a mess. Machines and supplies filled the yard. Stacks of timber, pipe, and missile-like rock props littered one side. Large black rolls of belting, battery packs the size of four-wheelers, and fire suppression equipment were scattered on the other side.

Haley stepped out of her car, hardly noticing the deafening noise. She didn't even glance at the source—giant ventilation fans, like jet engines, pressed against the face of the mountain pushing fresh air in the mine. The chaos and commotion didn't bug Haley. It was industry at work. And this was just the tip of the iceberg; the real operation took place 1800 feet below.

When Haley first hired on as a warehouse worker, they gave her a brief tour underground. It had been both terrifying and fascinating. It was there that miners used powerful technology to tunnel beneath millions of pounds of rock to harvest coal. It was there that they battled the mountain. And she wanted to be a part of it. Hopefully, her notice of hire was already waiting in her mail slot.

She put her hard hat on—a requirement to enter the warehouse— and walked into the building. She worked in the back room, which was set up like a hardware store with rows of large metal shelves holding everything from gloves and earplugs to tools and specialized equipment—all to be issued to the miners as needed. Instead of a checkout counter, there was an indoor window where the miners requested what they needed. Like a McDonald's that handed out hardware instead of hamburgers.

Today, Kayla Klip sat at the desk behind the window. Haley waved to her as she walked into the back room.

"You're here a bit early." Kayla pushed her hard hat back on her bleached hair and twisted her finger around one of her long curls. Despite her thirty-something years, Kayla disguised herself as a seventeen-year-old, right down to her double-thick mascara and dramatic eyeliner. Once, she admitted that if someone made a calendar of sexy women wearing hard hats, she'd be first in line to sign on as a model. Haley grimaced at the thought, but there was no doubt that Kayla would jump at the chance.

"I drove fast," Haley said. She stuck her purse in her designated cubby. "Kayla, have you heard any rumors about the mine closing down?"

"Nope. None of the men have mentioned anything, so it's probably not true. The only thing closed down around here is the belt line." Haley gave her a questioning look, so Kayla smiled like she knew everything and went on. "Someone threw a shovel in the belt line, and it bound up the coupler. They don't know who did it, and, of course, no one will admit to it."

"Really?" Haley stared at Kayla. "It might have taken them a few hours, but I think they got it fixed. At least I saw coal running on the line when I came in."

Haley turned and glanced at the mail slots—stacked boxes each labeled with a name. Her heart skipped a beat when she saw a paper in her slot. She pulled it out and read it. *Blah, blah, blah.* Where was a lighter and a little gasoline when she needed it? Haley dropped the notice regarding the extra freight truck in the trash can.

"Not what you were expecting?" Kayla asked.

"I was hoping to hear about the underground job."

Kayla flipped her hair over her shoulder. "You couldn't pay me enough to go underground. But I guess you were looking on the bright side—if you got the job, you'd be surrounded by a lot of strong men."

Of course, that's what Kayla would think about. If they gave out awards for flirting, she'd win the Oscar.

"I'm doing it for my own reasons, and that isn't one of them."

"You might want to get used to the idea of *not* doing it."

"What is that supposed to mean?"

Kayla picked up a small emery board and worked it around one of her fingernails. "I'm just saying you might not get the job."

Haley sat on the desk, forcing Kayla to look at her. "You know something; spill it."

Kayla pushed her chair back to give herself more space. "I went into the mine offices this morning to talk to Sherry when Mr. Branch gave her the list of the new hires. Your name wasn't on it."

Haley's mouth fell open. "There must be a mistake."

"Nope. Your name wasn't there, but Dean Bennet's was. Do you know him?"

"No." Haley felt a little lightheaded.

"He's that cute kid that works at the Subway in Walmart. He's only eighteen—too young to date . . . maybe. Anyway, I won't mind him coming to my window."

Haley almost grabbed Kayla by the shoulders. She wanted to shake some sense into her. "Who cares about what he looks like? Does he have any training or experience?"

"No, but he makes a good sandwich. Besides, the mine will pay for his training class."

Kayla began buffing her nails again. Haley thought about snatching the emery board out of her hand, but she didn't. "You're saying this kid is only eighteen, has no experience, and no training whatsoever?"

Kayla nodded. "Why does it matter?"

"You don't see that as a problem? He'll probably go underground expecting to find the seven dwarfs." Haley pushed herself off the desk and marched out the door.

"Where are you going?" Kayla called from the window. "You have to start your shift."

"I'm going over to the mine office to have a word with the boss."

Haley walked out of the building and across the gravel compound to one of the boxy trailers. Inside, Sherry sat at the front desk. Her face paled when she saw Haley.

"Hi, Sherry." Haley sweetened her tone and gave her an I-don't-bite smile. She actually liked the secretary and tried to imagine them hanging out together or exchanging small talk over a lunch break. As simple as it seemed, it was too much for Haley's comfort zone, so why did it feel like her future relied on becoming friends with Sherry? Even general conversation was difficult, so she jumped to the point. "Is Mr. Branch in?"

"He's talking with one of the engineers right now. Go ahead and wait in his office; I'll tell him you're here."

Haley walked down the hall to the room labeled *Mine Manager*. Mr. Branch's desk was littered with stacks of paper, and the bookshelf behind it was filled with technical books on mining. There were two leather chairs to accommodate guests, but Haley chose to stand.

She took a minute to look at the framed photos of Mr. Branch's family then turned to examine the four-foot paper map hanging on the wall. It was a detailed computer diagram of the mine. Each tunnel and block were labeled with measurements and specs. Even now she wanted to go down to explore the maze.

A moment later, Mr. Branch walked in. "Miss Carter, what can I do for you?" He stuck his hand out. Haley hesitated then took it.

Her insides shook. She didn't know if it was because she was mad that her name wasn't on the list, or because she was afraid to confront the big mine boss—not that Mr. Branch was big. He was average size, but his presence carried more clout than a normal man's. Everyone at the mine bowed to him, so to speak. At least everyone seemed to work twice as hard when he came by.

Haley swallowed and met his gaze. His gray eyes were sharp and calculating like those of a professor or an adept businessman. "Did you receive my application for the underground position?"

Mr. Branch moved to his desk and sat down. He motioned for her to do the same. Haley reluctantly complied. When Mr. Branch indicated for you to do something, you did it.

"Yes, I got your application."

Haley's heart pounded in the silence that followed. "But . . . I'm not on the list to be hired?"

"No." Mr. Branch leaned back, laced his fingers together, and rested them on his chest. "I'm sorry, but that was the subsequent result."

The knocking rhythm in Haley's chest kicked into overdrive. "Can you tell me why?"

"The men we are hiring are all qualified for the job."

"So am I." *Probably more than the rest of them*, she thought. "But isn't it a policy to hire in-house first?"

"We did hire someone in-house, however, we don't do that in every case."

Haley stiffened. She hadn't heard of anyone else at the mine putting in for the openings. As far as underground jobs went, these were the lowest on the totem pole—grunt jobs. She tucked her elbows against her, hoping it would help solidify her insides. "Considering my track record here, I thought I'd be selected."

"You're a good warehouseman, Miss Carter, but I don't think you're suited for underground work."

"Because I'm a woman?"

Mr. Branch's eyes flicked away momentarily. "It has nothing to do with gender. I'm just looking for good strong men that can do the work."

"There are female coal miners, Mr. Branch. Lila Canyon has a woman working underground. So does Deer Creek. And West Ridge, before they closed down." She clamped her mouth shut. It didn't feel right mentioning a mine that had closed down, like it was bad luck or something.

Mr. Branch's face hardened. "Miss Carter, I don't know how the other mines in the area conduct their hiring, but I run Price Canyon Mine, and if I say I don't want you working underground, then you're not going to work underground. It's that simple." He stood up and stuck his hand out to her, indicating that their meeting was over.

Haley clamored to her feet and shook his hand—she didn't dare not to. As she walked out, Sherry gave her a sympathetic look but didn't say anything.

Haley stepped outside and drew in a deep breath, trying to calm herself. She wouldn't be getting the job after all. But why? She was qualified. She could do it. There was no reason why she shouldn't have gotten it. It wouldn't have been a big deal except she really needed the extra money. Did Mr. Branch know how much it cost for a month in a care center? One single month? She would need to get a better job somewhere else, but without a good degree— No, this had been her best chance. And it was something she had really wanted to do.

She turned around and walked back inside the trailer. Sherry's face paled again. "Can I help you with something else?"

"I hope so. Can you tell me anything about the new jobs? Mr. Branch said they filled one of the positions with someone in-house."

Sherry nodded. "Bennie Butler."

"Bennie?" Haley's voice was louder than expected. She looked around, hoping the sound wouldn't bring Mr. Branch into the room. She leaned across the desk and lowered her voice. "You mean little Bennie who works maintenance vacuuming the offices at night and emptying garbage cans?"

"Yes."

"But he's only been working here for two months."

"Three," Sherry corrected.

"But Bennie can't even run a vacuum right. He came into the warehouse last week and took our shop vac because he ripped the cord out of the Hoover."

"I wondered what happened to it." Sherry shook her head. "I see your point, but I don't do the hiring."

"But if you did, would you hire me over Bennie?"

"In a heartbeat."

If only secretaries ran the industry. Haley tapped a finger on her chin thoughtfully. There was one more thing she could try. "Can you give me Don Wakefield's phone number?"

Sherry gasped. "You don't dare."

"Yes, I do."

"One call to Virginia headquarters coming up." Sherry picked up her phone receiver and handed it to Haley. "This is one conversation I want to listen in on."

CHAPTER 5

Haley was on hold for a long time before Mr. Wakefield came on the line. It took her a few additional seconds to catch her breath before she could speak. She explained how she had been overlooked for the underground job despite being qualified, and then waited for his response.

"Miss Carter," Mr. Wakefield's southern accent was deep and soothing, "I wish we could accommodate everyone with the positions they want, however, this industry doesn't run that way, and I trust Mr. Branch's decisions."

Haley felt the conversation spiraling down the drain. What else could she do short of begging and telling him she craved the job and wanted to be part of the real operation of mining? She couldn't get personal. She didn't want to be the mine's charity case and advertise that her family had been through a tragedy that had driven away her siblings and left her the sole provider for her disabled mother.

Haley cleared her throat. "I wouldn't complain, Mr. Wakefield, but this is unfair. I've worked for P.C. Mine for two years. I've already taken the training class, and I'm familiar with most of the tools and equipment."

"I understand, but—"

Haley cut in, "I don't think you *do* understand. I'm capable of doing the work, and I see no reason why I've been passed over other than the fact that I'm a woman."

There was a long pause on the other end. Haley hadn't said the words *gender discrimination*, but she had implied it, and it felt a like a lead ball in her stomach.

"I see." Mr. Wakefield paused again. Haley thought he had hung up. "Miss Carter," he finally said, "Mr. Branch is competent and proficient in running P.C. Mine, but I guarantee we will look into this matter. Someone will get back with you shortly."

There was a click on the other end, and Haley handed the phone back to Sherry, who must've overheard the whole conversation because her forehead wrinkled with a mixture of sympathy and optimism. Haley thanked her then walked outside, her hands still trembling.

Coal miners, getting ready to start the afternoon shift, trickled into the warehouse. Haley followed. Kayla glared at her as she entered the back room. "Your turn." She gestured to the window separating them from the line of miners waiting for their supplies. "This is your shift."

Haley logged into the computer then looked up at the miner standing at the window. It was Leech. "Channel locks and a flathead screwdriver," he demanded.

Haley walked to the first row of shelves and quickly found the tools. She had issued Leech a pair of channel locks yesterday and another one last week. He had to be losing them in the mine, either that or taking them home. Maybe that's how he got his nickname. She wrote the item numbers on her notepad then returned to the window and handed the tools to him. "What's your number?"

"8452."

Haley punched it into the computer to finish the process then turned to Kayla. "Aren't you leaving?"

"In a minute. I want to know how it went with Mr. Branch."

The next miner needed a pair of gloves and Kayla followed Haley to the bins where they were stored.

"I ended up calling Virginia headquarters," Haley said.

Kayla's eyes bulged. "You mean you talked to Mr. Wakefield?"

"I did."

"What did he say?"

"He was very cordial and said he would look into it."

"Well this will either get you that job, or it's going to land you in a lot of hot water."

Haley had already considered that.

Suddenly Kayla stepped in front of her. "I'll get the next one. Look who's in line." Kayla nodded toward the window. Jake Hunt was next in line. His dark hair stuck out from under his hard hat like a boy who was up to bat at a baseball game on a windy day. "Mmmm," Kayla hummed in her ear. "Do they come any better looking than that?"

Haley shrugged. She tried not to think about Jake in that way. She glanced at him but quickly averted her eyes when he turned his head in her direction. True, he wasn't bad looking if you liked that wholesome, honest-guy image. Unfortunately, nobody was as honest as they appeared. Sure, he visited his grandmother in the care center, but something was amiss with him. He was too smart to be working in the mine. He should've had a high paying tech job in some big city. Maybe he lacked ambition. That would be sad. Men like that tended to end up living in their parents' basement and spent too much time playing online games. She pushed the thought aside. Whatever Jake was, he was nice, she'd give him that.

Kayla flashed her best smile as Jake stepped up to the window. His expression crumpled into a grimace. "I need three feet of packing."

"Sure." Kayla twisted her finger around a curl. "Anything for you, Einstein." She walked over to Haley and pulled her between the rows of shelves. "I could stare at those dreamy, brown eyes forever."

"It's not the eyes. It's the smile."

"What?" Kayla looked confused.

Haley nodded toward the window. "It's his smile. You know—that grin that's so big it resembles the Cheshire Cat. He smiles and everything seems to disappear around him, leaving nothing but that big, beautiful grin."

"You're so right! I've always loved that about him." Kayla nudged her playfully. "I bet you five bucks he grins for me before he leaves the window."

Haley had already been watching the corners of his mouth. She wouldn't mind seeing it, but the way he was pressing his lips together, it wasn't likely to happen. Still, she wished for it. She'd never seen anyone's eyes light up as brightly as Jake's did. When he allowed it. And right now, he seemed a little irritated.

"Maybe you should forget about the smile and get him what he needs. Other miners are waiting."

"You just don't want to lose five bucks. Besides, he asked for packing, and I have no idea what that is."

Haley blinked several times in disbelief. "Packing rope. They put it around the cable where it goes into the motor, and it works as a fire seal."

Kayla shook her head. "Yeah, whatever. Show me where it is, and be prepared to cough up some money because that smile is mine." Haley showed her where the packing rope was, and a moment later Kayla hurried back to the window where Jake was waiting, lips still pressed together.

"Three feet of packing." She waved the end of the rope back and forth, teasing him. "Been working on a motor?"

Jake took the packing from her. "My number is—"

Kayla put her hand on his. "You don't have to tell me. I have *your* number memorized."

Jake pulled his hand away and looked over at Haley as if silently berating her for letting Kayla help him. Haley couldn't help but smile. Jake didn't.

As the next miner stepped up to the window, Kayla dipped into her purse then slapped a crisp bill on the desk. "I'll earn this back next time he comes to my window." She left without another word.

Haley finished handling the rush. She issued out a pump, safety glasses, a crescent wrench, and a valve within a matter of minutes. She liked keeping busy, but after the men went underground, things slowed down and only the occasional surface worker came in with requests.

A couple of hours into her shift, one of the surface men walked in and lingered in the doorway. She knew him as Wookie, and his excessive facial hair fit the name.

"Uh-oh." He pointed outside. Haley looked past him to see a black SUV pulling into the parking lot. "That's the second one today. I bet Mr. Branch is ready to hang himself."

Everyone at the mine recognized the black SUVs driven by the inspectors from the Mine Safety and Health Administration. In the coal industry, everyone referred to the organization as MSHA, pronounced "em-shaw."

Haley tensed. Normally she didn't mind the inspectors. They made sure regulations were being followed which kept the miners safe. But there was one MSHA inspector she didn't want to see. "Who is it?" she asked.

Wookie shrugged. "Don't know. Didn't get a good look at their face, but I think it's one of them women inspectors."

A jolt shot through Haley and she sat down. Out of all of the MSHA inspectors, there were two women, and that meant there was a fifty percent chance that this one wasn't Rivers, and a hundred percent chance of trouble either way. If it was Layla Harper, the rest of the day would be spent doing damage control. Layla left a wake of citations wherever she went. During her last visit, she wrote up the mine for no toilet paper in the bathroom stall. But Haley would still take Layla Harper over Rivers.

Wookie requested a pair of earplugs and a tube of grease, and Haley filled the order, all the while praying that the inspector wouldn't come into the warehouse. Haley had just sat down again when the outside door opened.

A slow cringe worked its way down Haley's back. Rivers Grey walked up to her window. Some mine inspectors earned nicknames like the miners, but not Rivers Grey. That was her real name. Her parents had a little bit of a hippie flair.

"Hi, it's good to see you," Haley said. It was a lie, but she said it with a smile.

Rivers' short blond hair stuck out from under her hard hat, and her safety glasses were pulled down to the tip of her nose, giving

Haley an unobstructed view of her glare. "You broke up with my brother!"

Before Haley could even think of a reply, Rivers left the window and walked through the door into the back room—Haley's territory. MSHA inspectors could go anywhere they wanted uninvited.

"I went out on a limb setting you up with Liam." Rivers sat her MSHA bag on the desk and folded her arms. "He was leery about dating someone from the mine because of his environmental principles, but I talked him into it anyway. Then you went ahead and broke his heart."

Haley rolled her chair away from the desk. "I didn't mean to hurt him."

"He sent you flowers, and you replied with that . . . that text!"

The temperature in the room seemed to shoot up. Haley didn't mention that she pureed the flowers and poured them down the drain. That kind of thing was better left unsaid.

"I told Liam I was coming up here today, and he asked me to talk to you."

"Did you come up just for that?"

"Of course not. I'm here on an EO8."

Haley nodded, but an EO8 wasn't good news either. That meant someone at the mine had noticed something unsafe and had called in a hazard complaint to MSHA. The calls were anonymous so the person wouldn't get in trouble, but it often meant more fines for the mine. Mr. Branch wouldn't be happy. The mine had received a lot of citations lately, so every time he saw a black SUV pull up, he was probably seeing dollar signs.

"I'm just waiting for someone from the safety department to take me underground." Rivers plucked a pen from the desk and read the mine logo on the side. Her eyes narrowed as if she found something displeasing about it. While Layla Harper was overly critical, it was unlikely that Rivers would write up the mine over an unsatisfactory ballpoint pen.

"Do you want to look around the warehouse while you wait?" Haley's offer wasn't risky. She kept the warehouse in order, but

Rivers didn't take the bait.

"Thanks, but I have better things to do. Like talking some sense into you."

Haley put her hand up to protest, but Roadrunner walked into the warehouse. "I'm lookin' for Miss Grey."

"Impeccable timing," Haley mumbled.

Roadrunner stepped up to the window and noticed Rivers. "You ready to go down, ma'am?"

"I guess."

Rivers grabbed her bag and headed out the door while Roadrunner tapped out a rapid beat on the window seal with the palms of his hands. He looked at Haley. "You're the talk of the mine office today, Miss Carter."

Rivers stopped, her head swiveling around. "What are you talking about? What's going on with Haley?"

Roadrunner stopped his tapping. "From what I hear, Haley is in bed with the EEOC. She's bringing out the big guns and using the Equal Employment Opportunity Commission to sue P.C. Mine for discrimination."

Haley's mouth fell open. "I'm not suing anyone!" She jumped to her feet. "I've never even talked with the EEOC."

Rivers pushed Roadrunner aside and leaned through the window. "What's this about?"

"Nothing." Haley felt the need to pound her head against the desk. "I applied for one of the underground jobs, but I didn't get it."

Rivers stared at her. "You want to go underground?"

Haley shrugged. "You work underground."

"I work for MSHA. It's completely different."

Haley didn't reply. Her last conversation with Liam was replaying in her head. *How many people do you think can die in a mine collapse or an explosion? When something goes wrong down there, it isn't just one or two people who are in danger—it's everyone.*

Roadrunner wasn't bouncing around anymore, and his quiet manner made the impact of her thoughts all the more tangible.

Haley took a deep breath. Coal was the root source of her income so she couldn't afford to share in the liberal opinions that ran through the Grey family. Rivers probably worked for MSHA for the thrill of doling out fines to the coal industry, but Haley actually needed miner's pay. "I applied for the job, and if they ever offer it to me, I'll take it."

Rivers didn't say anything, but her gaze turned stony. Then she pivoted on her heels and walked out, Roadrunner following in her wake.

Alone again, Haley sat at the desk and rubbed her temples. Fighting for the job might have been a mistake. Maybe she shouldn't have called headquarters. She didn't want people to think she was raising a discrimination suit. Perhaps she should go in and apologize to Mr. Branch and tell him she didn't want to cause problems. She looked at the clock. She'd have to wait until her shift was over.

Six hours into her shift, the outside door opened. It wasn't time for the next wave of miners, so Haley waited to see who would appear at her window. It was Mr. Branch. He walked forward, his hard hat perched cockeyed on his head, his expression so grim it frightened her.

He slapped a paper down on the window seal with a loud clap. "Looks like you got what you wanted."

Haley's insides trembled. She couldn't bring herself to take the paper. Mr. Branch must have seen her hesitation and pushed it toward her. "It's your notice of hire. And it's going to cost the mine over twenty-four thousand to remodel and section off a portion of the men's bathhouse so we can accommodate a woman."

He pointed a sharp finger at her. "Now you know the real reason I didn't want to hire you. This mine is spending enough in fees and citations; the last thing we need is to dump over twenty grand on you before you even step foot underground." He shook his head. "Mr. Wakefield insisted we put a rush on the women's bathhouse so you can start next week with the rest of the new miners. By tomorrow, we'll all be tiptoeing around a construction crew."

He paused in the doorway then turned and walked out. His glare lingered behind, permanently stuck in her mind like an unspoken threat.

CHAPTER 6

Haley climbed out of her car and glanced around. The parking lot behind her apartment building was vacant as usual, which was good—she didn't want anyone to see the bright orange hard hat she'd just bought. Everyone in Carbon County knew what the pumpkin-colored hats signified: new coal miner. In the mines, it was a bright beacon, warning everyone that the wearer was inexperienced, like a caution sign. Out of the mine, it signaled to everyone else that it was official—she was hired on—something she had tried to keep secret since Mr. Branch had given her the notice of hire last week. She was grateful she had gotten the job but with it came a twinge of guilt about the money being spent on the new bathhouse.

Haley draped her new coveralls over the hard hat, concealing the orange. She scanned the parking lot for Kim's silver Toyota. It wasn't there. Good, now all she had to do was get into the apartment and hide the hat in her room. The two-story brick building with its cracking mortar and peeling window seals had only one entrance from the back, a single battered metal door with squeaky hinges. It whined under protest, and Haley's head shot around just in time to see Mitch walk out. Ugh. Her new emergency contact person.

She tried to hide her ridiculous bundle behind her back and waited for him to walk past. He stopped outside the door and looked at her. His shirt was unevenly buttoned, and he wore the same coffee-stained khakis he had on every day. Haley stepped closer to her car. The coveralls had slipped exposing a sliver of orange, and she tried to shield it.

Finally, Mitch wandered down the alley that connected their apartment building with a handful of Main Street businesses. He glanced back several times, but he seemed to be more interested in inspecting the potholes in the cracked pavement. After a moment, he made his way to the back entrance of Farlaino's, a homey Italian café which had outlived all the other restaurants in the area. Haley expected him to go in the back door and ask for food, but he didn't. Instead, he paced back and forth, staring at the ground. A moment later, he stooped and picked something up. What was it? She wasn't sure until he pulled out a lighter. Mitch took the small object—a used cigarette—stuck it between his lips, and lit it up.

Haley cringed. But at least Mitch's attention was averted which gave her time to readjust the coveralls. Just then, Caleb's grandma pulled into the parking lot, and Kim's little Toyota turned in right behind her. What was this—rush hour? There was no time to waste now. She shoved the hard hat under her shirt, wadded the coveralls up in her arms, and bolted for the door.

Inside, she took the stairs two at a time. Thirty seconds—that was all she needed to get into the apartment and ditch the evidence. She stopped short when she hit the landing. Caleb was at the end of the hallway jerking on the doorknob to his apartment. He gave the door a solid kick, then turned toward her.

"You look pregnant." The comment was funny, but he didn't look amused.

"It's a present. I'm trying to hide it from Kim." Haley patted the hard lump under her shirt as she rushed to her door.

"I need help." He held up a bobby pin. "I've locked myself out, and I can't pick the lock."

Haley looked behind her at the stairwell. Kim would be coming up any moment. She slid her key in the lock, and looked back at Caleb. "Give me a minute—"

"Please? Gram will be home any second, and I'll be grounded for life if I'm not working on the dishes."

Haley groaned. "All right, all right." Picking the lock would only take a second. She had tried to teach him how to do it the last time he was locked out, but apparently, he needed a refresher course. She ran over to him. "Why are you getting home so late anyway?"

Caleb handed her the bobby pin which was already broke in half. "My friend caught a rattlesnake, and I had to go see it."

Haley knelt in front of the door and shoved one piece of the pin into the lock. "Rattlesnakes are dangerous, Caleb. You shouldn't be messing with them. Besides, they're illegal to keep."

The old hinges of the outside door creaked at the bottom of the stairway. Someone was on their way up. Haley quickly adjusted the makeshift tension wrench, then stuck the other thin bar in, feeling for each pin inside the tumbler. Footsteps sounded on the stairway. Her hand shook as she quickly jabbed in and out in a raking motion.

"Sam's dad was there," Caleb said. "And he thinks it's okay to keep the snake. Right now it's in their old iguana tank." He picked up his backpack and flung it over his shoulder.

The footsteps sounded louder, and the last pin clicked into place. Haley twisted the knob, opening the door. "I've got to run, Caleb."

She handed him the bobby pin pieces and dashed to her own apartment where her key still protruded from the lock. Kim topped the stairs just as Haley stepped inside. She swung the door shut behind her and locked it. That would buy her five seconds. She yanked the orange hard hat out from her shirt and ran for the closest hiding place—the broom closet in the kitchen. Kim's key turned in the lock. Haley threw her plunder in the closet and slammed the door.

"Why'd you lock me out?" Kim walked in and sat her expensive knockoff on the counter. "I was right behind you."

"Sorry. Didn't see you." Haley leaned against the closet. It wasn't uncommon for Kim to come home and start cleaning—not that the apartment needed to be cleaned, but Kim was OCD that way.

"Anything exciting happen today in the world of tourism?" Hopefully, this would be a good distraction.

"I'm making some headway with my coal mining attraction."

Haley raised a brow. She'd love to see coal mining draw in tourists, unfortunately, it didn't seem as promising as an amusement park or a national monument. But if there was a way to make coal attractive, maybe Kim would find it. The little town of Helper, just fifteen miles north, did pretty well. They had Big John, the world's largest coal miner statue, standing as tall as a two-story building. The town also had the Western Mining and Railroad Museum with several rooms dedicated to mining life in coal camps. If Kim could expand on something like that, it might draw a modest crowd.

Kim leaned against the counter, her expression turning serious. "I also saw Liam today."

"Is he checking up on me?"

"No. I stopped at Subway and he was there for lunch. We only talked for a minute. He says he misses you."

"You can save your breath if you're going to tell me to get back together with him."

"I know, and I told him as much. We all get how stubborn you are." She waved a hand in the air. Her bracelets—three or four of them—slid down her slender wrist. "By the way, Liam knows you're trying to get a job underground."

Haley's eyes flickered toward the broom closet. "I was working at the mine before I met him, and I'm not going to change now just to please him."

"I told him you wouldn't care what he thought and that he should move on." Kim pushed off of the counter and walked down the hall. "Not to be rude," she said over her shoulder, "but Liam is a nice guy, and he should find someone who doesn't turn his flowers into a drink."

When Haley heard the door to the bathroom shut, she grabbed the hard hat and coveralls from the broom closet and hurried toward her bedroom. She only made it two steps down the hallway when Kim sauntered out from the bathroom, running her fingers through her long, dark hair. Apparently, she had only gone in for a preen check.

Haley moved the hard hat behind her back, but Kim saw it.

"You got the job?"

There was no use hiding it now. "Um . . . yeah."

Kim took the hat and looked it over. "It took them long enough to decide."

"Not really. I've known for a week."

"Seriously? And you didn't tell me?"

Haley shrugged. "It's complicated, and I've lost some of my enthusiasm."

"That's understandable considering the mine might be closing."

"I asked around, and it's only gossip."

Kim flipped the hard hat upside down and examined the inside. "You know I don't like the idea of you working underground, but I guess I'll support you in whatever you decide to do."

"I'm going to do it, despite the lectures and the cold shoulders I've been getting. Despite, the rumor going around that I'm suing the mine—"

"Wait." Kim looked up at her. "People think you're suing?" She smirked. "That's not a bad idea. Some companies need a good lawsuit to keep them in line. It's lucky for P.C. Mine that they gave you the job before it went that far."

A frown pulled at Haley's lips. "But I wouldn't push things that far."

"It doesn't matter. This is yours now." Kim reached up and placed the hard hat on top of Haley's head. "You look more like the pumpkin than Cinderella, but it'll do."

Haley felt a touch of excitement. "Who cares about Cinderella— do I look like an official miner?"

Kim studied her for a moment. "You look like any other orange-hat worker. But I guess there is something about it . . ."

"I knew it. I look official." She grinned and gave Kim the *wassup* head nod. "Admit it, it's cool."

"What's a nice way to say this?" Kim sighed. "There is no nice way. You look stupid."

"No, I don't." Haley ducked into the bathroom and looked in the mirror and then reemerged. "I look stupid."

It was depressing, but admittedly, kind of funny. Kim just

nodded. "Just like a pumpkin head. Out of all the colors, why orange? It's hideous."

Haley took off the hat. "It's not like we're putting on a fashion show. Besides, in three months, I can graduate to a white hat."

Haley walked to her room, tossed the hard hat on her bed, and stared at it. Hopefully, she would last three months. She had a nagging feeling that it was going to be harder than she expected.

CHAPTER 7

The room smelled of tile and cement, but it was all hers. Haley looked around the new addition which was the women's bathhouse. Six lockers, a shower, sink, and a bathroom stall all confined in a twelve-by-fourteen foot space. It was small, but it was more than she'd hoped for. A few weeks ago, she had pictured herself waiting until all the miners were out of the men's locker room. Even then, she would have to post a guard outside while she used it, and that still wouldn't guarantee her privacy. She probably would've skipped showering to avoid the trouble.

Haley stripped out of her street clothes and stuck them in the end locker. The men had to label their lockers with their name and bring padlocks from home to secure them, but she wouldn't have to. She could pick a different locker every day if she wanted. Being the only female miner could have some perks—albeit small ones.

Once she was dressed, she looked at herself in the mirror. An anxious knot twisted in the pit of her stomach. It was as if she were about to give the performance of her life, and all eyes would be on her as she took the stage. Only this wasn't going to be glamorous; there was no Hollywood vogue here. This performer wore steel-toed boots, coveralls with reflective tape, and a bright orange hard hat.

Haley pulled the hat off. Walking into the lamp-house for the first time would draw enough attention, and she didn't need an orange pumpkin on her head to add to the anomaly. She took one last look in the mirror. No use putting it off any longer.

She only hesitated for a moment before walking into the lamp-house. The boxy building was a hub of activity. Men mingled around, getting ready for their shift, pulling their headlamps off the chargers and hooking them onto their belts. Others looked at the notice board or walked in and out of the foreman and maintenance offices, and another group gathered to drink coffee around the counter. They all wore similar coveralls, although theirs were stained and worn. Some paused to look at Haley as she stepped further into the room. Her decision to not wear the orange hard hat didn't make much of a difference. The further in she walked, the quieter the room grew—except for one voice.

"We should go on strike, that's what we should do!"

Haley's stomach churned. She looked at the cluster of men but couldn't see who was speaking. She hoped the conversation didn't have anything to do with her, but deep down, she knew it did.

"She'll never get the job done," the voice continued. "I've been in the mines for thirty years, and I've never had to work with a woman. There's no reason for it; this is a man's job. How many women steel workers are out there, or women construction workers? If they really held their own, like feminists claim they can, then we'd see equal numbers of women in these jobs."

It was the good ol' boy network in action. The room fell silent, and Haley could see the protester now. He had his back to her and wore a black helmet showing he was an experienced miner. "Certain trades are just not suited for the feminine sex."

Someone nudged him, and he turned and looked at her. It was Leech. He offered her a condescending smile. "I ain't afraid to talk in front of her. It's no secret. None of you want her underground either."

A few men mumbled in agreement.

Heat rushed into Haley's cheeks. Any moment now and her face would be as bright as her hard hat. She fought the urge to turn and walk out. She couldn't leave in defeat, but she couldn't just stand there either. What was she supposed to do? Mr. Branch had instructed her to meet the other new orange-hats in the lamp-house. She looked around, but there were no other hirees in the room.

Her stomach clenched, her mind trying to remember exactly what he had said. What if she had the time wrong? Someone behind her snickered, and a couple of other men joined in. With each passing moment, she felt how much of an outsider she really was. Her shoulders felt heavy. Her mouth grew dry, and a lump worked its way into her throat. She looked around one more time and then noticed Jake. He walked to the wall and pulled his headlamp from the large charging station and then met her gaze. After a moment, he gave a slight nod of his head toward the hallway.

Haley looked in that direction. Of course! The new miners would be meeting in one of the foreman offices. She looked back at Jake. If she could say thank you with a glance, she would, but he was busy hooking his lamp onto his helmet. She walked down the hallway and found the other orange-hats in the back corner office.

"We didn't think you would show," Bennie said as she walked in.

She still wondered how he would do with real mining equipment when he couldn't even handle a vacuum. "Sorry, I was told the lamp-house."

The other orange-hats looked at each other. There were four of them, which meant Mr. Branch had created another opening just for her. That made her uncomfortable. She didn't want any more special treatment.

"Sam Wilson called me and said we were meeting in his office." Haley guessed that this orange-hat was Dean Bennet. At least he fit Kayla's description of him. He was too young and had one of those pretty-boy faces.

"Me too," someone else said. This guy looked mid-twenties. He was stocky and could probably bench-press a mule.

Bennie nodded his head in agreement. Haley wondered what other information didn't get passed along to her. She noticed there wasn't a chair for her to sit in either. Without a word, she went into the next office and grabbed a chair.

Haley sat down with the others just as Sam walked in. He was an older miner with gray hair and permanent frown lines etched on his face. He looked at Haley and the lines deepened.

"I'm Sam Wilson," he said. "But you can all call me Boom. I'll be taking you through your last eight hours of training, and you'll be starting on your crew tomorrow." He handed out several papers. Remarkably, he had enough copies for all of them—including Haley.

For the next two hours, Boom droned on, explaining the ventilation plan, the roof plan, and the rules of the mine. At last, he dropped his papers on his desk and rubbed his hands together. "All right boys—I mean . . ." He let the words drop in awkward silence.

Haley groaned inwardly and slid down in her seat.

Boom motioned towards the door and tried again. "All right . . . crew, let's go to the warehouse and get your identification tags put on your belts."

Haley followed the others across the compound and into the warehouse. Kayla was at the window, and her face lit up as the guys walked in. Boom moved to the front of the group. "These men . . . um . . . and Miss Carter here,"—his eyes darted over to Haley—"are here to get their belts tagged."

"I'm all ready for you." Kayla held up the small stamping machine that would embed their names and the last four digits of their social security numbers into a small metal plate which would then be riveted to their leather belts. It was a primitive, yet effective, identification system despite its dark origins. When tragedy struck in a mine, bodies were often unidentifiable, and the tags were the solution.

Each orange-hat went in turn to the window and told Kayla their name and numbers then waited for her to stamp and rivet the tags. Haley was the last one.

"I'm going to miss you working back here," Kayla said.

Haley nodded, but what Kayla really meant was that she would miss having her around to help when she didn't know what something was or where to find it.

"I guess you're moving on to better things." Kayla raised her eyes to where Boom was. "Look at all the sugar daddies you're going to have. It will be so easy for you to get a man now. You'll be the only fish in the pond, so to speak."

Haley looked over her shoulder to see if the men had heard. They stood near the back wall and continued their own conversations. She turned back to Kayla. "I'm not doing this so I can get a man. In fact, I don't think there's a man in Carbon County I'd even consider dating."

Kayla looked affronted. "Not the dating type, are you?"

Truthfully, Haley had said it for the benefit of the other orange-hats—for those that were listening, if any. She wanted her position clear. She didn't want to worry about them, and she didn't want them to worry about her. Not in a personal way. Besides, if she was going to date someone, she'd have to find a guy she could actually become friends with—one that didn't know about her family's past—and that was unlikely to happen.

"Too bad," Kayla said. She leaned in and lowered her voice. "No one expects you to last long down there, so take advantage of the situation while you can, if you know what I mean."

Haley snatched her belt as soon as Kayla had riveted the tag.

Back at the lamp-house Boom gave them each an SCSR pack. The small aluminum box clipped onto their belts.

"You all know what these are. Self-contained self-rescuers. They will give you one hour of oxygen if the air in the mine goes bad. Do not go anywhere without it." He didn't go into detail about how to use them—that was covered in the thirty-two-hour classroom training they had previously taken. Afterward, he passed out a soft bag the size of a briefcase. "Here's your other one. New law requires you to pack two, and we don't want any more fines, so keep this within five hundred feet of you at all times."

Boom moved on to the headlamps. He demonstrated how to put them on the helmets and emphasized charging the battery after every shift. Bennie dropped his headlamp before he could hook it on, and it hit the cement floor with a loud crack.

"Watch it!" Boom yelled. The walls seemed to vibrate. There was no guessing where his nickname had stemmed from. "Those cost over eighty dollars apiece!" He glared at each of the orange-hats. "Take care of the equipment, you hear?" His frown lines seemed more menacing, and they all nodded in response.

Haley hooked hers on with no problem. A cord ran from the headlamp down to the battery pack on her belt. Her cord seemed extra long, hanging in a loop past her waist. It must have been made for a tall man. She thought about asking for one with a shorter cord, but Boom was still glaring at Bennie, and she didn't dare make the request.

Once they were all hooked up, Boom picked up a small box and pulled out a phone. "This is another safety feature. And yes, these phones work underground which is why they're so pricey. We're talking about a grand a piece." He looked directly at Haley. She squirmed under his gaze. But he didn't need to worry about her; she'd take care of her equipment. "Numbers are already loaded on it. You can call or text." He hesitated and then handed Haley the phone.

She clipped it on her belt and waited for the other orange-hats to receive theirs, but Boom didn't hand any more out.

"All right," he said. "Let's move on." He directed them to a wall where a large, white magnet board hung.

"But where are our phones?" Bennie asked.

Boom spun on his heels and glared at him. "Not everyone gets one. It depends on your circumstances."

Haley's cheeks burned red. She didn't ask to be singled out. She didn't want special treatment. She almost started to protest, but Boom pointed to the magnet board and went on with his lecture. "This is where we tag in, so we can see at a glance who is underground and who isn't."

The board was divided into sections and had over fifty orange and white rectangle magnets stuck to it in various places. Haley stepped closer and ran her eyes over them, pausing when she saw Jake's name. She looked away, irritated that it had even caught her attention.

"These are your tags." Boom pointed to five white magnets off to the side. They already have your name and the last four digits of your social." He reached over to another section of the board and pulled a magnet off and held it out for them to see. It had his name printed on it—Sam Wilson.

"The white indicates that you're surface side." He flipped the magnet over revealing the bright color on the other side. "Orange means you're underground. You'll be going down with me today so go ahead and tag in." He stuck his magnet back on the board under one of the divided sections, orange side out.

Haley's excitement mounted. She wanted to savor the moment. This was it. She was finally going under. She plucked her magnet off and rubbed her thumb across the lettering then smacked it back on the board orange side out.

They filed out of the lamp-house and headed to one of the mantrips—a stripped down, small Isuzu pickup truck that would take them into the mine. Mr. Branch walked across the yard, and Boom stopped the group and waited as the mine boss veered toward them.

"Taking them under?"

"Yes, sir." Boom gave a slight dip of his chin. For the first time that day, he had a smile on his face.

Mr. Branch nodded his approval then eyed each of the orange-hats. "You all listen to Boom and pay attention to what he tells you."

They all mumbled a response, except for Haley. She replied with an enthusiastic, "Yes, sir!" It sounded like she was in the military, but she wanted Mr. Branch to know she was going to do her best. She was going to be worth every penny they put into that bathhouse.

"Pile in, boys." Boom waved a hand toward the closest mantrip. Apparently, he had given up on trying to decide how to refer to the group with Haley there. She didn't mind. She was okay with being one of the guys—at least when it came to mining. She was going to make sure she was every bit as good as any of them.

"Miss Carter," Mr. Branch called to her. "Can I have a word?"

Haley gave a hesitant nod. Hopefully, he wasn't going to lecture her again for calling headquarters. Maybe he was simply going to offer some advice. Hopefully. She walked over to Mr. Branch.

His voice was quiet when he spoke. "I want to make something clear. One single mess-up from you, and you're done. Back in the warehouse."

Haley's excitement faded, replaced by a hollow, empty feeling.

"And just so you know, I have Mr. Wakefield's approval on this. If you don't cut it down there, you're gone."

Haley nodded. Mr. Branch gave her a not-so-friendly pat on the back and then walked away.

"What'd he want?" Bennie asked as she climbed into the back of the mantrip.

"Nothing." Haley looked over to the mine entrance where the blackness bore a hole into the mountainside. "He was just wishing me luck."

CHAPTER 8

The dark didn't bother Haley—at least it didn't until she turned around and watched the light fade from the portal. The mantrip tilted forward and they began their sharp descent, the light behind them growing ever more distant until it suddenly disappeared. It seemed as if they were burrowing down into the center of the earth. Haley reached up and turned her headlamp on.

She needed to be strong, to push her fears aside. There were plenty of people waiting to see if she would fail, and she would prove them wrong. She could do this. She was every bit as good as the other orange-hats. At least she hoped so.

The small Isuzu truck continued on through twenty minutes of darkness. The mine was a series of low-roofed passages which tunneled like a grid through the mountain. It resembled an underground city, carved out around huge blocks of coal called pillars which were left to support the earth above them. Small signs hung from the roof labeling each cross cut and passage. Despite the labels, it would be easy to get lost. Haley directed her headlamp to the signs. They were moving past cross cut sixty-three. How deep would they go?

At last, the mantrip slowed and turned down an entry labeled Ninth West. Boom drove past a couple of pillars then pulled near a cross cut and stopped. They were near a working section, and the entryway echoed with the deafening sound of electrical motors and grinding rock.

"All right, everyone out!" Boom called over the noise, his

headlamp shining on them.

Haley quickly climbed from the truck. The darkness was overwhelming. She couldn't see the walls on either side of her unless she turned her light directly at them. She looked up; the roof was only a foot above her head. She cringed. How many tons of mountain sat above them?

The short, wiry orange-hat—she couldn't remember his name, so she thought of him as No Name—was standing next to her. He stared at the roof too, probably thinking the same thing. He muttered something, but she couldn't hear it.

"Congratulations," Boom yelled. "You've passed your first test. You were brave enough to get out of the truck. You're either cut out for mining, or you're not. The first time under, you'll know which you are. And, yes, I've brought men down who couldn't bring themselves to get out and step foot into the muck."

He walked over to where their group was huddled together. Without warning, he thumped Bennie and Dean squarely on top of their helmets with his fist.

Bennie almost fell over from the blow. "What was that for?"

"First lesson for you orange-hats," Boom's voice was truly booming now, "keep your headlamps on when you're underground."

Haley hadn't noticed the mistake until now. It was hard to tell if your own light was on when you were standing next to someone who already had theirs lit up. She was glad she hadn't made the same blunder. She did her best to keep her attention on Boom, but a moment later she felt his fist pound down on her own helmet. A jarring pain shot down her neck and into her shoulders.

"And keep your lights out of people's eyes." Haley tipped her head down as he continued, "Look at men off to the side or at their chest so your light don't blind them."

The other orange-hats snickered. Haley directed her light across Bennie's and Dean's chests. There was enough spillover light to see their faces, and she glared at them. They had been reprimanded moments before, and she hadn't laughed at them.

"Let's go." Boom turned and walked into the darkness.

Haley followed. No Name seemed hesitant, almost scared. If she'd guess which of them wasn't cut out to be a miner, she'd guess it was him. She dropped her gaze to the ground, realizing how tight her own stomach was with anxiety.

The ground was a murky, gray sludge, and a chain link fence lined the coal walls. Everything was covered in a white powdery crust. Moose walked in front of her and had to hunch to keep his head from hitting the jumble of thick power cables and the water line that ran along the roof. The nickname Boom had given the big guy suited him—he seemed like a giant in the confined space.

He swiveled his head around. "It's weird to see white walls."

"It's rock dust." Bennie's know-it-all tone rose above the noise. "It's sprayed on the walls to keep the coal dust down like a fire suppressant."

Moose flashed his light into Bennie's face. "I know what it is. I just said it's weird."

Bennie shrugged. "Maybe I clarified because there's someone else who doesn't know." His headlamp tipped in Haley's direction.

She glared back at him. She wasn't going to be labeled as the dumb one on this crew. She opened her mouth, a harsh response jumping to mind, but she strangled it before it escaped. Instead, she took a deep breath and used a civil tone. "Sorry, Bennie, but I already know about rock dust. And those walls—they're called ribs."

"It's time to learn, boys," Boom called out. He pointed at a small box hanging from one of the cables overhead. "This here's our tracking system. You'll see one of these receivers every thousand feet. We call them breadcrumbs. It reads the trackers on your belt." He put a hand on the leather clip case hanging from his belt. "This is so Comspec can pinpoint where a miner is at all times."

Haley pictured Meg sitting in the Comspec trailer, surrounded by half a dozen computer monitors, and keeping track of all the information being fed into the processors. Meg could be watching her every move right now. Somehow that wasn't comforting.

"We don't have breadcrumbs in the bleeder sections." Boom waved his hand behind him. "So make sure you stay out of those areas."

That would be an easy rule to follow. The bleeder sections were the return tunnels at the back of the mine, and Haley had no intention of going there. That was where the bad air was channeled out, and she preferred fresh oxygen.

Boom moved to the left and grabbed a rope running along the roof. "If something happens and you need to walk out, this is your lifeline." He pointed out the cones attached to it. "If you can't see and you're walking blind, these let you know if you're going in the right direction. Two cones back-to-back signal a cash of self-rescuers." Boom pointed to the big plastic gray box. "Coming across one of these can save your life."

Moose shifted his weight and kicked his toe in the sludge. "Has that ever happened? Have the miners had to walk out before?"

"Twice a year we do a walk-out drill." A grim expression crossed Boom's face. "And yes, I've walked out myself during an emergency."

Haley remembered hearing of a few emergencies since she'd hired on in the warehouse. And there seemed to be more and more all the time—like maybe something was wrong. Maybe protection procedures were being overlooked. But she couldn't think about that now or she'd scare herself out of a job. She looked back at Boom.

"Safety precautions have been put in place to keep you men alive." Boom's light swiveled past Haley as he spoke. "Keep your wits about you at all times and make sure you understand the dangers. Methane gas is a constant threat. It's naturally released by the coal, and you can't see it, taste it, or smell it. It is explosive and if it builds up it only takes one spark to light up the whole mine. . ."

His words trailed off, and in the silence that followed, they all understood the ramifications.

"Carbon monoxide is another killer. That's why our ventilation system is so important. But bad air ain't the only problem. Bad roof kills just as easily. I've seen roof bolts sheer off and shoot out like a bullet." Boom pointed up at one of the roof bolts. A small square metal plate pressed against the ceiling with the bolt head sticking out. What they couldn't see was the six-foot shank embedded in the rock. The image of one of those shooting out at over a thousand feet per second was chilling.

Boom continued to point at the roof. "A ten-pound rock falling from the ceiling can disable a miner. Imagine what a four hundred pound rock can do. Make sure you know what kind of top you're working under. It's no secret P.C. has roof control problems and is prone to small cave-ins. We do our best to make it safe, but accidents happen.

"Besides roof falls, coal can pop out from the ribs." He ran his gloved hand along the chain link fence bordering the wall. "This will protect you most of the time, but as you saw coming in, not everything is chain linked. You'll be in areas that don't have any screening, so be careful."

Moose wrung his hands together as he looked around. "Yeah, but we'll all be working on the belt line, and it's safer there, isn't it?"

Boom focused his light to the side of Moose's head. "Most men start out on the belt line. You can't get in much trouble there." His face hardened. "But don't think it's easy. It's backbreaking work, and there are always dangers no matter where you are. You're between two sheets of rock. It's dangerous from the time you come in to when you go out."

Boom led them further down the entryway and showed them how to go through the air locks, talked about the curtains that hung between the cross cuts to control the airflow, and then took pleasure in showing them the porta-potty—a crude set up of a toilet seat on a bucket.

"No one uses it because no one wants to clean it," he said. "If you have to go, just find a spot in the gob and do your business." His light settled on Haley, and the other orange-hats looked at her as well.

If they were wondering if she'd be the first to use it, they had another thing coming. If the guys went to the bathroom in the mucky gob, so would she.

"What's next?" she asked. "As fascinating as this toilet is, I'd like to look at some mining equipment."

Boom grunted and then led them to the rock dusting equipment. It was covered in graffiti. Apparently, there were some bored miners with access to paint markers. Haley ignored the artistic drawings and listened to Boom as he gave a brief explanation of the mining process. They were able to see the miner, shuttle car, and roof bolter in action. Afterward, he drove them to another section where they saw the longwall operation. It was like coal mining on steroids. A large cutting head moved across a long panel of coal, dropping the black rock directly onto a conveyor belt. Haley wanted to stay and watch the process longer, but Boom directed them back to the truck.

"All right, boys. It looks like you'll be ready to go tomorrow. As for your assignments—"

"Yeah, we know," Moose said. "We'll all be working on the belt line."

Dean clapped a hand on his back. "You sound excited. Are you a little anxious to get started on the chain gang?"

Moose shrugged. "Sure. Aren't you?"

Haley didn't know about the rest of them, but she was excited—well, excited and little scared too. The anxiety to prove herself was growing stronger. It wouldn't be too hard to outwork No Name, Bennie, and pretty-boy Dean, but she wasn't so sure about Moose.

Boom stepped between them. "You'll all go down on the belt crew tomorrow, and your new crew boss will give you instructions there." He paused and then looked at Haley. "That is except for you. You'll be working in the continuous mining section on Bear's crew."

Haley's mouth fell open as if the air was being sucked out of her. The CM section? That's why she was the only one to get a phone—because she wouldn't be working with their group. But what about the belt line? And why wasn't she going to be with the other orange-hats?

Their lights settled on her and, quite literally, she was in the spotlight. Her head began to swim and knots formed in her stomach.

Dean chuckled. "Maybe they didn't want you on the belt because they couldn't call you a belt-*man* and still be politically correct."

The others laughed, but it died down as Haley stepped forward and focused her light on Boom's chest. "Why didn't I get put on the belt crew with everyone else?"

Boom shrugged. "Because I was told to put you on Bear's crew, so that's where you're going." He paused and a slight smile pulled at his lips. "And let me just say. . . good luck."

CHAPTER 9

The next morning, Haley sat in the back of the mantrip as it plunged deep into the earth. Three of the men on her new crew sat next to her, and three more sat in the cab. Jake wasn't among them, and that gave her a strange sense of disappointment. She stared at the roof, trying to ignore the conversation of the miners next to her. Once they left the light of day and descended into the darkness, they seemed a little more brash, their language more foul.

One of the miners elbowed her as he gave the punch line to a dirty joke. Haley shifted and turned away. "This sounds like a man's conversation; you can leave me out of it."

The truck slowed and then pulled into a cross cut and stopped. Haley was the last one to climb out.

"You gonna drag your butt over here?" It was Leech, the one who complained about her in the lamp-house the day before. He walked over to her, his head tilted to the side so it didn't rub against the roof. Haley steadied herself. It was bad luck that she'd been put on a crew with Leech. He shined his light directly into her face. "You got your SCSR bag and your lunch pail?"

Haley held both of them up. Leech chuckled. "What, no Barbie lunch box?"

She looked at her old metal lunch container. Kim bought it from an antique shop and surprised her with it that morning. It was a round bucket pail, the kind miners used nearly a hundred years ago. "Nope. What kind do you pack—Mickey Mouse?"

He flipped her off then punctuated the crude gesture with a glassy stare. When Haley didn't reply, he laughed. "Just remember, you're nothing more than a scab."

Whatever that meant. Haley shrugged it off and followed him down the intake passageway. The rest of the miners seemed to know what to do and went their various ways. Two of them dropped off into the next cross cut where the roof bolter was located. The rest of the men headed to the face where they would be mining coal. That's where Leech directed her.

Haley's spotted a light in the distance coming toward them. The shine of the reflective tape on the man's coveralls came into view long before his face did.

Leech nudged Haley forward. "Here's some fresh meat for you, Bear."

Haley had seen the crew boss plenty of times at the warehouse, but she hardly recognized him here. Men looked different underground, especially after the coal covered them. Bear had come down earlier with the fire boss, and his mustache and short beard were already coated with black dust. It clung to his cheeks, darkened his wrinkles, and smudged his thick, barrel-chested jacket.

He slowly ran his light down the length of her, his eyes moving over her new coveralls, and down to her steel-toed rubber boots before coming up and settling off to the side of her face. Men had given her the once-over before, and sometimes they smiled their approval, letting her know they liked what they saw. It always gave her the creeps, but this was worse. Bear's mustache pulled down into a frown. He did *not* approve of what he saw.

"Almost to retirement and they pull this on me."

"It wasn't my idea," Haley said. "I'd rather be on the belt line with the other orange-hats."

Bear's face hardened. "That's my preference too. Unfortunately, you're what we call a *special circumstance*." He walked into the darkness, and Haley followed.

Great beasts of equipment started to come to life. The continuous miner roared into the cut like a hungry monster. Within seconds, its rotating mechanical teeth began chewing away at the mountain. It digested the black rock via its conveyor belt and excreted it out the back into a graffiti-covered shuttle car which, when full, would bellow through the tunnel, taking the coal to the belt line.

Bear waved a hand through the dusty air. "Let's make one thing clear." His voice rose above the sound of the noise. "We have a quota to make, and I won't have you slowing us down."

"I don't plan on it, sir," Haley yelled back. "I'm here to work, same as everyone else."

"You think you're the same as everyone else? You've already put me in a predicament." Bear jabbed a finger into her chest a couple of times. "They pulled one of my operators and moved him to another crew in order to put you here. Demoted him to a low job, and in my way of thinkin', that ain't right. I could tolerate it if he was replaced by someone more experienced, but to be bumped by a newbie? That means I'm already shorthanded. Had to put my roof bolter on the shuttle car." He let out a string of expletives about how slow the man was.

Haley's face grew hot, and she thought about putting in the ear plugs she had stored in her pocket. Most guys didn't wear them unless they were right next to a piece of machinery that was unbearably noisy. Right now, Bear qualified.

"Let me tell you what you're *not* going to do." His light swiveled over to the shuttle car. The coal dust caked on his face intensified his troubled expression. "You ain't going to touch any equipment. Got it? Not the bolter, not the shuttle car, not the continuous miner. Nothing."

"Yes, sir."

"Those machines cost over half a million each, and if I see you lay a hand on any one of them, you'll be looking through the help wanted ads."

Haley gave a firm nod, and he continued.

"I don't have time to babysit you, so stay away from them completely. I don't want to find your crushed body around here because you failed to get out of the way of one."

Haley listened to the long list of *don'ts*, anxiously waiting for when he'd finally tell her what she *would* be doing. And that time came all too soon. Bear showed her the job and left her with a resounding, "Get to work!"

An hour later, sweat trickled down her face, cutting little trails through the coal dust that clung to her. She pushed her hands against the small of her aching back and wished he had taken longer in his lecture. Every muscle in her body hurt, and her legs trembled with exhaustion.

"You done yet?" Bear approached her, letting his light drop to the ground where the last three jacks lay at her feet.

"Almost." She tried to sound enthusiastic, but fatigue etched her voice.

"Get to work! I need some brattice hung, and I want it done before lunch."

He moved off, but two other lights flashed over her. The roof bolters had come out to get another load of bolts, which were stacked on a pallet not far from where she was. She noticed whenever someone was nearby, they directed their light onto her. They watched her with curiosity, wondering if she could do the work.

Haley arched her sore back then bent down and picked up one of the large jacks. It was all she could do to lift it.

Three more, she told herself.

The men's lights stayed on her as she struggled over to a low ridge of rock where the roof had collapsed. The area behind it was no longer being mined, but what remained of the old tunnel was still needed to help ventilate the mine. Haley set the jack on the ground and bent over to enter the collapsed passageway. The roof continued to slope down, and she had to crouch in a half squat as she dragged the jack behind her. The stale air was thick and hard to breathe, and every dusty particle seemed to stick to her damp skin.

Up ahead in the darkness, the small ball of light from Leech's headlamp turned on her. "What's taking all day? Did you stop for a coffee break?" He laughed at his own joke, the sound reverberating around her.

Haley replied with a grunt. The roof was so low now, she was forced to drop onto her hands and knees. She started crawling, her shoulders and arms burning with the exertion of pulling the weight of the jack alongside her. Leech had packed two jacks the first time they went in. She didn't know how he did it, but he seemed to manage them just fine. Since then, he had stayed there, letting her do all the work of going back and forth bringing the jacks in. His excuse was that he needed to get them into place—standing them upright and jacking them up to support the roof. That process only took a few minutes, and then he would sit and wait while she brought the next one in.

Haley pushed the jack toward him then turned to crawl back out. *Two more.*

"Don't be lazy," Leech called. "Get that jack over here!"

Haley turned, her light washing over him. He had his hand out toward the jack. It was four feet from him. *Four feet!* She thought of some choice names to call him but quickly pushed them to the back of her mind where they could simmer.

"Come on, little lady." His smile turned rancorous. "Afraid you'll break a nail?"

Getting defensive wouldn't help, so she gritted her teeth and turned to leave without a word.

"Do I need to tell Bear that you weren't working? Wouldn't even bring the jacks in all the way?"

Leech's threat hung in the stagnant air. So this was how it was going to be. They were all watching her, waiting for her to mess up, and the slightest discrepancy—no matter how small—would be blown out of proportion. They would use it against her, to prove she wasn't fit to be in the mine. But she was as capable as they were, and she needed to provide for her family the same as they did.

She turned and crawled back toward him. Grabbing the jack, she pushed it all the way over to him. Ignoring the screaming pain in her muscles, she lifted it upright and braced it directly in front of him.

"Anything else?" she asked.

He spit a wad of black tobacco juice out of his mouth. It landed on her boot and slid off into the gob. "Nope. I'll just sit here and take a siesta while you bring in the next one."

* * *

The other men were already eating their lunches when Haley and Leech crawled out from their confined workspace. Every muscle in her body hurt as she stood upright. It felt as though she had done a years' worth of physical labor in one morning. She dragged herself to the intake where the other men were. Her lunch box was the only one left on top of the transformer, the designated place where everyone kept their food.

Every light was on Haley as she walked past. She straightened herself and tried to put some energy into her step. Some of the men snickered and chuckled. She tried not to tighten her hands into fists, but this was beyond ridiculous. Couldn't she even get her lunch without drawing attention?

She grabbed the handle of her metal pail and turned to walk off, but the lunch box tugged back on her hand, not moving. Somehow it was stuck to the transformer. The mine echoed with laughter. Haley tensed. Jokes in the mine were common practice, especially with the orange-hats, but lunches were supposed to be sacred. Weren't they? If something happened to a miner's lunch, it wasn't like he could run out to a restaurant or call someone to bring food in. The prank was just another indication of how low she was on the totem pole.

Ignoring the laughter, Haley turned her attention back on the metal pail. Was it somehow riveted it to the transformer? She yanked on it again. This time it moved. It didn't break free, but it slid several inches. Laughter erupted through the mine again. Someone had magnetized her bucket. Haley's face burned red, but at least the coal dust masked her blush. She tugged on the handle again, making the container slide to the edge of the transformer until it popped free.

"There's a scab for you," one of the men called, and another bout of laughter followed.

Haley didn't know what he meant by the comment. Leech had called her a scab earlier too. Whatever it was, it was derogatory. She walked away from the group, up the intake, and into the next cross cut. When she was sure she was alone, she let her tired body sink to the ground. She wanted to pull her boots off and rub her aching feet, but she was too tired to even try. Besides, the hollow in her stomach demanded attention.

She pulled her lunch pail into her lap. *Clink. Clink.* Two metal buttons on her jacket attached themselves to the bucket. She left it there and pulled the lid off. Her light illuminated the inside of the pail, and she let out a guttural moan. It was gone. Her two sandwiches, her chips, the apple, even her brownie were gone. In their place sat a large lump of coal. She grabbed it and hurled it into the darkness, then yanked the bucket free from her buttons, slammed the lid on it, and dropped it onto the ground next to her. Her jaw was tight, but she didn't have time to feel the full anger of the prank; a light turned the corner, and she lifted her head to see Bear.

Suddenly, she felt the need to look busy. She grabbed her battery pack and began adjusting the long cord so it wasn't caught behind her back. Bear looked down at her lunch pail.

"You gonna eat?" A strange smile crossed his face.

Haley glanced at the bucket. Was he there to watch her open it, so he could have a good laugh?

"I guess I should." She picked up the lunch pail and put her fingers under the ridge of the lid, ready to pry it open. Bear's eyes twinkled in anticipation. But she wouldn't let him have the pleasure. She sat the pail back on the ground. "On second thought, I'm not that hungry. I think I'll save it for later."

The glimmer left his eyes. "You have a lot of work ahead of you. You better eat now to keep your strength up."

"I'm really not hungry. I had a *huge* breakfast."

Bear's face hardened. "All right. Well, if you aren't going to eat, then you might as well get to work."

Haley's jaw tensed. *Get to work* must've been Bear's favorite three words in the whole world.

~ 65 ~

The crew boss motioned behind him. "Go hang that brattice back up in the next entry. Scarecrow tore it down with the shuttle car, and we're losing airflow. You should be finished by the time the rest of us get done with lunch. After that, I'll give you some real work to do."

CHAPTER 10

Haley made it to the end of the shift and, amazingly, was still alive—if only just barely. She forced her stiff joints to move as she walked down to join the other men. Bear stood next to the transformer, wrapping someone's hand with gauze. From what she heard, there had been a mishap with the roof bolter.

As she moved closer, all lights turned on her. She smiled, hoping it would make her feel included, but it was about as persuasive as handing a lollipop to a bouncer at a New York nightclub. These guys weren't going to include her in their inner circle, and right now she was too tired to care.

Bear had been true to his promise of giving Haley some real work after her non-lunch. She hung the brattice like he had asked, and then the rest of her shift consisted of hanging fiberglass tubes. She could hardly stand upright now and was more exhausted than she'd ever been in her entire life.

As Bear finished his wrap job, Haley made her way through the group to retrieve her lunch pail. It wasn't on the ground where she had left it, but it was sitting on the transformer again. Great. She grabbed it and did the jerk-slide movement until it freed itself from the metal. There were a few chuckles, but no one said anything to her.

Bear led the group back to the mantrip, shoving the first aid kit under his arm and tromping up the intake. He made a crude comment about the night crew and the shabby repair job they had done on the roof bolter. Despite the inventive use of adverbs, it brought out the boss's Neanderthal qualities. He really was a bear—savage and thick-skinned.

When the crew reached the small Isuzu pickup, Bear elbowed Leech, and a shared expression passed between them. The boss climbed into the driver's seat while Leech turned to Haley, his light lingering on her helmet. Despite the black smudges, her hard hat still looked undeniably new. It was naked compared to the other men's sticker-clad helmets and had yet to earn the normal marks, stains, and scratches.

Leech's gaze moved down her body. Her headlamp illuminated his malicious grin—black lips parting to reveal a white toothy smirk. "You gonna leave your breather?" He pointed back toward the coalface where they'd come from.

Haley gasped, realizing she had left her SCSR bag sitting next to the transformer. As painful as it was, she jogged back down the intake to the work area. It was like she was asking her body to do a ten-meter sprint after finishing a marathon, but she needed to hurry. It was bad enough that her orange hat was a large target screaming *pick on me*; she didn't need to make the bull's-eye any bigger by making rookie mistakes.

She reached the transformer and stared at the empty space where she had left the SCSR bag. It wasn't there. The mine echoed with Leech's laughter, and the others joined in.

Haley clenched her teeth. "Very funny."

She spun around, turning her headlamp in every direction, her face burning so hot that the coal dust coating it should have erupted into flames. At last, she spotted the small case on top of the shuttle car—one of the machines Bear adamantly told her never to touch.

The men's laughter merged into taunts when they saw her hesitation. She didn't want to disobey her boss on the first day, but there was no way around it; the men were waiting to see what she would do.

Taking a deep breath, she climbed up and scrambled across the machine. When the bag was within reach, she grabbed it and climbed down, careful not to touch any controls. As she ran back, the mantrip started driving away.

"Too slow, Scab," one of the men called.

Haley stopped and squared her shoulders, refusing to show any signs of humiliation. She wasn't going to make a fool of herself by running after them. It was just another joke and, in a few seconds, they would stop and let her catch up. She waited. The truck continued on, the men's laughter fading. A moment later their lights disappeared in the darkness. Tightness constricted Haley's chest. She blinked rapidly, forbidding even the smallest of tears to make an appearance. They weren't going to stop. They were leaving her behind.

CHAPTER 11

Haley started up the dark tunnel. They left her. They had *really* left her. What a horrible prank. It wasn't even funny.

What was she supposed to do now? It was illegal to leave her in the mine by herself, wasn't it? It had to be against safety regulations. Her training hadn't gone over *How to Deal with a Crew that Hates You*. And there wasn't a *What to Do in Case your Crew Abandons You in the Mine* section in the handbook.

If Leech was there, she'd punch him. He wasn't, so she did the next best thing. She yanked off her hard hat, threw it on the ground, and kicked it. The light beam shot wildly around as the hat bounced like an orange turtle on its back. But it couldn't go anywhere. It reached the end of its cord and sprang back, hitting her in the knee.

She let out a yelp and cupped a hand over her new injury. It probably served her right for breaking one of the cardinal rules of helmet wearing. She snatched up the offending hat and smacked it on her head as she weighed her options.

She could call the surface, but that would require talking to Meg in Comspec. If she did that, everyone in the office would know what happened. Meg was friendly, but she had a big mouth and loved gossip. It would be too humiliating. No, Hayley would walk out before she'd call the surface for a ride. Then again, her muscles were already crying out with each step. She stopped and looked over her shoulder. The beltmen. Maybe she could get a ride with the belt crew. If she hurried she could catch them.

She forced her legs to move as she jogged toward the belt line.

Maybe with some luck, she could talk them into letting her drive their mantrip. The driver's seat was a coveted position and, as distasteful as it was, she was willing to turn on some feminine charm to get it. It would all be worth it to see the expressions on Bear's crew as she drove up to the bathhouse. The thought of their prank backfiring made her smile.

She hadn't gone far when she found the other crew about to climb into another beat-up Isuzu truck. The infamous orange helmets glistening in her light beam was a welcoming sight. Her headlamp flashed across their blackened faces but the coal dust obscured their features. She could tell Moose from his height, but Bennie, Dean, and No Name all looked the same. Moose hobbled toward the truck, favoring one leg.

"What happened?" she asked.

Moose turned his light on her. "A chunk of coal came off the belt line. I guess I wasn't watching as closely as I should have."

"You gonna be okay?"

He nodded. "It put a gash in my shin, so I'll need a few stitches. I didn't think coal could get through these coveralls."

Haley's light moved down to where a layer of bandages stuck out through the tear in his pant leg.

"And what about you? What are you doing here?" It was Bennie talking to her now, although the only way she could tell was his voice.

"I just came over to see if I could catch a ride with you." She tried to sound casual, but with her thoughts on the driver's seat, she let the feminine softness come out in her voice.

"Why? Did you miss your own ride?"

Her lamp swiveled to illuminate the face of the man speaking. A tall figure walked toward her; the only black-hat on the crew. The dark smudges across his face weren't enough to conceal his identity. It was Jake.

What was he doing here with the orange-hats? He stepped closer to her, his headlamp pointed to the side, keeping the light out of her eyes. Suddenly all thoughts of feminine charm flew out the window.

She wouldn't be driving the mantrip after all.

"Well?" Jake asked. "Did you miss your ride?" He stuck something in the pocket of his jacket but didn't take his eyes off her. There was no smile. Maybe his day had been as rough as hers.

"Umm . . . yeah." The other men stared at her, but she didn't elaborate.

At last, Jake shrugged and motioned for her to get in the cab. She climbed in on the passenger side, hoping he wouldn't be the one driving, but she knew he would be—the only black hat on a crew of pumpkin heads wouldn't pass up his seniority to be a passenger.

Haley scooted to the center of the seat and waited for one of the other newbies to climb in next to her. Despite the small size, the cab could fit three men, or two men and a woman, in her case. She wouldn't be behind the wheel, but the cab was still a step above the back of the truck.

Jake climbed into the driver's seat, and her lunch pail promptly attached itself to something on his belt with a loud click.

"Sorry." Haley tugged on the pail, but it didn't come loose.

Jake raised an eyebrow. She tugged again, feeling his belt move with each jerk. She pressed her hand against his side as a brace and yanked on it again. It broke free and snapped onto the buttons of her own jacket.

"Going through initiation?"

Haley wrapped her arms around her lunch bucket. "If that's what you call it." She glanced away. It felt awkward being so close to him. Like those couples where the girl sits in the middle of the truck to be next to her boyfriend. Haley made fun of people like that. It always looked silly, like the truck was off balance.

"Looks like it's just you and me." Jake stuck the key in the ignition and started it up.

"What?" Haley looked at him but tried to direct her light off to the side. His face was close to hers in the confined cab, a black smudge creased the ridge of his right cheek, and she couldn't help but notice that their hips were touching.

Jake gave a short nod, gesturing to her. "Shut the door and scoot over. You're not riding there."

Haley turned and saw that the other four guys had all opted to ride in the back. It wasn't a big deal, but it was still disappointing. It was another form of rejection. She slid over, pulled the door shut, and leaned against it, giving Jake plenty of room.

She tried to watch the road in front of them, but she couldn't help but catch a few glimpses of Jake. It was unfair how attractive he looked even with the powdering of coal dust and dark smudges. A black line had formed around the ridges of his eyes giving him the appearance of an Egyptian prince as much as a Utah coal miner. Haley forced herself to watch the road. A girl who was never going to date again shouldn't have thoughts about how attractive certain guys were.

"How'd your first day go?" he asked.

"Like you said, I'm going through initiation."

"That can be tough on Bear's crew. Some of those guys can be relentless when it comes to jokes. That's one thing I won't miss, but I can't say I enjoy being on the belt line either."

Haley's head jerked around. A tight knot grew in her chest. It was him. Jake was the one Bear had referred to, the one who had been bumped to a lower job in order to make room for her. A part of her hoped she was wrong, but she knew she wasn't. The knot in her chest solidified like a chunk of coal and sunk to her stomach. It might not have bugged her so much if it was anyone else, but Jake was nice.

She angled her head so she could study his face in her peripheral vision. There was no sign of malice in his expression, but she wanted to know if he blamed her. "Did they tell you why you had to move to the belt line?"

He shrugged. "They're always moving the guys around to where they need them. It's like musical chairs. It's just part of the job."

It was a nice answer, but it wasn't completely true. It wasn't like he was moved because he changed shifts or something. Jake had been moved from a machine operator to the belt line to work with the pumpkin-heads—the crew she should have been assigned to it weren't for her *special circumstances*. It was worse than being demoted. He was going to spend ten hours a day shoveling his guts out with a bunch of idiot newbies because of her. But he was nice enough not to blame her—at least to her face. It wouldn't be so bad if he was fairly new himself, but he had worked there for years.

"Exactly how long have you been at P.C. Mine?" she asked.

Jake lifted a hand off the steering wheel, his light illuminating red blisters on his palm. He rubbed them then grabbed the wheel again. "Six years."

Haley's suddenly felt heavy and slumped in her seat. Six years only to be bumped to the bottom of the barrel. He must have started working for the mine before he had even graduated high school.

She still had a hard time picturing him doing anything other than sitting behind a computer screen designing software and hacking Warner Brothers in his spare time so he could watch movies before they were released. That's how he was as a teenager. The mad scientist side of him had been more prevalent back then.

She thought about the homecoming dance and felt another surge of guilt. She didn't do dances, so when he asked, she told him she was going to be out of town. It had been a lie. Maybe if she could redo it—no. There was no going back, and sadly she was even more antisocial now.

The truck approached the mine entrance, and the light gradually increased until the late afternoon sun flooded over them. The men from Bear's crew stood next to the bathhouse laughing. They had waited to see how she would get out of the mine. Of course, Bear wasn't with them. With so many witnesses, he would've been obligated to stop the harassment, and she was sure he enjoyed it too much to do that.

The truck slowed as Jake pulled in and parked. Leech grinned at her and directed a not-so-unique hand gesture in her direction.

"I guess your high school popularity didn't follow you here," Jake said.

"I wasn't popular. You know that."

He rubbed one of his blisters then looked at her. "You were

friends with Kim, and she was popular."

"It didn't rub off on me."

"Are you still roommates with her?"

"Yes."

"At least you have a friend that's been with you for all these years, and you only need one good friend. To me, that's popular."

Haley nodded thoughtfully. He was probably right, all she needed was just *one* good friend. Kim really wasn't very friendly, but they did get along. But maybe she could find someone else she could get close to. Not that she knew how to do that. It wasn't like she was in junior high where she could walk up to the cool misfit in science class and ask to be friends.

As an adult, she was so busy with the daily grind that finding extra time to build a relationship with anyone would be hard. Her one attempt with Liam had failed, and she wasn't the type of person to hang out in bars or at the coffee shop in order to meet people. In fact, you couldn't pay her to randomly approach a stranger—male or female. Just thinking about it left a sour taste in her mouth like the enamel was being pulled off her teeth.

She wondered if Jake had anyone close like that. She remembered watching him walk the hallways alone in high school. She should've agreed to go to the dance with him.

Haley thanked Jake for the ride and climbed out of the truck. She held her head high as she walked past Leech and the other men, showing off her blackened helmet with its new scuff marks. Granted, the pumpkin was only scarred because she had thrown it on the ground and kicked it, but at least it looked more seasoned than the other orange-hats.

The men snickered as she passed by, but she ignored it. The company had hired her on and she was a miner—same as them. They would just have to get used to it.

Inside the lamp-house, Haley tagged out, flipping her magnet to the white side, then stuck her lamp on the charging station. When she walked outside, the men were still there as if they were waiting for a grand finale. She could feel the weight of their eyes following her as she headed to the woman's bathhouse—like cats waiting to pounce on their prey. It made her skin crawl. She wouldn't let it get to her though. The shift was over, so what else could they do to her?

CHAPTER 12

Haley stepped into the new bathhouse and locked the deadbolt behind her. She wasn't taking any chances, especially with vultures hanging around outside. After double-checking the door to make sure it was secure, she went to the sink and washed her hands. She didn't want to tarnish anything with black fingerprints.

She scrubbed the coal dust off and then looked in the mirror. The black-smudged, distorted face staring back at her caught her off guard. She looked like them. She was a miner. The swirling gray water was additional proof that she had done the job. She watched the grime drain away and let out a long breath, trying to relax her sore muscles. It was nice to have a private place to herself, and right now the bland tiled room felt like a luxurious hotel spa.

Once her hands were clean, she went to her locker and pulled out her Wonder Woman beach towel. She'd bought it off a clearance rack, but considering what she'd accomplished today, it felt appropriate. She laid the towel on the bench then noticed something tucked in the bottom of the locker. Pushing her clean clothes aside, she leaned in to get a better view. It was a small gift basket wrapped in pink cellophane and tied with a coral-pink bow. The tag on the handle clearly read: HALEY.

The layers of pink cellophane obscured the contents, but she thought of the vultures outside and decided to treat the package as a loaded weapon. Keeping the basket at arms' distance, she took it out and set it next to the towel. Was this the grand finale the guys were waiting for? After what she had experienced today, the pretty basket was just as likely to jump up and attack her as it was to sit there. She poked it gingerly then caught the sweet scent of roses. Ugh. She leaned back and eyed it skeptically. Hopefully, it wasn't another let's-get-back-together gift from Liam. She pulled the ribbon and stripped off the cellophane.

A large plush towel was nestled in the basket along with what looked like a bar of hand-made soap infused with rose petals. She picked up the soap and examined it. She really didn't mind the sweet aroma. It was just the whole romantic image that usually came with it that she opposed. And this basket didn't look romantic, it looked cheesy—which wasn't Liam's style. Maybe someone from the mine gave it to her. Someone who didn't oppose her working underground or maybe even admired her for doing it. Sherry? Or one of the Comspec ladies? Not likely. She picked up the plush towel which revealed a small note pressed against the bottom of the basket. It was handwritten and simply said: Enjoy your shower.

That was . . . creepy.

Haley unfolded the towel and searched it. She didn't know what she was looking for—a hidden camera, prickly thorns, or itching powder—but there was nothing. She took the bar of soap and snapped it in half, expecting to find a dead mouse or something stuck in the middle, but there was nothing—just silky-smooth soap. Perhaps it was innocent after all. Someone was actually trying to be nice to her. Maybe.

After another thorough examination proved nothing malevolent, she decided to take it for what it was—a towel and some soap. There'd be time to figure out who the sender was later. Right now, she needed a hot shower to wash the soreness from her muscles. She stripped off her dirty coveralls, surprised to see where the coal dust had accumulated on her body.

The plush towel stayed on the bench; she was still feeling the Wonder Woman vibe. Grabbing her washcloth, shampoo, and conditioner, she walked to the shower and turned the knob on full. Instantly, a bright-red spray shot out the showerhead like blood pouring out onto the pale-white tiles. She jumped back, but not before her bare legs were splattered with crimson droplets. The horror-like scene pushed adrenaline through her veins before the smell of cherries rose up in the air. Not blood. Kool-Aid. Someone had put Kool-Aid in the showerhead.

Enjoy your shower, huh? "Is that the best you vultures can do?" she yelled toward the door.

They were probably mad about the pricey bathhouse. She didn't feel great about the money being spent either, but she had as much right to clean up as they did. If their plan was to have her run screaming from the shower in nothing but her towel, they had failed. She wouldn't be scared off so easily. She waited for the water to run clear, then stepped in without trepidation.

Black dust ran in rivulets down her legs and pooled around her feet, turning the water gray. For several minutes, she stood unmoving, letting the hot water massage her sore muscles. Finally, she grabbed her shampoo and squeezed an extra-large dollop directly on her head and began scrubbing. Closing her eyes, she worked up a lather, then took the washcloth and started scrubbing her face. It was complete bliss which was only interrupted when someone knocked on the door. She intended to ignore it, but a loud voice followed.

"Enjoying your shower? You're sure taking a long time. You afraid to come out and show us what you look like?" A cackle of laughter sounded from beyond the door.

Haley quickly tipped her head back to rinse the suds from her face and opened her eyes. The first thing she noticed was the water swirling around her feet. It was no longer gray, but blue. Really blue. Unnaturally blue. She stripped a handful of lather out of her hair. It was a wad of blue suds. But worse, her hands were blue. She looked at the showerhead. The water was running clear. She stuck her hand in the stream and tried to wash the color off, but nothing happened. The blue didn't even fade. Yanking her shampoo off the self, she twisted the lid off and squeezed the bottle, emptying its contents onto the white tile at her feet. It looked like blue pudding. Haley groaned remembering she had scrubbed her face with it as well.

She clamped her mouth tight until her jaw ached and stared at the door. The vultures were out there, waiting for her to come out of her new, specially-made-for-her bathhouse like a creature emerging from the Blue Lagoon. The luxury she had previously felt was gone. The message was clear. She had pushed too hard to get this job, and they were going to make her pay for it.

She dropped she shampoo bottle on the tile and walked to her locker. It didn't matter that she hadn't rinsed off. The damage was done. She pulled her clean clothes on over her wet body, big blue dots appearing on her white Hollister shirt from her dripping hair. It would be pointless to wipe them up—the stain would always be there. She shoved her shoes on over her bare feet, stuffed her socks into her back pocket and trudged out the door, not caring that she'd left the shower running.

Laughter erupted as soon as she stepped out the door. The men were there waiting for the grand finale. She noticed the crowd had grown. Apparently, they had told others about the prank. Bear was there along with the orange-hats from the belt line, and a couple of men who worked the tipple. A pang of disappointment went through her when she saw Jake. He wasn't laughing with the rest of them, but he was there, and that was enough.

If they wanted a grand finale, she'd give it to them. She snapped her heels together and gave a flourished bow. The whoops and cheers increased. She stuck her chin in the air and walked casually away like she couldn't care less.

CHAPTER 13

Haley had officially seen her first alien. Fairly young, sandy-brown hair with plumb-colored highlights, lovely lavender skin, and . . . angry eyes. She jerked her gaze away from the vanity mirror on the back of her visor and pulled the key from the ignition. With a quick look around to make sure no one was watching, she slipped out of her car.

The smell of stale cigarette smoke and dank garbage assaulted her nose, and for those reasons, the parking spot next to the dumpster behind her apartment building was usually vacant. Today, the stench was a small price to pay for the cover the large bin provided. She didn't want anyone else to have a close encounter with the extraterrestrial from apartment 4B.

Haley edged along the back side of the dumpster. The squeaking hinges on the apartment building door whined, warning her to stay put. She peered around the corner to see who was there. Mitch, with his signature coffee-stained khakis and impeccable timing.

She stepped back to make sure he wouldn't see her, hoping he'd leave. Mitch didn't own a car. It was more like a boat on four wheels—an olive-green Buick LeSaber from the Jurassic period—but he seldom drove it. He walked almost everywhere, which was probably how he maintained his lean, wiry frame. When Haley didn't hear the rattle of his car engine, she ventured a peek to see where he'd gone.

He was still there, behind Farlaino's Cafe, inspecting the crumbling pavement for used cigarettes. It wasn't long before he stooped, picked up a nub and lit it. He pulled in a deep breath and slowly blew the smoke into the air as he turned his pale-blue eyes on her.

It was unnerving. Almost as if he had sensed she was there.

Ducking her head, she stepped out from behind the dumpster and hurried to the apartment building. Thankfully, she managed to get upstairs without running into anyone else. Mitch seeing her was enough. Hopefully, he didn't get a good look at her blue face. Once inside her apartment, she grabbed some vinegar and a box of baking soda—anything with stain removal potential. For good measure, she added a bottle of Mr. Clean to her arsenal and then headed to the bathroom to examine herself in the mirror.

Whatever the guys had put in the shampoo had been effective. The stain appeared more purple than blue, and it covered nearly every part of her face, not to mention her hands. Food coloring? Or perhaps some kind of chemical? She inspected her fingers then turned on the faucet, pumped a fist full of liquid soap into her hand, dumped some baking soda on it, and began scrubbing. The suds turned a violet-blue, but when she rinsed the lather off, the color had only muted a little.

She shouldn't have let it set on her skin so long. If she'd stayed at the mine and finished showering, it might not have been as bad. She turned the shower on and jumped in with the determination to scrub her skin raw if necessary.

Nearly twenty minutes later, she tossed the empty baking soda box out onto the floor. The water swirling around her feet ran clear, but she'd given up hope of getting her skin back to its normal color. The violet-blue pigment was still there, despite the rough scrubbing. What was she supposed to do now? It'd be horrible going back to the mine tomorrow looking like a blueberry. For a minute, she contemplated other options. Gasoline? Or maybe turpentine. She grabbed a towel and was drying off, mulling over the idea of soaking in a tub of petrol when she heard someone open the front door to the apartment.

She froze. Kim had told her that she would be at the office until eight finishing up her new brochure on coal mining. She picked up her watch. Six thirty-five. Quiet footfalls sounded down the hallway past the bathroom.

"Kim, is that you?"

There was no answer.

She took a deep breath, trying to settle the uneasiness wriggling up into her chest. She distinctly remembered locking the front door. Fear of her father had instilled that habit in her. *Caleb*, she thought. Maybe he mastered his lock picking technique and needed an afterschool snack. She shook her head. That was unlikely. Besides, Caleb had promised to only use the skill to get into his own apartment.

"Kim?" she called louder.

Still no answer, but soft footsteps padded down the hallway again, pausing outside the bathroom door. Haley took a step back, a chill moving down her neck. She stared at the doorknob and waited for it to turn like she had seen in horror movies—slowly moving as the intruder tried to get to his victim.

She swallowed her apprehension and forced herself to reach out check the doorknob, making sure it was locked. It was, but somehow she didn't feel any safer. She looked at her pile of clothes on the floor, realizing her cell phone wasn't there. It was on the kitchen counter with her keys. She closed her eyes and silently berated herself. Then as quickly as they came, the footsteps retreated until all was silent again.

Her hands shook as she pulled her clothes on, then pressed her ear to the door, listening. It wasn't long before she heard a soft thud—the sound of the front door closing. She waited several more minutes. All was quiet.

Suddenly things clicked in her mind. It was Mitch. It had to be. Kim said she trusted him enough to give him the spare key to their apartment. She had said something about him always being home and that he would be a reliable person in an emergency. It was insane, and this proved it.

But if it was Mitch, what did he want? Had he gone through their bedrooms, looking for money and valuables? And how would she protect herself if he still happened to be in the apartment? He was probably a good thirty years older than she was, but he appeared strong for his age—lean and hard. She didn't know how he managed it with his drinking habits. Probably genetics. Still, if his intentions were to hurt her, there was no doubt he was tough enough to do it. If she didn't end up dead, she was going to kill Kim. What had she been thinking, giving a spare key to the creepy neighbor?

It was another minute before she mustered the courage to open the door a crack. She cocked her head to the side, straining to hear the slightest sound. Beyond her own uneven breath, there was nothing.

"Hello?" she called out. "Is anyone here?" Nothing. "I'm calling the police." It was a lame threat. She would have already called if she had her phone.

She stepped out of the bathroom and looked up and down the short hallway. She could see into her bedroom and nothing seemed out of place. The door to Kim's room was shut. She was certain that Mitch, or whoever the intruder was, had left, but she wouldn't be able to relax until she looked around the apartment and saw for herself that there was no Jason or Freddy Krueger hiding in the corners.

She tiptoed into the living room. There weren't any places a person could hide except for the broom closet in the kitchen. She grabbed her phone and a glass plate from the dish drainer. It wasn't a great weapon, but it would do. Holding the plate up, she took a deep breath and yanked the closet door open.

Haley saw movement and jumped back with a scream. The plate dropped and shattered on the linoleum floor, as a broom toppled out at her. She clutched at her heart. There was no one in the closet. Just the vacuum, Kim's cart of cleaning supplies, and the assailant broom. It must have been resting unsteadily against the door. She pocketed her phone just as the sound of keys jingled outside the apartment door. Whoever had been there was coming back. She picked up the broom and grabbed a fly swatter for added measure.

Her breath faltered as she watched the doorknob turn. Raising both makeshift weapons, she readied herself. The door opened. A cool sweat broke out on her brow as the intruder stepped inside. Haley swung, only managing to stop herself just before she made contact. It wasn't Mitch as she expected. It was Kim.

Her roommate threw her arms up to protect herself. "Aaaahhhh! What are you doing?"

Haley lowered the flyswatter. "I thought you were an intruder!" she shouted back. "For heaven's sake, Kim, call me when you decide to come home early. You know how freaky it is when you think you're alone and you're not."

"Okay." Kim dropped her arms and cautiously looked up at Haley. Her mouth fell open. "Holy Smurf! What happened? You're blue!"

Haley lifted her hands, examining her new pigment. She had almost forgotten about it. "Some of the guys played a practical joke on me at work. Is it really that bad?"

Kim stared at her with wide eyes. "No. It's not that noticeable . . . if you were sitting with the Blue Man Group."

"Ugh." Haley's shoulders slumped. "I don't know what to do. It won't wash off."

Kim walked around her looking at the broken plate on the kitchen floor. "What happened here?" She took the broom from Haley and began sweeping up the shards.

"Sorry. The broom jumped out at me, and I had to defend myself."

"Seriously? Why are you so jumpy?"

"I told you. I thought you were Mitch breaking into our apartment."

"And why would Mitch want to break in here?"

"I don't know? You gave him a key—"

Kim glanced up at her. "He's not that kind of person. Maybe if you didn't skip all of those apartment tenant meetings or the neighborhood Christmas party, you'd know him a little better. He drinks a bit, but he's actually a nice guy. I trust him. I wouldn't have given him a key otherwise."

Haley gave an exaggerated sigh. "But something about him rubs me the wrong way. Does a guy that goes around picking up used cigarettes sound like someone trustworthy?"

Kim continued sweeping. "You don't trust *any* male over the age of ten."

"Twelve," Haley said. "But let's forget about it. I'm just glad it was you and not the boogieman. Why are you home so early anyway? I thought you were putting the final touches on your coal mining brochure."

Kim dumped a dustpan full of broken glass into the garbage and went back for another pass. "The brochure can wait. I changed my plans for tonight." The corner of Kim's lip pulled up in a sly smile. "I have a date."

Haley rolled her eyes. "This isn't leading into another lecture on relationships, is it?"

"Here, hold this." Kim pushed the dustpan into her hand. "You might've declared a war on dating, but that doesn't mean the rest of us women have to enlist."

"I never said you couldn't date. You go right ahead and entangle your own life if you want to. Just warn me about your plans next time so I don't beat you with the broom as you walk in. Why didn't you answer me when I called out to you earlier?"

Kim looked up from the neat pile of glass crumbs. "What do you mean?"

"You know. About fifteen minutes ago, when you walked past the bathroom, and I called to you to see who was there."

Kim shook her head. "This is the first and only time I've been in the apartment since I left for work this morning."

Haley set the dustpan down. "That wasn't you?" She looked down the hall to where the door to her bedroom was still open. "Someone was in here."

"Are you sure you weren't hearing things?" Kim started walking down the hall, and Haley hurried to catch up with her.

"What are you doing? We should call the police."

Kim continued on without even so much as a fly swatter for protection. Then again, she always did like to take control and do things her own way.

"I'm just taking a look." She ducked her head in the bathroom. "No one in here." She moved to her room, opened the door to peer inside, then shook her head. At last, she turned and stepped into Haley's room and looked around. "No one in here either. But this is cute. Who gave it to you?" Kim picked up a small gift bag from off her dresser.

Haley's heart skipped a beat. "That...was not...here...before." She punctuated each word then sat on the edge of her bed, trying to quell the nauseous feeling rising in her stomach. She had already received one gift today, and that was enough.

Kim paced around the room like a nervous cat, checking in the closet, and looking under the bed. Finally, she stopped and looked inside the bag. "I'm certain this didn't come from Mitch. It looks like a nice gift, and I can't see him doing the whole neighborly thing like gift bags. Look." Kim pulled out a package of Lindt truffles. "Your favorite kind of chocolate. Mitch wouldn't have known that. And a book on coal mining." Kim held up a thin paperback book. "There's a note here too. 'Congratulations on your new job and good luck.' It's not signed, and there's nothing else in here. Do you have any idea who it's from? Liam maybe? Did you give him a key to our apartment?"

"No. I took my key back from him."

Haley took the book while Kim continued to examine the bag for evidence. At last, she set it on the dresser. "I'm trying not to panic about this. Whoever it was, they didn't ransack the place. I guess if we have an intruder, at least they left chocolate." She paced in a circle again. "Most likely the person left the bag outside the door, and Mitch brought it in so it wouldn't get stolen. I'll talk to him and see if he knows anything."

"Good. Because I don't want him playing Santa Claus." Haley held the book up. The cover featured an old black-and-white picture of coal miners—some of them were young boys. They had antique

~ 87 ~

headlamps and blackened faces, their expressions grim. Finally, she read the title. *Most Fatal Coal Mining Disasters of All Time.* She shuddered. Was it a threat? Someone warning her to stay away?

"I need comfort." Kim unwrapped one of the Lindt truffles and popped it into her mouth.

Haley lunged at her, trying to stop her. "Don't eat that!"

"Don't worry." Kim's words came out muffled. "You can have the rest."

"But something might be wrong with them."

Kim stopped chewing and immediately spit the chocolate into the wrapper. "What do you mean?"

Haley showed her the cover of the book. "I think someone's trying to threaten me. Who would give me a book on mining disasters unless they wanted to scare me away from my job? Some of those miners are really cruel. I mean look at me. I'm blue. They could've put something in the truffles as well."

"You think someone from the mine is trying to scare you into quitting?"

Haley nodded. "Yes. Or I guess it could be Liam. I know he doesn't want me working there."

"All right. I'll talk to Mitch and find out what he knows, and if he brought this in for somebody." Kim paused and looked at her. "What are you going to do if this really is a threat?"

Haley shrugged. "Try to stick it out. But I don't know if I can take much more of this. I just hope I can handle the humiliation of showing up to work looking like a Smurf."

"Have you considered quitting?"

Haley desperately wished the answer was no, but truthfully, the thought had crossed her mind. When she didn't answer, Kim understood and a glint of *I told you so* flashed in her eyes.

Haley shook her head. "No. I can't give up."

She looked at the book again. This time, she noticed the men in the picture were holding a makeshift cot. It was behind them, almost obscured by the others in the picture, but she could make out the form of a body covered by a tattered blanket. A dead miner.

CHAPTER 14

"I see you came back for more, Scab."

Haley knew Bear was addressing her, but she ignored him, which was potentially dangerous considering he was now her boss. *Scab.* That's what they had called her yesterday. Did he think she was some kind of crusty, old sore? She hoped the nickname wouldn't stick.

Bear stepped closer and thumped her on the back with his big, burly paw, almost knocking the breath from her. "Feeling a little blue today?" He let out a roar, laughing at his own joke.

The door opened and two men walked into the lamp-house. As if on cue, they looked at her and started laughing. They couldn't have heard Bear's joke so they were probably just enjoying the fact that she was still blue. She took a deep breath and tried to reassure herself. She could handle this. She was strong enough to take anything they dished out.

She turned and faced Bear. There was darkness behind his bemused grin. His beard didn't hide the shrewd and calculating turn of his lips or the hatred that gleamed in his eyes. She wanted to walk away, but she responded by smiling politely, knowing it would only irritate him more. "And how are you today, Mr. Karlson?"

His eye twitched. He was probably surprised she actually knew his real name. The door opened again and several more men walked in. Jake was with them. She watched for his reaction at seeing her, but he was talking with Moose, asking about his injured leg.

She walked to the announcement board and pretended to study

the accident reports and citations pinned there. A minute later, Jake was still busy. Oh, well. She wasn't sure why she wanted to talk to him anyway. Maybe it was the simple fact that he was nice, and right now she could do with some nice.

She turned to leave and reached for the doorknob just as Leech stepped in front of her. She jerked her hand back to keep from touching him. They hadn't even started their shift, yet he still looked dirty to her. It wasn't that he was coated in coal dust, but there was something that seemed grimy about him just under the skin.

"Morning." Leech's voice was calm, but she still braced herself for whatever was coming next. "I have to say, I'm surprised to see you back here."

"Really? Why's that?" She kept a steady eye on him, doing her best to forget that she was blue.

"Well, I . . ." Leech stammered then scratched his head. "I mean no offense, but I thought you had figured it out—women shouldn't be coal miners."

The chattering in the lamp-house died down, and Haley was all too aware that her response would be heard by everyone in the room. This wasn't necessarily a bad thing. It would save her the time of giving each of them the same speech. "Thank you for your unsolicited opinion, but I'm here and I'm not leaving." She pushed past Leech and walked outside without looking back.

"All right! Where's my hard hat?" Bear's voice boomed out as the door closed behind her. Haley stopped, a slight smile creasing her lips. Finally, Bear had fallen victim to one of their relentless practical jokes. It was about time. He was probably long overdue for his fair share.

Suddenly the door to the lamp-house flew open and the crew boss's large figure stepped out. "Haley!" he growled. "What'd you do with my hat?"

"You're blaming me?"

"Yeah, I am. Now, where is it?"

Haley gathered every ounce of courage she possessed, which wasn't much. She hated confrontation, and her insides were trembling so much she was sure it would register as a small earthquake on the mine monitoring equipment.

"Does it look like I have your hard hat?" She narrowed her eyes, trying to return his glare in full force, but then again, with her stained face, maybe she just resembled a mad blueberry. "Does it look like I walked out with your hat?" She held her hands up in an open gesture, showing him that the only things she held were an SCSR bag and her lunch box, which was now a plastic container— no way could they magnetize this. "If you still don't believe me, go ahead—search my locker, search my car. I don't have it."

Bear stared at her for a moment. She could sense danger behind those dark eyes, and all at once, she was certain he was the one who had given her the book on mining disasters. As her boss, he would have access to her personal records. It would've been easy for him to get her address. It terrified her to think that he might have even picked the lock himself and gone into her room, but she wasn't going to let on that she was scared. She pulled her shoulders back, trying to stand a little taller, trying not to be intimidated. She had resolved to do this job, and that's what she was going to do for as long as it lasted.

"Enough of this!" Bear stepped back with a huff. "It's time to get to work!" He spun on his heels and stomped back to the lamp-house just as Jake and the other beltmen emerged.

"So someone pranked old Bear, huh?" Jake stopped next to her while the others continued on to the nearest mantrip. He hadn't shaved, but the day-old stubble wasn't unattractive.

"Not that he doesn't deserve it, but maybe Bear simply misplaced his hat."

Jake shook his head. "Miners don't misplace their gear. He was pranked all right." A hint of a smile pulled at the corner of his mouth, teasing her. She wanted to see it bloom into his famous grin. But he held it back. "Was it you?" he asked.

Haley laughed. "As much as I'd like to claim it, do you really think I'd pull a trick on my boss—and on my second day no less?"

Jake eyed her carefully. "Right. It was probably someone from the night shift taking revenge because he's always complaining about them."

"Probably." Haley turned her head so Jake would stop looking at her blue pigment.

As if he read her thoughts, he let out a soft chuckle. "Don't worry, you look good in blue."

At least he was being nice about it. "I painted my nails to match." She lifted a hand showing off her bright blue nails which accentuated her stained fingers perfectly. She had borrowed the fingernail polish from Kim.

He laughed. The sound had a nice ring to it.

"I tried to wash it off," she admitted. She rubbed the back of her hand. "Whatever they put in the shampoo was pretty strong."

Jake ran his eyes over her, slow and steady. She expected to cringe under his examination, but there was nothing judgmental in his gaze. "I wouldn't worry. It was probably Methylene Blue or Crystal Violet."

Haley shifted her lunch box under her arm. "And what are those?"

"Nothing serious—just really strong dyes. If so, the color should wear off in a day or two. In the meantime, you can start a new fad. Blue is in, you know."

"Really? Then I should get a blue ribbon for best in style."

Jake was on the verge of smiling, and her hopes rose again, but his expression flattened when a group of longwall miners and the rest of Bear's crew walked out of the lamp-house. Bear was in the middle of the group, wearing a new hard hat. He ignored her, but the rest of the men had no shame in staring at her.

"Yep, blue is a great color," Haley muttered.

The last man passed by, and she waited for Jake to follow them. It wasn't fair to assume the worst of him, but from her experience, most men were like that. She turned to go when she felt a hand on her arm.

"It's my favorite color," Jake said quietly.

Haley suddenly felt overly warm. He must've sensed her

uneasiness and removed his hand. She smiled, trying to lighten the mood. "Too bad blue isn't popular around here."

"I don't know about that." Jake nodded toward the men's bathhouse. "Old Mater was singing Blue Bayou in the locker room this morning."

"Most likely as an insult to me."

Jake looked over to where the men had gathered near the mantrips. "Never did like that song much. I tend to lean more old country. You know . . . 'Baby's Got Her Blue Jeans On.'" His mouth twitched, but he still didn't break into the smile she was hoping for.

Maybe there was more to his comment than just the blue reference. Haley had a pair of worn blue jeans that were a little more form-fitting than they used to be. In fact, she'd had them on when she saw him at the care center. Maybe it was time to get rid of them. Oh well, the only thing attracting attention on her now was the reflective tape on her coveralls. Not exactly alluring, and she was okay with that.

"Thanks, Jake. I'm not here to win any popularity contests. I only want to be treated the same as any other miner. No better, and no worse."

"It will happen." He paused as more men walked by. "In the meantime, don't let them get to you."

"So you're telling me, don't be so blue?"

Jake must've appreciated her witty response because a smile flashed across his face. As brief as it was, it was still a nuclear reaction, his enthusiasm bubbling over into an ear-to-ear grin, giving him an absurdly boyish look that brightened his whole countenance. Unfortunately, he restrained it too quickly, but she still felt like she had accomplished something for the day.

"Exactly," he said. "Just be smart about things. Deep Blue smart."

Haley raised an eyebrow. "I love the whole blue thing we have going here, but I have no idea what Deep Blue is."

Jake's eyes brightened, and his grin appeared again, turning him into a teenager posing as an adult. Haley wanted to do something, but cheering would be inappropriate. Jake was more energetic now, leaning forward, his face alight with excitement. "Deep Blue—it's intelligence, ingenuity, and cleverness all wrapped up in a box."

"It? You mean it's an object, not an adjective?"

"Computer," Jake said. "Deep Blue was the first data processing computer to win a chess tournament against a reigning world-champion chess player. It's old school now, but it was brilliant in its day."

Again Haley wondered how he ended up working in the coal mine. She could relate to Deep Blue though. Not that she was smart like a super computer, but this job was like a giant chess match, pitting her against some of the best players, and she hoped she wasn't outmatched.

"Looks like they're ready to go down." Jake motioned to the mantrips.

"Yeah, we better get going." Haley started walking but couldn't resist darting a glance over her shoulder at the dirty lump pile near the tipple. Sitting on top was Bear's hard hat, partially buried in the filthy coal. She smiled slyly. Maybe it was childish, but they had started it, and she wasn't going to let them have the advantage. She could play this game along with the best of them.

CHAPTER 15

Haley climbed out of the truck and lagged behind as she followed the men down the dark intake. Her violet-blue pigment had been the only subject of conversation during the twenty-minute ride into the mine, so she trailed behind to rally her emotions and to get her game face on. As soon as she sat her new plastic lunch box on the transformer, Bear turned his light on her. She glanced up at his new hard hat and smiled.

He didn't return the gesture. "You'll be working with Stump today."

"Stump?" She almost jumped for joy. She didn't know much about the miner other than he'd been in the warehouse plenty of times. He was the quiet sort. But she was elated she didn't have to work with Leech again.

"You're gonna be timbering," Bear continued.

Haley's elation deflated like a balloon. Timbering was hard work—something she wasn't sure she'd be able to do considering how sore she was from yesterday. She had muscle aches in places she didn't know she had muscles. She absentmindedly rubbed a twinge from her back as she listened to Bear give her and Stump further instructions. As always, he ended with his coined phrase, "Get to work!"

Haley followed Stump up the intake. He was a short man who walked with a bowlegged limp. He looked cumbersome when she saw him in the warehouse, but down here he moved through the darkness with the grace of a cat, looking more at ease in the mine than he did on the surface.

They walked past Wing Nut and Leech who were flipping switches on the bolting machine and cussing like, well, miners.

"Somethin' wrong?" Stump asked.

Wing Nut thumped the machine with his fist. "We've only got lights. Nothin' else on this damn thing works." Haley wasn't sure how Wing Nut got his nickname. He didn't seem very mechanically minded.

She followed Stump as he circled the machine. Surprisingly, she had a hard time keeping up with him; he was so adept to the dark surroundings. He seemed to glide around with ease while she stumbled in the gob and tripped on the cable. It was obvious he wasn't in a hurry to start timbering. She didn't mind the delay either, but to Stump's credit, his reasons were nobler than hers. He was going to lend a hand and, unlike her, he seemed to anticipate what was needed. He removed the controller box panel and after a quick examination, he started to pull the jacket off the cable.

"Here's the problem," he said. "Bad splice. This cable has been run over so many times it looks like someone took a chainsaw to it."

Haley stood next to him, wanting to help but not sure how. It was a painful reminder that she wasn't a real miner yet. At least not like him.

A light flashed behind them, and Stump put the cable down. "That's our cue to move on before Bear comes and gives us an earful." He gave some pointers to Wing Nut and then led Haley to another section.

"This is where we'll be working. . ." Stump's words trailed off as he examined the roof inches above their heads. A frown creased his lips.

Haley followed his line of sight, trying to see what he was seeing. "What is it?" she finally asked.

"The bolts." He pointed to the end of a bolt sticking out from the roof. "Them ain't cable bolts; them are regular bolts."

Cable bolts were extra-long and could extend up to sixteen feet inside the rock to give the roof extra support while regular bolts only averaged six feet.

"Were they supposed to use cable bolts here?"

"Yeah. Didn't you hear them talkin' about it yesterday? And for good reason too. Look at that top." Stump pointed to the roof. "See that brown coloring?"

Haley wouldn't have noticed it on her own, but now that he pointed it out, she could see it. It was a muddy clay-like color, and even she knew that clay-like rock wasn't good to bolt into.

Stump shook his head and cursed. "I have half a mind to call in a hazard complaint. I don't know what Bear's thinking, sending us out here to work under bad top that ain't been bolted properly."

A prick of fear edged its way through Haley. "Does Bear know the wrong bolts were used?"

"Bear knows all right. The bosses have a meeting every day before shift starts and you can bet he's filled in on all these details. What I don't understand is why he'd send us to timber this section before the problem gets fixed."

The uneasiness spreading through Haley worked its way up into her throat. "You don't think he'd put us in harm's way, do you?"

Stump shook his head. "He's never done anything like that before."

"He's never had a woman working for him before," Haley muttered. She kicked her boot in the mucky coal. "So what are we going to do? Can we tell Cross about it?" As one of the safety men, Cross could handle things like this fairly easy.

Stump shrugged. "Yeah, but nothing might come of it. They might just tell us that they needed the section timbered because the roof needed the extra support. It's not the first time the wrong bolts have been used. We'll just watch it. It's not bad top that kills you, it's good top."

Haley flashed her light on him. "That doesn't make sense. How can good top kill?"

"With good top, you grow complacent, don't watch it. But with bad top, you're always keeping an eye on it. You're more careful. Let's get to work, and when Bear comes around we'll ask him about the bolts."

It didn't take long for Haley to forget about the roof; it took all of her concentration to keep her body going. After they took measurements, they shoveled out the holes for the timbers. The wooden posts couldn't stand on loose coal, so Haley shoveled her guts out trying to get each hole cleaned to Stump's specifications. After the last one, she put the shovel down and pressed her fist into her aching back.

"You hurtin'?" Stump didn't wait for an answer. "Let's go get the posts."

Haley mumbled under her breath. How could he work like that at his age and not complain? Trying not to drag her feet, she followed him on the long walk to the intake where the timber was piled. They would have to carry each post, one at a time, through a three-foot mandoor and then another two hundred feet back to where the holes were. There, she and Stump would cut the timbers to size before they wedged them up to brace the roof.

Haley ran a finger over the blisters on her hand, then pulled her gloves back on and bent down to pick up one of the posts. A groan escaped her lips as she stood, her muscles cramping.

Stump's light turned on her. "Too much for you?"

"No. I can get it. I'm just a little sore." It was an understatement. Every part of her body was screaming.

Stump nodded. "That's expected. You can't work in these conditions and not hurt. Nothing else to expect when you're carving a hard living out of solid rock."

He hoisted one of the timbers under his arm and headed to the mandoor. Haley followed, but one end of her post fell to the ground and she ended up dragging it to the door.

Stump turned and watched her. "These timbers have been sitting outside; they're a little waterlogged so you'll have to put your back into it."

Pain shot through her, but Haley picked up the heavy post again. Despite her effort, she was slow and lagged behind. She was about a hundred feet behind Stump when she heard the boom.

Like a terrifying clap of thunder, the explosion echoed around her. The blast hit, peppering her with small chunks of coal. The force of it tore the timber from her arms and threw her to the ground. She lay there, hands covering her face to block the shooting debris, her eyes pinched shut, expecting the mountain to collapse on top of her. Then everything fell silent.

It took a second before she realized Stump was cussing and running toward her, his feet pounding in the gob. She opened her eyes and rolled over, choking on the thick dust. Her helmet lay a couple of feet from her, its light turned up, reflecting off the swirling gray cloud that filled the tunnel. She put her trembling hands on the ground and pushed herself onto her hands and knees and vomited.

At last, Stump's light cut through to her.

"You all right?"

She wiped her mouth with the back of her gloved hand, still gagging on the coal dust.

He touched her shoulder and directed his light down her body until it rested on a massive rock inches from her feet. It was the size of a tire and probably weighed over two hundred pounds. Haley stared at it, unsure of where it came from. There were two more chunks the size of basketballs further out.

Stump swore again then turned his light back on her. "Say somethin'. Are you okay?"

She finally managed a nod. She wasn't hurt—at least she didn't think so. Just scared. She pulled her glove off and felt her cheek. It stung from where bits of coal had hit her, but there didn't seem to be any blood.

"What happened?" she asked. "Did the roof fall?"

"Nope. The rib blew." Stump pointed to the wall behind her. It didn't have the chain link fencing like some of the other sections. "We call it a bounce," Stump said. "The mountain is always moving, and we're down so deep it can't withstand all the pressure. Sometimes it just blows out the ribs."

Three lights appeared in the distance. The other miners must have heard the small explosion. They ran toward her, looking like firefighters making their way through a cloud of smoke, their bouncing headlamps shooting beams of lights in all directions.

Haley pulled herself up and put her helmet back on. Her whole body trembled, but she forced herself to walk.

The men drew near. "What did you do?" Bear growled.

"Nothing!" Haley turned to face him. "I was packing a timber and the rib blew." She looked at the other two miners: Leech and Wing Nut. Leech seemed to have an oddly pleasant look on his face.

"She's not hurt," Stump added.

Bear didn't seem to care much about that. In fact, there seemed to be a hint of disappointment in his face. He turned away, hiding his expression as he looked at the rib and grumbled something about orange-hats needing to be watched so they didn't hurt themselves.

While Bear examined the wall, Haley swallowed the grit in her throat and tried not to cough. She wished she had brought a dust mask with her, but then again, she didn't know if she would wear it. The other men didn't like to use them.

A moment later, Bear walked back to her. "Everything looks all right now." He kicked his toe against the large rock that had nearly crushed her. "I don't need any lost-time accidents from this crew, you hear me?"

Her hands tightened into fists, which seemed to increase the tremors in her body. It wasn't like this was her fault, but she nodded anyway. "Yes, sir."

"Watch yourself, Scab, or you'll be done quicker than you started."

The hot, dust-clogged air seemed to thicken around her as she took the chastisement.

Bear's face didn't show any signs of sympathy. "Meet me in the lamp-house after the shift. I'm fillin' out an Unsafe Work Observation form on you."

Haley's mouth fell open, but she closed it when she tasted coal on her tongue. "You're writing me up? For what? If there was an accident, that'd be one thing, but I didn't do anything wrong—"

Bear shined his light in her eyes. "And for challenging me, I'm going to post it on the board too."

Haley's jaw clamped tight. Accident reports were posted on the board at the lamp-house for everyone to see—but not Unsafe Work Observations. Those were usually kept in a miner's personnel file, but she hadn't even done anything unsafe. Bear just wanted to humiliate her and give more fodder to the men.

He rocked forward on the balls of his feet, seeming pleased with himself. "You probably want the rest of the shift off, but we don't work like that, girly, so pull yourself together and get those timbers up."

She looked at the other miners, hoping someone would see the injustice and defend her. Stump stepped next to Bear and nodded his head up at the roof. "And what about this bad top? Why weren't the cable bolts used?"

Haley's heart fell. So that was the end of it—no one was going to stand up for her. She would've argued the point herself, but it would probably get her into more trouble.

Bear's light flickered across her for the briefest moment before he looked at the roof. "They didn't have any cable bolts down here. We have them now, but the bolter just broke down again."

Wing Nut nodded and held his hands out with a shrug. "We fixed the splice, but something else is wrong. Something electrical. Einstein fixed it last time. He has a phone. Maybe we can call him and tell him to come take a look at it."

Haley felt a small surge go through her at the mention of Jake's nickname.

Bear rubbed his beard and finally nodded. "Get him over here." He pointed to Haley. "Don't think this means you're getting a break. Get back to work!"

Haley's light washed over the roof and the blown-out rib. "Is it even safe?"

Bear didn't answer. There was a tug at the edge of his lips, the strange smile nearly imperceptible behind his beard. At that moment, he looked like his namesake. A bear that had just caught a fish and was about to devour it. His eyes narrowed. "There you go again, Ms. Carter, acting like a scab. Now, are you going to work"—his smile widened—"or is this your quitting day?"

CHAPTER 16

"Like the boss said, let's get back to work." Stump walked away, packing the timber Haley had dropped.

She jogged to keep up with him then waited until they were out of earshot of the other men before she spoke. "Do you think it's okay for Bear to write me up for an Unsafe Work Observation?"

"I'm sure he's just teasing, Scab."

Haley tried to take the timber from him, but he wouldn't give it to her. "Why does everyone keep calling me Scab?"

"I suppose it's your nickname for now because you act like a scab."

Haley wasn't even sure what it meant, but she didn't want to appear ignorant, so she tried to work her way around it. "And how do I *not* act like a scab?"

"You start working like a real miner. Now go get another post."

A few minutes later she crossed paths with him as she walked toward the section, timber under her arm. Fear for her safety still ebbed up from the pit of her stomach, but she refused to go home a quitter.

Struggling to carry the post, she hurried along as best she could, but it wasn't until her next trip that she finally caught up with Stump and tried to match his stride. When they set their loads down, he nodded his approval. "At some point, you just might earn a new nickname."

"Are you admitting I'm a good worker?"

There was a long pause before he answered. "Better than some."

"Better than Leech," she muttered. Stump smiled then shot a stream of tobacco juice out the side of his mouth. Haley wrinkled her nose. Smoking wasn't allowed in the mine, so most of the men chewed—something she wasn't going to get used to anytime soon.

She forgot all about the unsavory habit when the noise of machinery filled the air. A moment later the roof bolter came charging around the corner, but it wasn't Leech or Wing Nut driving. It was Jake.

His light settled briefly on Haley before he went to work. After bolting a section, he handed the controls over to Wing Nut and walked over to where she and Stump were working.

"Overdoing it, aren't you?" Stump pointed to the new bolt pattern on the roof. They only need to be spaced five feet apart. You put in double that."

Haley looked at bolt spacing, noticing it for the first time.

Stump directed his headlamp at Jake again. "What were you thinkin', Einstein? Concerned for our safety?"

Jake's light flickered across Haley. "I thought that's what Bear wanted. Why don't you go tell Wing Nut to space them farther apart?"

Stump nodded and hurried off.

Haley felt her stomach twist at being left alone with Jake. His light focused off to the side of her head. She worried about her blue pigment then realized she was covered with enough coal dust that it would mask the color. He seemed just as bad, the dust clinging to his day-old stubble making him look more rugged and tough than usual. When she felt her heartbeat quicken, she looked away, directing her light up to the roof. "Thanks for the extra bolts, but you really don't need to watch out for me."

He shrugged. "I just want you to be safe. You never know when something is going to happen."

"And you think putting in extra bolts where I'm working is the answer?"

"Not entirely. I hope they help, but bolts are never the complete answer. If the roof cracks above them, it will all come down anyway, and like you saw today, there are other dangers."

"Does everyone know about the rib blowing out and nearly killing me?"

"Pretty much."

Haley felt another flash of irritation. "There was no damage done, and like I said, I can look after myself. So, don't assume that I need any special treatment. Besides, I don't want the other guys to get the wrong idea."

Jake held her gaze. The kindness behind his eyes dissolved into frustration. "You don't want anyone to think I like you." Haley didn't say anything. Jake kicked at a muddy lump with his boot. "It's no secret I had a crush on you in high school, I admit it. I liked that you always had a cause: fundraisers, student rights, and all those after school committees. You were ready to take on anything. Your conviction, your purpose—I liked that about you. It doesn't surprise me that you pushed for this job and that you're stubborn enough to do it. But this"—Jake pointed at the roof bolts—"this isn't because I have a crush on you. I don't care if you don't want my help, but down here, we watch out for each other."

Stump walked back to join them. "Wing Nut is spacing the bolts like they should be. And he said he told you the same thing, but you wouldn't listen."

Jake shrugged. "Guess I misunderstood." He looked at Haley for a long moment before walking away.

Stump's light flashed back and forth between Haley and Jake. As soon as they were alone, he laughed. "I saw what was going on there." A grin split across his face. "And you think the teasing was bad before, wait 'til the rest of the crew hear about this."

Haley rounded on him. "And what exactly are you talking about?"

He pointed to the roof. "Look at all these extra bolts." Stump rubbed his hands together in excitement, and a sudden dread settled over Haley. Lunchtime was going to be unbearable if she had to listen to all the men chide her about Jake.

"Just keep your mouth shut. Jake put in extra bolts, but it wasn't because he likes me. He just wants everyone to be safe."

"Oh, yeah? He's never double-bolted a roof for any of us before. And maybe you don't like him, but he sure likes you."

"You're jumping to conclusions."

"Am I? It's not like Einstein to waste supplies." Stump looked up at the newly secured roof and grinned.

Haley's mind worked furiously to come up with a viable excuse. There was no way she'd let the teasing get worse. "He did it because that's the deal we made."

Stump eyed her curiously. "What deal?"

"I asked him to look out for me when he could." She felt terrible about the lie. Jake really was looking out for her, and she was twisting it into something else.

Stump waved a hand in disbelief. "That ain't true."

"Why? Because you don't think any miner would do that for me? Because I have a target on my back, and no one wants a woman underground?"

Stump tipped his hat low over his eyes. "Can't blame us. Ain't nobody gonna stick their neck out and risk getting caught in the fire when you probably won't last long down here anyway."

"I'll outlast the other orange-hats that hired on, you'll see."

"Until you prove it, no one, not even Einstein, would agree to watch out for you."

"I'm paying him," she said.

Stump's firm look shifted to uncertainty. "Ain't no miner got extra money for stuff like that."

He was right. No one would give away part of their paycheck for something like that. Especially her. Haley fidgeted with her belt. "I pay him in meals." It was the stupidest excuse, but Stump's eyebrows rose curiously and she rushed on, "I pack him a lunch twice a week. I make a mean lasagna and the best homemade chocolate chip cookies you'll ever taste."

He rubbed a hand across his mouth. "I've never heard of anyone makin' a deal like that. Einstein doesn't even work around you, so what are you paying him for—just to be nice whenever he crosses your path?"

"Isn't that enough? The way everyone's been treating me . . ." She pulled off a glove, directing her light over her blue-stained fingers. "I think I could use a friend. Just one single person who doesn't think my working here is a joke."

Her words seemed to have a sobering effect. For the briefest moment, it looked like Stump understood. If Haley could buy a little compassion with a few lunches she really would. But with Jake, she didn't have to. He was kind all on his own, and she had refused it. She looked up at the roof bolts and couldn't help but picture his rough face with his day-old stubble.

Something stirred inside her, and suddenly she wanted to get back to work. "Let's get these timbers in."

She walked over and picked up one of the heavy posts. An aching pain shot through her. It was almost enough to wipe out the emotions twisting in inside her, but not quite. She heaved again and set the timber in the prepared hole. She needed to work harder.

A few hours later, Stump insisted they stop. Reluctantly, she followed him to the transformer where they grabbed their lunch boxes. Her hard plastic box didn't have any problems coming off the transformer today. Too tired to move off into one of the side cuts to be by herself, she sank to the ground next to Stump, and then opened the box and pulled out her sandwich. Something was wrong. There were black fingerprints on the Ziploc bag. She examined the sandwich through the plastic. It seemed thicker than normal. She gave it a squeeze. Thick black goo seeped out from the sides, pressing against the baggie. Grease. Someone had filled her sandwich with mechanic's grease.

The men laughed, including Stump. Did the jokes never end with them? She dropped the sandwich into Stump's lap and stood up. He clamped his mouth shut and gave her an apologetic look, but it was too late. She walked into the darkness, taking her nearly empty lunch box with her.

At the next intersection, she quickly ducked around the corner and walked for several minutes. At last, she looked around, orienting herself. No one was around, but it wouldn't take much for someone to find her if they came looking, and she needed time alone.

She eyed a small mandoor separating the entry from the return. Beyond it, the bad air was being moved out of the mine. She knew the rules. For the most part, the return was off limits to all but the fire boss, and she clearly remembered Boom's warning to stay out of the bleeder sections. But she wasn't in the mood to be compliant. Besides, it was the only place she could go that would guarantee her privacy. She looked around, then opened the door and slipped through into the forbidden section.

The air was breathable, although considerably more hot and stagnant. She dropped to the ground and opened her lunch box. What was left consisted of an apple and a small bag of chips that someone had smashed. At least the crumbs would still be edible, but it would do little to appease her growling stomach. Working at the mine was proving to be a good weight loss program. She picked up the smashed bag of chips and saw that someone had used a paint marker to write across it.

Scabs don't last long. Quit while you can.

Haley tore open the bag, accidently spilling the crushed chips onto her lap. She picked up what she could and ate them, and then brushed the remaining fragments into the darkness. Who was the note from? Bear? Leech? It could be anyone. They all hated her. And after what she said to Jake, she wouldn't be surprised if he hated her too.

CHAPTER 17

The board in the lamp-house was about five feet across and four feet tall. Haley stood in front of it with her hands on her hips. It was the first time she took careful notice of it. It was a wall of papers displaying the ventilation and roof control plans for the mine along with violations, citations, awards, and accident reports. She was only examining it now because she wanted to see if there were any other personal reports tacked on it. Bear had followed through on his threat to fill out an Unsafe Work Observation, and she had spent the last ten minutes in Cross's office listening to him tell the safety specialist how unsafe she was. Soon the report would be posted on the board for all to see.

Not surprisingly, there weren't any Unsafe Work Observations, but there were a few accident reports. One man had his hand crushed when a pipe rolled off the stack he was unloading. And another miner threw his back out while putting bolts in the roof bolter. They were unfortunate accidents but not as humiliating as having an Unsafe Work Observation posted.

Haley looked for Moose's accident report from when a lump of coal fell off the belt, cutting his leg. It wasn't there. That was a good sign. Maybe it took longer to post the reports than she thought. At least it would give her another day before the humiliation started. With that happy thought on her mind, she headed to the bathhouse.

It was raining outside. Not heavy, but just enough to give the mine a gray, washed-out appearance. It felt as though she had stepped into a scene from the Great Depression. She hurried to the bathhouse, and this time had no trouble with unexpected surprises.

It was still raining when she headed home. Fat droplets plopped down on the windshield, blurring the road between swipes from the wipers. When she turned into the parking lot behind her building, she noticed that someone had left a large sack of garbage next to the dumpster. Seriously, would it take that much more effort to have put it in the bin?

She parked her car in the only available space and hurried across the lot as the sharp, icy rain pelted her. As she ran past the dumpster, she glanced at the discarded garbage sack. She stopped short, her heart flipping in her chest. It wasn't a sack of garbage, but a person. In fact, it was Mitch, his back laying against the large dirty bin, head lulled to the side.

"Oh, please don't be dead." Haley propped her lunch box on the edge of the dumpster and dug through her pockets for her cell phone, preparing to dial 911. She bent over, feeling for a pulse, her own heart racing as she expected the worst. His skin was cold and clammy, but surprisingly, there was still life in it. Her blue fingers found his carotid artery. It was still throbbing strongly.

"Mitch." She tapped his cheek with her hand. The acrid smell of alcohol cut through the moist air. She wrinkled her nose and pulled away. He wasn't dead, just dead drunk. His hair was flattened by the rain and his clothes were soaked through, both indicating he had been passed out for some time.

Haley nudged him with the toe of her shoe. "Mitch!"
Nothing.
She nudged him again. "Mitch! Get up."
He let out a groan but didn't move. The pelting rain ran down his face and into his whiskers. He probably didn't even know he was outside.

"You're such an idiot." The words were quiet, but she hoped he heard them. She had seen her own father this intoxicated on several occasions. With him, it might have been better if he had died out in a ditch somewhere, but not Mitch. As much as she disliked him, he didn't deserve that fate.

Her sore muscles protested as she bent down and slid an arm around his waist. He was so cold. A chill ran through her, but she held him tight and hoisted him to his feet. She wouldn't have been able to if he'd been a larger man, but his wiry frame probably didn't top 150 pounds including his wet clothes.

"Come on," she said, lurching him forward. He fell against the dumpster, knocking her lunch box inside as the lid slammed shut. "Great." Haley pulled him upright again. "You're fishing that out for me as soon as you're sober."

At last, Haley managed to get him in the building. He stumbled along, moaning. She got him up the stairs and was tempted to drop him right there; the stench of alcohol was almost unbearable. It seemed to eek out from every inch of him, and there was another odor. She was afraid to admit it, but it was probably urine.

"You takin' me home, Suzzy?" His words were slurred.

"I'm not Suzzy, I'm Haley. Now stand up straight." She kicked his foot over so he could take more of his own weight and tugged him along. She dragged him to the end of the hall and tried his door. It opened. "Come on."

She prodded and pulled until she got him into the apartment. The rank scent of stale cigarettes combined with rotting food and dirty laundry wafted over her. His entire apartment smelled like a giant unwashed gym sock. She glanced around and wasn't too surprised by the mess. A box of half-eaten Little Cesar's pizza sat on the coffee table along with several magazines, and three coffee cups obscuring the view of the old, stained couch behind them.

Mitch probably wanted to lie down, but the couch was heaped with clothes, and she wasn't about to clear it off. There was no way she was going to venture into his bedroom either, so she dragged him over to the thrift store La-Z-Boy in the corner. She picked up the pile of mail from off the armrest and settled him into the flea-bitten recliner.

He grunted and looked up at her with watery eyes. "You gonna abduct me?"

"What are you talking about, Mitch?" She dropped his mail on top of the overfilled ashtray on the end table. Too bad the spent cigarettes weren't lit; the place could've done with a good burning.

He raised a hand and pointed it at her. "Are you going to abduct me? Take me to your planet?" He laughed then started coughing. It was a hard cough, deep in his chest like he had smoked too many cigarettes.

"You're drunk, Mitch."

"And you're blue."

She reached down and pulled the reclining bar up, jerking the chair into a lying position. "Get some sleep."

She turned to leave when she saw the bookshelf next to the door. Unlike the rest of the room, it was cleaned and organized. An antique miner's lunch pail, similar to the one Kim had bought her, sat on the top. Next to it was a vintage tin for blasting caps. The next shelf held three antique miners' hats. One was a leather and canvas cap. It resembled an old baseball cap except for the carbide lamp attached above the brim. The other two were turtle shell mining helmets from the early 1900s.

Haley walked over to examine them. The other shelves were filled with similar items. Growing up in coal country, she had seen antique mining gear, but this small personal collection was impressive. Mitch must have been a miner at some time. Only someone with the love of it would put effort and money into obtaining a collection like this.

"You like that stuff?" Mitch's words slid into each other. "I heard you're working underground."

Haley reached out and touched one of the carbide lamps, tracing her finger along the edge of the silver dish-like reflector. "Yeah, but I can't imagine working in a coal mine with an open flame on my head."

Mitch chuckled. "I hear you're on Bear's crew."

She almost couldn't understand him, but he said Bear's name like he knew the crew boss personally. She looked over her shoulder. "How did you know I was working with Bear?"

Mitch didn't answer. He leaned over the side of the chair, swayed a little, and laughed. "Did they give ya a nickname yet?"

"You didn't tell me how you knew I was on Bear's crew."

"Come on." He slumped back in the chair. "Tell me. What'd they stick you with? Goldilocks? Princess? Or Mother Goose?"

Haley glared at him. "Scab."

Mitch slapped his knee. "Scab!" He tipped his head back and laughed so hard tears formed in his eyes.

Haley turned and left just as he started to choke. She hesitated at the door, wondering if she should go back and thump him on the back, but he regained his breath with a cough. That was convenient. She had already done her good deed for the day anyway.

She pulled the door shut behind her and walked down the hallway, still listening to his bouts of laughter interrupted by the nicotine hacking fits that rattled his chest.

CHAPTER 18

"Haley. It's been a long time."

Haley had almost reached her apartment when she heard the voice. This day was moving from bad to worse.

Liam stood at the top of the stairs. His sandy blond hair was wet from the rain, his tanned face moist. She wasn't deceived by his handsome appearance, and an uneasy feeling crept over her.

"What are you doing here?"

"I want to talk. We haven't even had a conversation since I sent the flowers." He took a step closer letting his eyes wandered over her, taking in her odd coloring, but he didn't say anything. Someone must've already told him about it. Maybe Kim . . . or even Rivers?

"Well, I don't like flowers. And I don't want any gifts from you. Speaking of which, were you the one who left the bag in my room with the chocolates and the book?"

His eyebrows rose. "What bag?"

"It's just something someone left for me. I'm trying to narrow down my list of suspects."

"Someone else is giving you gifts?"

Haley cringed. Hopefully, he wouldn't twist her words and assume she was trying to make him jealous. That was something her dad did with her mom.

"Look, this isn't a good time. I just got off work, and I'm tired." She stuck her key in the lock and opened the door, but Liam put his arm in front of her, blocking her.

"That's one of the things we need to talk about. I wish you'd quit.

Look what they're doing to you." He nodded to her, obviously referring to her stained skin.

Haley stepped away. She could've pushed past him, but what if he followed her inside? She didn't want to be alone in the apartment with him. "What I do is none of your business."

Liam masked his irritation with a controlled smile. "I hated it when you worked in the warehouse, and now this? We should be phasing out coal plants, not contributing to the problem."

"Sounds like this is more about your environmental campaign than it is about me."

Liam shrugged. "I just don't understand how you can support that industry, knowing what it's doing to our society. Ninety-six thousand pounds of mercury being released into our atmosphere every year from coal plants. The CO_2 is—"

"Just stop," Haley broke in. "Don't quote me statistics. So the CO_2 levels have been rising, but so has the human lifespan. Explain that. More gasses and we're living longer. Maybe it's good for us. Think of all the plants; they live off of CO_2. The more in the air, the more green growth. We're saving the world by feeding one plant at a time."

His body tensed. "You know that's not true."

He was probably right, but this was her job, and it was paying for her mother's therapy. He couldn't expect her to jump on the environmentalist wagon.

Liam leaned in. "I just don't want my girlfriend to be a part of something so controversial."

A flood of heat rushed through her body. He had always used the term *girlfriend* too liberally. "Excuse me? We broke up, remember?"

"That's the other thing we need to talk about."

"There's nothing to discuss. We're not dating anymore."

He ran his fingers through his hair and leaned against the wall. His sagging shoulders made him appear pitiful—which was probably what he wanted. "What did I do this time?"

She shook her head, trying to clear her thoughts. Admittedly she had trust issues with men, but there was no need to expatiate on every individual reason for severing the relationship. She gritted her teeth and leveled her eyes on him.

"We're not discussing this." The words came out harsher than she intended, but that was okay. She needed to be forceful. She didn't want a repeat of the other times she'd tried to break up with him. He would get her talking, and before she knew it, they'd be back together.

Liam stuffed his hands in his pockets and stared at her with a dull expression. "At least give me an explanation." He put a hand on her shoulder, stroking her neck with his thumb. She wanted to cringe away from his touch, but she couldn't let him know how much it bothered her. She stood still, and Liam's eyes softened. "Haley, I'll do anything to get you to talk to me. Anything."

Was he placating her? That was another tactic her dad would use. Liam's thumb stroked her neck again, causing her skin to crawl. She pulled away and walked downstairs. She needed to be out in the open. The hallway was too enclosed—too much like the closet she used to be forced into for punishment.

She pushed the thin metal door open and stepped outside. The rain had slowed to a light drizzle. Liam seemed reluctant to follow her out, but unfortunately, his hesitation only lasted a moment. Haley stopped next to the dumpster, her face brightening with an idea.

She patted the metal bin. "If you'll do anything, then climb in here and get my lunch box. It fell in by accident." Liam didn't move. "So what about that whole *I'll do anything to get you to talk to me* speech? I guess you really didn't mean it."

She turned and started to walk around the side of the building when he called to her. She looked back. It was a mistake. Liam had the lid to the dumpster open. A nauseous feeling rose into her throat. He was going to do it.

"How did your lunch box *accidentally* fall in here?"

"It was transported by an alien ship."

He rolled his eyes. "Whatever. But just to show you how serious

I am—" He hopped up and sat on the edge. A moment later, he stuck his foot inside and lifted her lunch box out with the toe of his shoe. "Good enough?" He tossed it down to her. "Now that I practically went dumpster diving for you, let's talk." Liam started climbing down.

"Stop. Just stay right there." Liam froze and looked at her. Haley's fingers tightened around the handle of her lunch box. Maybe it was a little mean, but she didn't want him within touching distance.

"What? You won't talk to me unless I stay here?" He pointed to the dumpster.

She nodded.

"But why? You want to humiliate me, is that it?"

His words stung. She wasn't like that. She wasn't cruel. Her father was, but she wasn't, was she? She tipped her head up toward the gray sky and took a deep breath. "I need some distance. Just stay there and we'll talk."

"Fine." He pulled a leg up, resting his arm on his knee. Only Liam could look totally casual on top of a dumpster. "I want you back, Haley, and I hope this proves that I'll do whatever it takes."

He was doing what she asked, but it still felt like *she* was the one being manipulated. "We're still not getting back together."

"That's what you say now, but—"

She resisted the urge to walk over and shove him in. "We aren't getting back together—ever."

"Then explain why. I can't fix things unless you tell me what's wrong."

Kim would've told her that she owed him at least that much. She didn't agree, but it was probably the nice thing to do. "We aren't good together. I tried, Liam. I really did. I would've backed out sooner, but I didn't want to hurt your feelings."

"That's not a reason. I need specifics."

So much for sparing his feelings. Haley walked closer. "All right. We're too different. Politically, socially, emotionally. You move too fast for me. You're obsessed with the idea of commitment but not to me."

Haley heard footsteps and looked up to see Caleb's grandma walking out from the building and across the parking lot. She looked at Haley with a raised eyebrow. It wasn't audible, but her expression clearly said, *Don't mind me, dear. Carry on with your conversation with the crazy man on the dumpster.*

"Great," Haley muttered. Caleb's grandma climbed into her car and had to turn the ignition over four or five times before it took. A moment later, she drove out of the parking lot.

"Opposites attract." Liam held his hand out. "And how can you say I move too fast? We've only kissed a few times."

Haley cringed at the memory. "That's only one facet of a relationship. There are other areas, and you're too domineering for my tastes."

"But that's something we can work with. Give it time."

"You're not listening." She raised her voice. "There is no *we*."

Liam's eyes grew hard and determined. "Are you sure you're not running away because you don't want to face other issues? If you could just trust me more—"

Haley shook her head. "I know I've got problems, but so do you. That day in the Walmart parking lot when I first tried to break up with you. You jumped into my car and refused to get out. You yelled at me, and then you . . . you raised your hand."

"But I wasn't going to hit you. I'd never do that."

"But it looked like it, and it scared me. You were so angry, and I just can't deal with that."

"I didn't mean to let it go that far. I'll never do it again."

Haley wasn't buying it. Her dad wasn't a hitter when he first married her mom. It came over time, and he had made countless promises never to do it again. In the end, the only thing that stopped him was prison. True, Liam might never go that far, but she could see the signs of a poisonous relationship. And Liam was toxic.

"I swear, Haley, I didn't mean to. You knew what kind of week I'd had, and I wasn't thinking. How many times do I have to tell you I'm sorry?"

"You don't have to apologize anymore. We're done."

Liam kicked his foot against the dumpster with a loud bang. "You can't mean that." His eyes flashed, dark and moody.

Haley took a step back, her insides trembling. "I do mean it."

"Listen." His face transformed, and suddenly he smiled at her like nothing was wrong. "Give it some time. Think about it."

It didn't matter what he said; no amount of talking would change her mind. She should've never let Rivers talk her into dating him in the first place. She didn't trust Liam then, and even less so now.

"I'm sorry. I frightened you." His voice was soft. "I'm just like any other guy. I get mad and frustrated at times, but I hope you know I'd never hurt you. Give me another chance and I'll work on my temper. I'm a better person when I'm with you. You make me try harder." He looked at her, his eyes pleading. "Our relationship is worth saving." He pulled his feet under him, balancing on the edge of the dumpster, ready to leap down.

Haley tensed. Maybe it was true. Maybe he'd never turn violent. But listening to his apologies and promises, it reminded her too much of her parents.

"Just leave me alone." She stepped forward, slamming her hands against the dumpster, all of her fear and frustration smacking out through the palms of her hands. The bin shifted. Liam threw his arms out, but lost his balance and toppled in.

Haley stepped back, a breathless "oops" passing through her parted lips as Liam's flailing hands, and twisting body disappeared. The lid slammed shut on top of him. She heard him thrashing against trash bags, cussing her. She ran. Not toward the building. She wasn't about to be caught in there with him. She ran to her car, her heart pounding. A moment later, she sped out of the lot before Liam could even gather his footing and open the lid.

CHAPTER 19

Haley slid her pink vinyl chair closer to her mother to see if that would coax a response out of her. "If I had any friends, Mom, I'd be venting to them instead of you."

Her mother took her hand and opened her mouth as if she wanted to say something.

"Go ahead," Haley encouraged. "Tell me what you think."

Her mother darted a nervous glance around the room. "I don't mind listening, Brooke." There was a long pause. "But I can't give advice about men."

Of course not. Haley patted her mother's hand. She wouldn't ask that of her, but at least she was talking.

Soft footsteps sounded at the door and Haley looked up. Kim walked into the room. "I thought I'd find you here, and I'm glad you're discussing your relationship problems with someone."

She must've been standing in the doorway for some time. Haley shifted in her seat. "I don't have any relationships. I broke it off with Liam, remember?"

"Is that why I found him climbing out of the dumpster?"

Haley couldn't help but smile. "What can I say? Liam finally found where he belongs."

"Good girl, Brooke," her mother added.

Haley wasn't sure if her mother knew what she was saying, but she liked it.

Kim rocked her weight onto one hip. "I don't think it's good to encourage her, Mrs. Carter." She glared at both of them through a double layer of mascara. It was amazing how she could give an entire lecture with one look.

"If it's any consolation," Haley said, "the whole thing was an accident."

"Is that your story?" Kim started pacing back and forth in the tiny room. "I was walking across the parking lot when suddenly the lid to the dumpster flies open. Do you know what goes through a woman's mind at a moment like that? Slasher movies, that's what. Then Liam pops up like a possessed jack-in-the-box." Kim grabbed at the front of her blouse as if to demonstrate the heart attack she'd had. "He told me *you* pushed him in."

Haley's mouth twitched. "He always did give me more credit than I deserved. But really, it was an accident. I didn't mean for him to fall in. But I swear, if Liam comes back, I *will* push him in."

"That will never happen. I called Joe from the city, and he's getting rid of the dumpster."

Haley stood up. "No way! Where are we supposed to put our trash?"

"If you're referring to Liam, he's not trash." Kim walked to the wall-mounted sanitizer dispenser and pumped two squirts into her hand as if all this talk about garbage had tainted her. "I told Joe to bring out a few city garbage cans for our building. He owed me a favor anyway, and I hated that stinking dumpster."

Haley rubbed her forehead. "Why does it seem like everyone in this town owes you a favor?"

"Because I work it that way, and since I smoothed things over with Liam, you owe me a favor too."

"Brooke, is it getting dark in here?" Her mother squinted up at the lights.

"No, Mom." Haley put a reassuring hand on her shoulder. Hopefully, she wasn't paying attention to the conversation. She didn't want her getting confused or upset.

"No one asked you to smooth things over," Haley said to Kim, her voice lowering to a whisper. "Liam fell in all on his own. I only shoved the bin because he was being creepy. Like crazy stalker kind of creepy."

Kim shook her head. "I can't believe how you're acting. It's more than you shoving Liam into the dumpster." She dropped her voice to barely a whisper. "Are you sure you're not turning into your dad?"

Every muscle in Haley's body tensed. Her eyes darted to her mother, making sure she hadn't heard. Luckily, she hadn't. "That's not fair." That was all she said.

She wasn't going to discuss what it was really like to be shoved in a bin. As a child, her regular punishments for any minor infraction was being confined to the broom closet in the basement for hours at a time. Her longest lockup had lasted thirty-two hours. No food or water, sitting on a cold cement floor with no room to move. That was being locked up. Her brother broke curfew by an hour one night and spent the next three days in the closet. Okay, maybe he had been out getting stoned with his friends, but the beating he got, plus three days in lockdown wasn't the right punishment. Haley had slid handfuls of ice chips and some Jolly Ranchers under the door to him.

Kim glared at her but must have known better than to carry on the conversation in front of present company. She leaned over, meeting Mrs. Carter's confused, watery gaze. "Would you like to go into the dining room? When I came in there was a group of kids getting ready to sing. They're the Musical Majors, and I hear they put on a good program."

Her mother lifted her head. "I like singing."

"Good." Kim helped her to her feet and patiently walked her into the hallway.

Haley stared at her mother's rubber-soled slippers scuffing along the plastic tiles. Her vision blurred and her chest grew tight. Her mother was too young to shuffle like that. Brain damage could do that though.

Out in the hall, Kim flagged down a nurse—a male nurse.

"Oh, no." Haley ran out, but it was too late. Her mother was already whining, cowering against the wall, trying to get away.

"Sorry," the nurse said, backing up. "I usually try not to get too close to her."

Haley nodded. It wasn't his fault. Her mother had that reaction with all men. "It's all right, Mom." She wrapped her arms around her mother's shoulders, attempting to calm her. She tried to pull away, but Haley gathered her into a warm embrace until she began to relax. Cindy hurried down the hall to help.

"I'll take her to the dining room." She took Mrs. Carter's hand. "Come on, you know me. Let's go watch the kids sing."

As soon as they were gone, Kim stepped back inside the room and waited for Haley to join her. "Sorry about that. I wasn't thinking." Kim rolled her eyes up to the ceiling. "Now where were we?" Her posture grew rigid. "I'm just trying to help you, Haley. And as far as Liam goes, I know he's not perfect, but he's the only guy you've ever dated—your one and only attempt at having a normal relationship. I really didn't want you to lose that."

Kim folded her arms and continued. "Someday you'll have to take a leap of faith and trust a guy, but, now that I think about it, maybe you're not ready for that. Maybe you're more like your mom, at least you share the same aversion." Her eyes drifted to the hallway.

"I get it." Haley threw her hands in the air. "This is just another way of saying I'm socially broken."

"You're the one who seems determined to push people away. I guess was wrong about expecting you to date, and we should just leave well enough alone until you can behave yourself."

The words stung. Haley had gone through therapy after the *accident*. Her counselor had tried to help her reconnect socially. Even now Haley was resolved to try harder at building friendships, but it sounded like Kim expected her to *stay* broken.

She shrugged a shoulder like it didn't bother her. "I can be single for the rest of my life and still be happy. History is dotted with single women. Look at Joan of Arc."

Kim's face went deadpan. "Joan of Arc was burned at the stake."

That wasn't the effect Haley was going for. "It doesn't matter.

The point is I'm fine by myself. I don't need anyone, especially a man."

Kim rested a hand on the serving cart, then thought better of it and had to pump another squirt of sanitizer onto her palm. "Sorry I tried to persuade you to get back together with Liam. But I think you're right. You should hold off on falling in love."

Finally, Kim was seeing things her way. At least she wouldn't be so pushy.

Someone sped past the door. Haley barely caught a glimpse of him and was pretty sure it was Jake going to visit his Grandma Hunt who happened to be in the room two doors down from her mother's. Haley knew because she'd checked that morning before going to work. She even stopped in and said hello. But that was quite literally all she said before she got nervous and left. Mrs. Hunt had probably thought she was one of the nurses.

"That's it then?" Kim asked. "No guys until you learn to play nice?"

Haley nodded. "I'm a no-guy gal."

"Alright. I guess this is for the best. No more dates, no more flowers being blended to a pulp, no more dumpsters."

Haley tipped her head in agreement. "My only goal is to do my job and stay alive so I can pay for all of this." She waved a hand, gesturing to the room.

Soft footsteps sounded down the hall. "Hold onto me; I don't want to fall." The sweet elderly voice grew closer.

"Don't worry. I've got you."

That was Jake's voice. Haley stood back in the shadows, waiting for them to pass by, but unwilling to let him see her. She felt too guilty about how she had treated him at work after he had double bolted the roof for her. He was probably still mad at her anyway.

"Come on." Grandma Hunt's voice was closer now. "We're going *too* slow. At this rate, I'll miss the music program."

Haley's lips pulled to the side in an amused smirk. It sounded like Grandma Hunt had some sass. The two figures passed in front of the door, Jake's arm wrapped around the stooped, frail figure of his grandma. They came, they went. Jake never looked into the room, but his image burned itself into Haley's mind. The way he held his grandmother's arm, gentle and caring. The way he kept his attention on her. The way he patiently moved, his slow steps guiding hers. Haley was taken aback by it. She wanted to hold onto the moment, to find a special place in her mind and store it, so whenever she doubted the goodness of men, she could pull it out and remember.

"Let's go," Kim said, pulling her from her thoughts. "We can forget about Liam and go home and celebrate your nunhood."

"Fine. You're buying ice cream then." Kim shot her a look then rolled her eyes which meant she would comply. Haley should've held out for more. Nunhood should at least deserve chocolate too.

CHAPTER 20

The air was cold. Haley pulled the collar of her jacket up and tucked her chin into it as she hunkered down in the back of the mantrip. It was always cold coming out of the mine. Going in wasn't so bad, but coming out meant going against the airflow. It mirrored her life. She was going against the flow, and that's why the men treated her so coldly. She wouldn't complain though. Today hadn't been so bad. Of course, her Unsafe Work report was posted that morning—even though Moose's accident report wasn't there yet—but beyond that, the day was pretty good. Except for the part where she nearly starved.

Someone got in her lunch box again and ate all her food. She had even kept the box with her while she worked, but someone still managed to get in it without her seeing. But she had come prepared. She had stashed some cheese sticks and jerky in the pocket of her jacket which saved her from starving. All in all, not a bad day.

Wing Nut and Shark sat next to her, talking. For once, it wasn't a lewd conversation, but they seemed determined to keep her out of it nonetheless. Every now and then, Stump looked at her, his eyebrows gathered together in an apologetic look. She appreciated the gesture, but she really didn't mind being left out.

At last, they pulled into the parking lot. Before the truck had even come to a complete stop, the men piled out.

"That scab's gonna peel off any day now," Leech called. "I can feel it."

Jake walked toward her from the men's bathhouse giving Leech a sidelong look as he passed. He was already showered and wearing his street clothes, which meant he must have some place to go. He usually wasn't that quick to get out of the mine.

He stopped when he reached Haley. His eyes still had a slight black outline to them—the telltale sign of a miner. It was hard to get the coal dust out from between the eyelashes, but Haley just considered it her own version of permanent eyeliner. It didn't look bad on Jake either. She mentally chided herself for the thought.

"Are they still giving you a hard time?" he asked.

"Should I expect anything less? I *am* the only orange-hat on their crew."

Jake gave a stiff nod and turned to leave.

A twinge of guilt shot through her. Maybe he was in a hurry, but maybe he was upset with how she had treated him.

"I'm sorry," she called after him. "For being so rude yesterday. I really did appreciate you thinking of me. I mean . . . not that you think about me, but you did think about my safety. You know . . . the roof bolts?" She stopped. The more she talked, the more she sounded incapable of coherent speech. She should just hang a handicap sign on her lips.

Jake's expression didn't change. "You're welcome. But next time I try to help you out, I expect you to pay."

"What do you mean?" she asked.

"I hear that's our deal. I'm nice to you and you pay up with some lasagna or something."

Haley blanched. "I'm sorry. I only said that so the guys wouldn't tease me."

"I get it." He tipped his head down to look at her. "I know how bad it can be. And anyone who's different gets the worst of it."

Haley tapped her new plastic lunch box against her knee. She would always be different, so did that mean she was doomed to mistreatment for as long as she worked underground? Would she be relegated to packing her lunch in her pocket for the next year? Always doomed to be a scab—whatever that was.

"Can you tell me something?" She waited for his nod. "There's an inside joke going around, and I seem to be left out of the loop. What exactly is a scab?"

Jake's eyes darted away momentarily as if ashamed. "A temporary worker," he finally said. "In the old days when the miners would go on strike, the mine owners would round up farmers and other inexperienced men to cover the work. They were called scabs."

Haley nodded. So that's what she was—someone unfamiliar and unqualified for the job, and they didn't expect her to last long.

Jake gave her a friendly nudge. "Look at the bright side. At least the blue is starting to wear off."

There was a slight pull at the corner of his lips. She anticipated more, hoping for the signature smile. She wanted to see how it lit up his face and radiated happiness, but it wasn't to happen today. She rubbed the back of her hand where only a slight blue tint remained. She had stuck to a three-showers-a-day routine to get it this far. "It's still not wearing off quick enough."

"Yeah, that was a mean prank. Miners can get carried away sometimes."

He reached into the breast pocket of his shirt and pulled out a pen and a business card. The other miners didn't carry pens in their pockets. She didn't mind the touch of nerdiness though. She kind of liked it.

He wrote something on the back of the card and handed it to her. "If the teasing gets too bad, or if you just need to talk, give me a call. No lasagna required."

Haley looked at the number. It was written in small neat handwriting. She flipped the card over. "Southeast Paint?" She knew the local business; it was only a block from her apartment.

"I helped my parents paint their house a couple weeks ago, and that's where we bought supplies."

Haley flicked the corner of the card with her fingernail. The thought that he still might be living with his parents popped in her head, but she quickly dismissed it. For some reason, she didn't want to think of him as the perpetual live-in, the guy that took over his mom's basement and stayed up all night playing online games. Just thinking about it felt like she was betraying him.

"Well, thanks." She wasn't sure what else to say. Jake had just given her his phone number, and she could feel the heat creeping into her cheeks. She ducked her head to hide it. "I guess I better go tag out."

It's nothing, she thought as she marched off to the lamp-house. She looked down at the card. "It's nothing more than it seems. If the teasing gets too bad—, I call him." She shook her head. It was never going to get that bad. Whatever they dished out, she could handle on her own.

Just as she stepped into the lamp-house, Bear waved her over to the notice board. He slid an arm around her shoulder as if they were old friends, but it felt more like a snake about to strangle her than a gesture of friendship. She tried to keep her groan inaudible.

He tapped his knuckle on the Unsafe Work Observation report as if she hadn't seen it hanging there earlier.

"See this?" He didn't wait for a reply. "It's no secret I don't like you, but let me be honest. If I ever sign off on another report with your name on it, I'm going to put in a complaint to Mr. Branch. And that will be enough to put you back in the warehouse." His brow rose as if that would take the ridicule out of his words. "It's no fault of your own. I'm just old and comfortable with my regular crew where I can break quota every day. I don't need a pumpkin head who can't lift her own weight slowing us down and distracting my boys." He paused. "Oh, and by the way, the same goes for any injury. The first scratch you get that so much as requires a Band-Aid, you're gone."

Haley wanted to tell him that he'd have to fake another report if that were going to happen. She wanted to pull out from under his arm and tell him how stupid his new hard hat looked. But she didn't. Instead, she stood there, trying her best to rein in her thoughts. Bear's threat didn't matter anyway. It wasn't anything new.

Finally, he left, and she walked to the other side of the room and tagged out. *Be tough*, she thought as she pushed the numb feeling away. Their threats couldn't get to her. Despite her inner pep talk, her shoulders slumped. She could do this, but for today—today, she was done.

When she walked outside, Bear was standing with a group of men by the bath house, and she couldn't bring herself to walk past them. In fact, it seemed like the perfect time to veer across the parking lot. It didn't matter how dirty she was; she wasn't sticking around any longer. She walked to her car, snatched the spare key taped behind her license plate, and drove to the care center.

"Mrs. Frackle," Haley said as she entered her mother's room. The therapist was madly typing on a mini laptop. "I didn't know you'd still be here."

She looked at her mother's schedule taped next to the door. Apparently, their session started at three which meant it had lasted over two hours. It was going to be pricey. "How's Mom doing?"

Mrs. Frackle looked up at the clock and made a note. "We've made some good progress . . ." Her words trailed off. She brushed a gray curl away from her eyes and squinted. "My dear, are you sick? You don't look well."

Haley brushed at her coveralls then grabbed several tissues from her mother's bedside table and wiped her face and hands. "Sorry. It's just coal dust. I left work in a hurry, and I haven't showered yet."

"I see. But below the coal dust, you look a little green—"

"Blue, actually."

"Brooke, is that you?"

Haley bent down and kissed her mother's cheek. "It's me, Mom. Haley. Remember?"

"She's doing much better." Mrs. Frackle shut her laptop then piled some papers on top of it. "In fact, we've talked about several events that happened before the accident. She even reminisced about your ninth grade school play."

Haley's heart leaped in her chest. "She really talked about me? I'm the only one that took drama, so I guess she does remember . . ."

A shadow crossed Mrs. Frackle's face. "Well, it was definitely about your play. She talked about how cute it was when you forgot your lines." She paused and then lowered her voice to a whisper. "But she still referred to you as your sister, Brooke."

It was a crushing blow. Haley took her mother's face in her hands and looked into her watery eyes. "Come on, I need you. Please. It's okay to remember."

"I am, sweetheart. I remember everything." She leaned back and stared at Haley. "You're filthy, dear. Did you just climb out of a dust bin?"

"I came from the mine. I told you I was working underground."

Her mother lifted a hand, touching her parted lips in surprise. "But I don't want you to be in the dark."

Haley stared at her. Was she really referring to her? Was she subtly admitting to the times Haley had been locked away in the closet, and now she didn't want her in the mine because of the similarities? Maybe that was part of the reason Haley took the job in the first place. The mine was a dark space she could take control of. She wasn't completely helpless there. Unlike the closet at home where the confines were so tight her elbows bumped the walls, the mine offered her a chance to conquer that part of her past.

"I'm not afraid of the dark, Mom."

"I know, Brooke, but I am. Now be a good girl and open the curtains."

Mrs. Frackle looked at the open curtains then jotted down a note. "It's taking time, but we *are* going in the right direction." She stood up and walked to the doorway then motioned for Haley to join her. "Discussing your ninth grade play is a huge breakthrough, even if she is still calling you Brooke. She's not ready to remember the trauma of that night and admit that you witnessed it. Understand, she has a lot of shame attached to it."

Mrs. Frackle let her eyes drift over to Haley's mother. "On a different note, I've been doing our sessions here at the care center because your mother's insurance paid for it that way, but now that you're taking on the expense yourself, would you like me to start seeing her in my office? It will save you thirty dollars a session."

Haley nodded. "Yes. And thank you for bringing that to my attention."

"That's what I'm here for. I want to help. I already talked to nurse Cindy." She leaned in to whisper. "She said you'd appreciate the savings because she thinks you'll be quitting your job before long. So I want to help any way I can."

Haley nodded. "I appreciate it. And don't concern yourself about my job. It's going fine. In fact, things couldn't be better."

CHAPTER 21

Haley opened the door to her apartment and instantly knew something was wrong.

The room was unnaturally cool. A breeze rushed over her, ruffling her hair, and her eyes went to the broken window then shot back to the lump of coal that lay in the middle of the floor. It was only the size of a softball, but it loomed before her, dominating the entire space.

Haley let out a series of short breaths to calm herself. She'd experienced anxiety attacks before. She stepped further into the room, glass crunching underfoot, unable to take her eyes off of the menacing black rock. There were dozens of people who didn't approve of her working underground, but who would go this far? It was one thing to tease and prank her at work, but in her own home?

Someone had broken into the apartment before, but they had left chocolates—okay, it was chocolates with a threat, but that was still far cry from coal through a window. This . . . this went beyond joking. This was personal. Someone had crossed the line into pure malicious harassment. She dropped her lunch box on the floor and walked around the room.

She stared at the lump of coal for a long time. When she finally went to pick it up, a shard of glass pierced her finger. She pulled back and looked at the wound. Blood seeped out of the cut, but she pushed the pain away and grabbed the coal to examine it. There wasn't a note attached, but she understood the message perfectly. *Scabs don't last long. Quit while you can.* The threats were growing more personal and more violent. But was it worth quitting her job over? She still wanted to prove herself, and she also needed the money. But if she stayed on, what would she be risking?

* * *

Haley rushed into the parking lot as Kim climbed out of her silver Toyota. "I need to tell you something before you go into the apartment."

Kim looked at Haley's dirty clothes and wrinkled her nose. "What? That you've decided to quit showering in protest?"

"No." Haley glanced at the building. "I'm talking about a *big* mess."

Kim walked around her. "I know all about it."

"You do?" Haley followed her inside.

Kim paused at the top of the stairs. "Yes. When Liam comes to my office and talks to me for an hour, pining on about you, I'd say that's a big mess."

Haley stared at her. "But I'm talking about the window."

Kim flipped the hair out of her eyes. "And I'm talking about Liam. Apparently putting him in the dumpster didn't scare him off. He still wants to be with you. But don't worry, I did my best to convince him to leave you alone. I even offered to take him out myself—anything to stop him from making a fool of himself."

Kim opened the door. "Wait!" Haley tried to block her, but Kim pushed past.

"I'm telling you, you have got some serious . . . " Kim stopped and stared at the broken window. "Problems."

"I tried to tell you."

"What happened?"

"Someone threw a chunk of coal through the window." Haley bent down and started picking up the larger shards of glass. "I'll clean it up right now."

"Coal? Haley, this is a hate crime. Did you call the police?"

"I did. That's why the mess is still here. An officer just left. He

~ 133 ~

took the coal with him and said he'd look into it."

Kim walked around the room, wringing her hands. "What are the police going to do? The list of suspects will include half the people at P.C. Mine."

"And I got the impression the officer doesn't want to put much effort into it. The miners are always playing pranks on each other."

"This goes way beyond a work-related joke." Kim held her hands out. "Has anything like this happened to the other orange-hats?"

"Probably not, but it's only natural I'd be taunted more—"

"Seriously, Haley. I get that you're the only woman working underground there, but this is beyond ridiculous." Kim grabbed an old phone book that had been sitting in her magazine rack and thumbed through it. A moment later she punched a number into her phone and handed it to Haley.

Haley hesitated. She hated how presumptuous Kim was. "Who am I supposed to be taking to?" She held the phone out, staring at it.

"It's Becky Hill. She works underground at Lila Canyon. Talk to her; she might have some insight."

Haley pressed the phone to her ear. It rang several times then Becky's voice sounded on the other end. "Hello?" She sounded sweet. Not like a coal miner.

"Hi, Becky. This is Haley Carter. I don't think we've ever met, but I work underground at P.C. Mine, and I was wondering if you could give me some advice."

"Sure. I heard P.C. hired a woman miner. You're working in the CM section, aren't you?"

"Yes."

"How are you liking it?"

"Umm... I'm having a few issues." Haley explained her predicament about how the men had been treating her. Becky listened quietly. She probably sensed Haley's uneasiness, but she was patient. Haley finished by telling her about the coal thrown through her window. "Is this normal? I mean just because I'm a woman and because I'm an orange-hat—"

"No," Becky cut in, her voice tight with concern. "That's not normal. Nothing that bad has ever happened to me. The guys I work with are pretty decent. I mean they have their moments, and I've endured some teasing, but *nothing* like that. I guess, for me, it's like any other job. Good and bad, you know? I make no overtures to the men, and they make none to me. I choose to work in the mine, so I deal with what comes with it, but for me, it's been different."

Haley sighed. "I wish I could say the same. I wouldn't complain, but considering what happened—"

"Yeah, I'd definitely talk to someone about the coal. There are a still some male chauvinists out there, and it sounds like you found one. But all miners aren't like that. They do stick together though. Kind of like follow the leader."

That's what Haley worried about. And the leader, in this case, was Bear.

"It's really not a bad job if you can stand the environment," Becky continued. "What you need to do is talk to your crew boss, and if that doesn't go anywhere, then talk to Mr. Branch. He should put a stop to it."

Haley thanked Becky then ended the call.

"Well?" Kim asked. "What'd she say?"

"That I'm toast." Haley's eyes drifted to the broken window.

Kim waved a hand in front of her. "Did she give you any advice on how to handle it?"

"She said to talk to Mr. Branch, but the mine doesn't want any more problems dealing with me. It'll just prove that I'm more of a liability for them, and they'll put me back in the warehouse."

"Then don't bring it up with Mr. Branch. Isn't there someone else you can talk to?"

Haley pulled the Southeaster Paint business card out of her pocket and turned it over to look at Jake's number. A small pocket of excitement stirred inside her. She wanted to call him—which was exactly why she shouldn't. She stuffed the card back into her pocket. It was too tempting, and she needed to guard herself.

"You better pick someone to talk to about it, or I will." Kim pulled out the vacuum and plugged it in.

"Alright. I think I know someone that might help. At least I think so."

"Good. Who is it?"

Haley buried the emotions that were all tied up around thoughts of Jake. "It's . . . um . . . Mitch," she finally said. "I think he used to be a coal miner. He might be able to give me some advice."

"Good idea. And he didn't just work at a coal mine—he owned one."

Haley stared at her. "He used to own a mine? I thought that kind of thing made you rich. How did he end up like he is?"

Kim shrugged. "Why don't you ask him?"

With that, the vacuum roared to life and began to devour the remains of Haley's hate crime.

CHAPTER 22

Haley adjusted the load in her arms and knocked on the door. She had to knock two more times before Mitch answered. She held out two loaded grocery sacks to him, but he just looked at them skeptically. "What's that?"

"I picked some things up at the store for you." Haley held the sacks out further. "Some food, a new pair of pants, and a shirt. I'm pretty sure they'll fit—"

"I don't need your charity." Mitch started to close the door, but Haley stuck her foot in the way.

"It's not charity. It's an exchange."

He eyed one of the bags. A box of Hostess donuts stuck out the top and the rest of the sack bulged with frozen pizzas. He rubbed the stubble on his chin. "Exchange for what?"

"Some advice."

"I already told Kim. I didn't put any gift bag into your apartment. I never saw anyone. I don't know how it got there."

Haley nodded. "And that's why I *really* need your advice."

He looked at the bags. "And what if my two cents ain't worth taking?"

"You'll get to keep the stuff anyway."

His eyes ogled both bags now. Finally, he nodded and stepped aside, motioning for her to come in. "Have a seat." He took the sacks into the kitchen and began to unload his plunder.

Haley looked around. Nothing had changed since the last time she'd been there. She pushed the pile of clothes to the side of the couch and sat down.

"What kind of advice do you want?" Mitch held a gooey donut up one up with his nicotine-stained fingers. "Want one?" He looked relieved when she shook her head.

"I'm having some issues at the mine."

Mitch put the donut down and slowly pushed it away from him. "I don't know anything about mining." He walked into the front room shaking his head. "I can't help you. Sorry if you're disappointed, but you made the deal, not me. I get to keep the stuff, and now you get to leave."

Leaving wasn't an option. Haley didn't spend her hard earned money on him only to be kicked out before she had even explained the situation. She leaned back on the couch and rested her arm on top of the pile of clothes as if she were settling in for a long movie at a friend's house. She wanted to appear confident, but really, she was just hoping there weren't any cockroaches hiding in the pile of laundry.

"There's another sack in the hallway," she said.

Mitch walked to the door and looked out. A moment later he stepped back in, holding it in his hand. This one had brownies and a variety of frozen Banquet dinners—the insurance policy she'd purchased.

"That sack comes with its own price," Haley said.

The eager look on Mitch's face fell. "What price?"

"Honesty."

Mitch's jaw tightened as he agonized over the new deal. She really did want his advice, which was why she'd gone to the effort to bribe him. Besides, after she had seen his apartment, she knew he could use the help. If she could get him to talk, it'd be worth the cheap meals and the trip she took to the sale rack in the men's department.

Mitch stuck his hand in the sack and looked through the contents. He must have found something he liked because he began to rub his chin greedily.

"All right. I'll give you ten minutes of honesty, and then we're done."

"Fair enough." Haley gladly removed her arm from his clothes pile and explained the ruthless taunting going on at the mine and how it had followed her home. "I'm hoping it doesn't escalate into something even more violent. This is completely unheard of, right? I mean it's not common for men to do this kind of stuff outside of the mine, to threaten others at home."

"Yes, and no." Mitch plopped himself down in the stained La-Z-Boy and looked longingly at the ashtray on the side table. "It could escalate. It all depends on how deep this problem goes. The coal industry has a lot riding on it, so miners have a way of taking things to the extreme. Look at the Molly Maguires. They were a secret group of miners who used terrorist tactics to get what they wanted. In the end, twenty men were hanged. And look at Ludlow. That problem escalated until forty were dead, including women and children."

Haley slumped back on the couch. "Yeah, but those things happened forever ago. Miners don't do things like that in this day and age."

Mitch raised an eyebrow. "Oh? You don't think so? You think miners have somehow lost their spine over the years? That they don't push for what they want or for how they think things should be? You're talking about an industry that has the power to sway a presidential election. And you can bet those dynamics trickle down into each individual miner."

Mitch shook a finger at her and continued. "Most men in this country don't even have what it takes to work underground. They don't have the nerve. But, you take the men here in Carbon County, mining is their way of life. They belong to secret society. They're tough, and they've got each other's backs. Don't think for one minute that they're going to let you come into their world and disrupt their secret pack without putting you to the test. And they'll take things as far as they want to make their point."

"And how do I get the pranks to stop?"

"It's a coal mine, honey, they never stop. That's like telling a comedian to stop telling jokes."

"Okay, then how do I get into their secret society?"

Mitch picked at a loose thread on the edge of his armchair. "It's like being jumped into a gang. If you survive, you're in. You've got to prove yourself. And with you being a girl, you've got more to prove. With luck, this problem only goes as deep as gender politics, and hopefully, no one has anything else against you."

"Besides me being a woman, I can't think of anything that would make them hate me. And I've been trying to prove myself. I'm pulling my own weight down there, so how long is it going to take for them to accept me?"

Mitch shrugged.

"So that's it?" Haley stood up and shoved her hands in her back pockets. "You're telling me that things could continue to escalate, and I'm supposed to keep taking it?"

"Not necessarily. From a business standpoint, the mine is supposed to keep a cap on that type of misbehavior. If you bring a complaint up against someone, it's a good chance you can get him fired. That will make the men hate you more, but they'll leave you alone. All you have to do is talk to your shift boss. That's Bear, isn't it?"

Haley nodded.

"Just tell him what's going on and who you suspect is doing it."

Haley kicked at a dirty sock lying under the coffee table. "And what if I suspect that Bear is one of the guys behind it?"

There was a long pause as Mitch pressed his lips together like a vice.

"You know Bear, don't you?" Haley asked.

He leaned forward in his chair and locked his eyes on her. "Yes, I know him. So my advice to you is—watch your back because things might get a lot worse from here."

CHAPTER 23

A robot. That's what Haley tried to become. Nothing more than a robot. No emotions, just a working machine. She showed up at the mine, still sore from the day before, she did the work, she went home. Nothing else. She only talked to the men on the crew if they addressed her first, and even then, sometimes she didn't respond. She lost ten pounds, and her muscles grew harder. Kim said she was starting to look like a supermodel, but Haley knew better. Coal mines didn't turn out supermodels, they turned out hard, callous men. And she was becoming one of them.

For the most part, she grew immune to their teasing. But some things still got under her skin—like the blatant mistreatment of her lunches.

Tuesday

After four hours of work, Haley was starving. She sat on the ground and opened the small metal toolbox with its lift-out tray. She had used her regular lunch box as a decoy, while the toolbox hid her real stash. She removed the top section of tools then gasped when she found the lower compartment empty. There wasn't so much as a crumb. Sneaky coal miners! How did they do it?

"Lost your tools?" Wing Nut asked as he walked by. He peered over her shoulder into the vacant box.

She nodded then pulled some jerky sticks from her pocket. Tomorrow she'd up her game.

Wednesday

Haley nestled her small plastic lunch box under the passenger seat of the belt crew's mantrip. No one had emerged from the lamphouse yet, but she still looked around to make sure no one was watching. Once the box was hidden, she went to the other truck. Come lunch time, she would have to take a short walk over to the belt line, but at least the lunch thief wouldn't think to look there.

Four hours later, Haley stared at the remaining shards of her plastic lunch box. She didn't have to walk to the belt line after all. Someone had saved her the trouble and had brought it to her. The shuttle car was still parked on top of it. She sat down and pulled the jerky out of her pocket. Oh yes, they were good. But she was better. Just wait until tomorrow!

Thursday

Haley set the small fireproof safe on top of the transformer. She pulled a chain through the newly made hole then fished it through the safe's handle and padlocked it. There was a possibility she'd get in trouble for drilling a hole in the edge of the transformer, but it would be worth it. She picked up the industrial strength drill she had used and pulled the trigger, revving the motor. "Try to get into it now, boys."

Four hours later: Haley stared at the roof. "You've got to be kidding me."

She should've remembered that the warehouse issued bolt cutters which could easily cut through a padlock. But this? It was a fireproof safe for heaven's sake. Was nothing indestructible?

She pulled the jerky from her pocket, but couldn't take her light away from where the fireproof safe was now roof bolted to the ceiling above her. This one was going to be hard to top.

Friday

It wasn't that Haley was a bad welder, just inexperienced. Granted her bead wasn't the smoothest. Okay, it actually looked like drops of metal boogers, but it would hold. She stood back and admired her work. Her new metal lunch box, which was technically a small safe for a handgun complete with a built-in combination lock was now welded solid to a graffiti-covered generator. It wasn't going anywhere.

Four hours later Haley stared at the small gun safe.

Stump had helped her that morning by measuring the gas with a multi-meter, letting her know that the readings were within the standards that OSHA had set. Then he had rock-dusted the area and had stood by with the fire extinguisher—all of which allowed her to weld in the mine. Apparently, the same precautions made it safe to use a torch as well. Her lunch box was still welded to the generator, but only half of it remained. The top was completely gone.

She took some jerky sticks from her pocket and picked up the slip of paper left in the safe. It was a page from an operator's manual, and someone had used a paint marker to write across it.

Too late scab. You should've quit while you could.

She contemplated the new threat as she finished her jerky. Eating pocket snacks every day was getting old, and she had spent a lot of money on lunch containers. If this kept up much longer, she would have to keep an eye on the help wanted ads.

A dark figure rounded the corner. Her light reflected off the silver stripes on his jacket just before his face came into view. It was Bear.

"Shark's got the flu and has been puking all morning. I had to send him top side. That means I'm short a man. I'm putting Leech on the miner and you're going to be his helper."

Haley followed Bear back to where the other men were finishing up their lunches. Leech opened a small cooler and pulled out several bottles of pop. "The Coke man gave these to me when he was fillin' up the vending machine yesterday."

He tossed a bottle to Bear and then preceded to hand the rest out to the other men. His eyes roamed over Haley—not in a greedy, lusting way, but in a cruel, scrutinizing-every-flaw kind of way. "I guess the scab needs one too."

He pulled another Coke bottle out and tossed it to her.

Haley caught it, her mouth dropping open in disbelief. Was

Leech actually attempting to be nice? It didn't make sense. He and Bear were her top two suspects for stealing her lunches and leaving the threatening notes. The only thing she hadn't determined was if Bear was giving Leech the orders or if Leech was the mastermind and Bear was just enjoying the show.

She sat the Coke down next to her SCSR bag. "You should drink it," Leech said. "I'm gonna work ya hard, and you'll need the caffeine."

She was thirsty, but she wouldn't give him the satisfaction. "Don't worry about me. I'm ready when you are."

Bear slapped his knee. "All right boys, you heard the scab. She says she's ready, so . . . Get to work!"

The men groaned and put away their lunches then headed off in different directions. A minute later, the continuous miner roared to life. The beast-like mining machine drank its life source through a large cable that ran from the transformer. Leech squatted off to the side of the cut with a control box balanced on his knee, directing the large vehicle by remote. Haley's job was to watch the cable and pull it out of the way whenever Leech had to back up, making way for the roof bolters to go in and pin up the roof.

It wasn't an easy job, but she was beginning to learn that nothing was easy in the mine. The cable was so thick she could barely get her hands around it, and it was heavy. As big as it was, it could still get tangled. Within the first fifteen minutes, it twisted into a knot which shortened its reach length. When Leech pushed the miner forward, the power cut off.

"What happened, Scab?" His voice bellowed through the darkness. Haley was already doing her best to fix it.

She pulled the cable out in a line and dropped it back on the ground. "That should take care of it."

"Nope! I still don't have power!"

Haley ran alongside the massive cord, examining it as she went. When she reached the transformer, she found the head had been pulled out. Luckily, the prongs weren't bent, and she shoved it back in and heard the miner roar to life. Dodging an oncoming shuttle car, she ran back to her post.

Leech was pushing the machine further into the cut and her job was to follow, but she could only go so far. The roof wasn't bolted where the miner was, and she had been told to stay at least two bolts back from any unsupported top. Leech kept cutting in further. She waited for him to stop. The shuttle car eased in behind the miner until it was full. A moment later, it roared past her as it went to deliver its load to the feeder near the belt line.

Leech continued moving the miner far beyond where the last bolts were as if daring her to go into the unsupported area. Haley took a couple of awkward steps forward, keeping her eye on the roof. She looked over at Leech, but he just stared back, his eyes full of venom. A rancorous smile pulled at his mouth. He didn't say anything, but she could imagine his thoughts—*Go ahead, Scab. I dare you.*

But she didn't dare. She wasn't going to do this anymore. Leech could watch his own cable. She turned and walked away but had only gone a few steps when she heard the electric motor whine. When she looked over her shoulder, the monstrous machine was charging toward her. She leaped out of the way just as it plowed into the rib next to her. Her helmet went flying and her head knocked hard against the wall. Pain shot through the back of her skull, and she crumpled to the ground. The miner moved away, and part of the wall sloughed down next to her.

"Sorry about that, Scab!" Leech called over the noise. "I guess it got away from me. Must be your lucky day, and to make it up to you, I won't even tell Bear about this. Wouldn't want you to have to fill out another report."

Haley found her helmet and gingerly placed it back on her injured head and walked past him.

"Where you going?"

"Bathroom."

Leech laughed. "Yeah, you probably need to change your pants after that scare."

Wet, sticky blood was running down her neck by the time she reached the porta-potty. Luckily there was half a roll of toilet paper there. She pulled the cardboard tube out of the center and pressed the whole wad of paper against the gash in her head. After a few minutes, she moved off into the darkness. What was it—three hours until the end of the shift? She couldn't finish working with an injury like this, but she wasn't about to tell anyone about it either. Bear said one scratch and she'd be back in the warehouse.

What she needed to do was to hide out and keep pressure on her wound. Sneaking off during a shift wasn't unheard of. Stump had told her about a guy who was notorious for hiding and taking naps. She walked to the nearest door leading to the bleeder section and went through it. The air grew hot and stale around her, but at least no one would find her. She sat down and held the makeshift bandage on her head.

Bear didn't say anything to her when she showed back up just in time to climb into the mantrip. He was arguing with Wing Nut about the roof bolter and hardly even glanced at her. That was good. Maybe she'd keep her job after all. Eventually, if things didn't get better, she'd consider quitting, but she wouldn't be bullied away. If she was going to leave, she'd do it on her own terms.

She sat in the back of the truck and carefully balanced her helmet on her head, concealing the wad of toilet paper which was plastered to her blood-soaked hair. The road out of the mine wasn't smooth, and after a few minutes, the makeshift bandage dislodged under her hat, and a new trickle of blood made its way down Haley's neck. Stinging pain pulsed around the injury with every bump.

"Does someone have any pain reliever?" she asked.

Leech was in the cab, so it was a safe enough question to ask without being teased.

Stump finally nodded. "Like I told you before, you can't work down here without hurtin'."

"It's nothing. Just a headache."

Stump pulled a small pouch from his jacket and handed it to her. It was one of the over-the-counter medication packets that were readily available in the Lamp house.

"Thanks." Haley looked at the familiar ibuprofen label. She

wanted something stronger, but this would have to do. She downed the pills with the Coke Leech had given her earlier, and slowly sipped the bottle dry while the mantrip made its way to the surface.

At last, the men piled out. Leech climbed out and leaned against the truck. His eyes narrowed as if he were studying her. Then he grabbed the empty Coke bottle from her hand and thumped it on her helmet. Her head seemed to explode. "You finally drank the Coke and didn't even give me so much as a thanks." He thumped her with it again then hurried away.

Haley followed, but her head started throbbing. Her movements seemed slow and awkward as if she didn't have any balance. She stumbled to the lamp-house and went directly to the tag-out board. It took her a moment to focus well enough to find her name and flip the magnet to the white side.

She unhooked her lamp, without removing her helmet, and tried to place it on the charger. It took three tries before she got it. Her eyes blurred and her head spun. Something was definitely wrong. She didn't think her head injury had been that bad. It had happened hours ago, and she hadn't felt dizzy until recently. Why was she having such a delayed reaction?

She stumbled outside and made her way into the bathhouse. The room seemed to turn around her. She sat on the bench for a minute, but the dizziness intensified. Laying down would be better; she needed to get home, now. She opened her locker, grabbed her cell phone and keys, and made her way outside to the parking lot.

Trying to keep the ground under her feet, she leaned against the door of her car. This was bad. She wouldn't be able to drive home in this condition. She felt drowsy and tried to force her eyes to focus. They didn't, and she swayed. Someone walked past her. It was a blur of tan shirt and blue pants. Whoever it was climbed into a red truck—Jake's truck. She couldn't see him clearly, but it had to be him. She stumbled in that direction and fell against his passenger door with a thud. The engine was on, but the truck didn't move, at least not physically. In her mind, thought, it was tilting. Maybe it was her. She slid her hand along the door to the handle then opened it and pulled herself inside.

"What's going on," Jake asked. "Are you okay?"

"No. Can you give me a ride home?" Her words came out in one long slur.

"What's wrong?"

"I just need to go home." Haley's head dropped back against the seat and her helmet toppled into her lap.

Jake nearly leaped across the cab to her. He reached out and touched the makeshift bandage. "How did this happen?"

"Is it bad?"

Jake lifted the corner of the blood-soaked paper. "It's bleeding. Let me go get Rabbit. He's an EMT."

Haley lifted her hand, trying to stop him. "No. Don't. Just take me home." It was harder to talk now, and she couldn't keep her eyes open.

"You need to go to the hospital."

"No hospital. Promise me." She wasn't sure if her words were clear enough. Maybe she was having a reaction to the ibuprofen. She tried to reach into her pocket, to show Jake the medication packet, but she couldn't control her hands anymore. Jake helped her and reached into her pocket and pulled out the small wrapper.

"You think it's this?"

She nodded.

"You still need a hospital."

She couldn't even turn her head in his direction now, let alone open her eyes. Her mind was drifting away too. She just needed to let go of everything and go to sleep. She tried to focus her thoughts one more time. Jake had said something about a hospital. She couldn't go to the hospital. If she did, it would get back to the mine and go into her report. She would lose her job. She opened her mouth to try to explain to him, but all she could do was mutter, "No . . . hospital."

CHAPTER 24

There was a second heartbeat in Haley's head—at least that's what it felt like—a dark rhythm pounding inside her skull. She rolled over and opened one eye. Slowly things came into focus. A cherry wood nightstand. A wrought iron lamp. A short, stocky glass of water. She blinked. There was a fancy digital alarm clock too. She stared at the display. Saturday, 6:42 AM.

She pinched her eyes closed. Saturday? And where was she? She forced both eyes open and looked around the pristine room—a hotel room. It wasn't the cheap we'll-leave-the-light-on-for-you kind, but something a step above. It was nice. A padded upholstered armchair sat in the corner, and an open door off to the side gave a limited view into the bathroom. All she could see was part of the marble countertop and the neatly folded plush towels hanging on a rack next to the sink.

She pushed herself up onto one elbow, completely disoriented now. How did she get there? The pain in her head amplified and she rubbed her forehead, trying to remember. She had been in the mine and had cut her head. Instinctively, she reached for the injury, but her fingers didn't meet with blood-crusted hair. There was a soft bandage.

She tried to remember more. Leech almost running her over with the miner, hiding out until her shift was over, riding out of the mine in the back of the mantrip. There was nothing after that, yet here she was in a hotel room on Saturday morning.

Haley peeled back the duvet and sat up on the edge of the bed.

She was dressed in her light-blue Hanes thermals. Anyone would've guessed they were her pajamas, but they were the clothes she wore under her coveralls, a miner's trick to ward off the underground cold. She looked around but couldn't see her work clothes. As filthy as they were, she didn't expect them to be lying around the pristine room. She put a hand on the nightstand to balance herself and stood up. She needed to go home, but walking out in what looked like pajamas would be awkward. Her coveralls had to be there somewhere—maybe in the bathroom?

The door opened and Haley jumped. The sudden movement escalated the pounding in her skull, and she nearly closed her eyes to alleviate the pain, but the sight of Mitch walking in stopped her. Instead, her eyes widened in disbelief, but it was him. Fifty-something, lean and wiry, scruffy with three-day-old whiskers—it was Mitch.

Her mouth fell open. "Wh. . . What?" It was all she could say. What was she doing in a hotel with her vagabond neighbor?

"You feelin' better?"

"What?" She still couldn't find any suitable words. Mitch walked toward her. She put her hand up, warning him to stop. "Don't come any closer."

He kept coming. Haley took a step back and looked down at her thermals. They were decent enough, but she still felt insecure.

"Just relax. I've been married twice, and seeing a woman dressed in long underwear is nothing new to me."

Haley grabbed the nearest thing—the stocky glass of water from the nightstand—and hurled it at him. Water shot across the floor and the glass hit his shin with a dull thunk.

"Owww!" Mitch yelled and bent over, nursing his sore leg. "If you didn't want help, you could've said as much!"

"If you received mixed signals in 'don't come any closer' that's your own fault."

"Fine. Never liked helping damsels in distress anyway." Mitch turned around and limped out, slamming the door behind him.

Haley had to steady her breath while her mind reeled in

confusion. She needed to go home, which hopefully wasn't very far. She walked to the window and pulled back the heavy drapes to look outside. The morning sun was peeking over the eastern horizon. She blinked at it for a second then looked around. She was on the second floor, but it wasn't a hotel. It was a house.

She looked over her shoulder at the room again. It certainly looked like a hotel room. But outside it was definitely a house. There was a lawn, a driveway—where her rusted yellow Bug happened to be parked—and a row of houses across the street.

"Where am I?" Clothes or no clothes, she was leaving. She wobbled her way to the door, pulled it open, and jumped when she saw Jake standing there. She slammed the door and leaned on it. Mitch, and now Jake? What was going on?

"Whoa, Haley. Take it easy," Jake said from the hallway. "Are you okay?"

Slowly she opened the door. "What are you doing here?"

"I live here."

She shook her head. "I don't understand."

"It's simple. I own this house."

"Your house?"

"Yes."

Haley's heart seemed to be pounding harder, but that was reasonable considering the mounds of confusion sweeping over her. "*This* is your house? As in you own your own house?"

Jake's brow wrinkled. "Living the American Dream; is there a problem with that?"

"No." Why did she ever think he lived in his parents' basement? She bent over and sucked in a deep breath. Being here was *too* personal, and her head hurt from trying to think through the fog.

Jake moved forward. She didn't look up, so she focused on his shoes. A gray pair of Adidas.

"I think you should lie down." He put a hand on her back. "Is there something about this being my house that upsets you?"

Haley sucked in another long breath then straightened and tried to look casual—something that was hard to do when she was standing in nothing but her thermals. "No. I just didn't expect you to live in a hotel." She waved a hand, gesturing to the room.

Jake shrugged. "Yeah, me neither. My mom used to work for Marriott, and she wanted to help decorate."

Haley pinched the bridge of her nose to dull her headache. "Understandable. But what I'm really having a hard time with is— how did I get here?"

"You don't remember getting into my truck at the mine yesterday?"

She looked at him. "No. I never got in your truck."

"What's the last thing you remember?"

"I was in the back of the mantrip. I took some ibuprofen. I think I remember when we got to the surface. But nothing after that."

Jake's brow came down as if he were studying an unsolvable problem. "Here." He held his arms out to her. It was the first time she realized he was holding something. "Hope you don't mind. Your coveralls were coated in coal dust and blood, so these will have to do." He handed her a folded pair of jeans and a T-shirt. "They might be big on you, but it's either this or put back on your dirty work clothes."

She hesitated, but there didn't seem to be another option, and she didn't want to go around in her thermals. She took the bundle and hurried into the bathroom, locking the door behind her.

"By the way," she called loud enough so Jake could hear. "Where did my work clothes end up?"

"Everything is still in my truck. . ." He paused. "Don't tell me you're worried about that."

"What? I shouldn't worry about some guy undressing me while I'm unconscious?"

"Don't flatter yourself." His voice was closer as if he was standing right outside the door. "It wasn't like that, and I wouldn't have considered it if you didn't have something on underneath. It was like pulling off a coat; not even worthy of Hollywood fodder. Besides, do you know how bad you were bleeding? Coal dust and injuries don't go well together. It's bad enough it's all over my truck, we weren't going to let you lay in it."

"We?"

"Mitch and I."

Haley leaned against the counter and rubbed her forehead.

"I wanted to take you to the hospital," Jake continued, "but you were pretty adamant I didn't." There was a soft thud against the door. She guessed Jake was leaning against it. "Are you going to tell me how you split your head open?"

"I still have a lot of questions myself. I remember some things, but then it gets fuzzy, and . . . I don't know, and now I'm here. It doesn't make sense—"

"It's all right." Jake's voice was calm and reassuring. "Get dressed, and then we'll talk."

Haley looked down at the clothes in her arms. As much as she wanted to keep the door between them, she couldn't stay in the bathroom forever. Reluctantly she started to dress. She had to roll the waist down on the Levis so they would stay on, but the shirt fit surprisingly well. She recognized it. She'd seen Jake wear it before. It had been black at one time, but it was now soft and faded, and the white Captain America symbol printed on the front was worn and cracked.

She stepped out of the bathroom, trying to ignore the fact that she was wearing his clothes. As soon as she looked at him, his mouth twitched like he was trying not to smile. Even that little hint, the slight movement at the edge of his mouth, gave her a sense of accomplishment.

Haley felt heat move into her cheeks, and she turned away. "I need to figure this out, so first, tell me why Mitch is here."

Jake pulled her cell phone from his pants pocket and gave it to her. "You were on the verge of passing out in my truck and refusing to go to the hospital, so I took your phone and looked in your contacts to find someone to call. Mitch was listed under *emergency*."

Haley nearly choked. "That's why he's here? Kim put his number in my phone, and I forgot to remove it."

"So you don't like him. Is that why he came limping downstairs saying you beat him up?"

"I . . . threw a cup at him." She pointed to the glass lying near the wall. She felt bad about the water on the floor, but Jake didn't seem to mind.

"You should thank Kim because it's a good thing Mitch showed up. He said if you didn't want to go to the hospital, then we should honor that. As it turned out, he was a huge help. He used to be a miner, you know, and he's like a first aid ninja." Jake motioned to her head. "He did a good job patching you up. It could've used some stitches, but he put Steri-Strips on it. It should heal okay if you're careful."

Haley started rubbing the hem of his Captain America shirt. It was soft, like her own personal comfort blanket. "It's not that I hate Mitch," she said. "I just don't know him very well."

"I'm not surprised. You always liked to keep your distance. "

Haley felt a pang of guilt, remembering his attempts at trying to befriend her in high school.

Jake looked away for a long moment. "Sorry. I'm just tired and I have a ton of questions running through my mind."

He had every right to say whatever he wanted. He'd done so much for her, and she probably sounded ungrateful and nitpicky. "I'm the one that should be sorry," Haley said. "I should be thanking you for taking care of me. Maybe between the two of us, we can figure everything out."

Jake gestured towards her head. "How did you get the cut?"

Haley told him that she thought Leech was trying to run over with the miner and that she'd hit her head while trying to dodge it.

Jake's face hardened as he listened. "And you didn't tell Bear?"

"No. He said if I get another report written up on me, he'll have me fired."

"Are you sure you didn't misunderstand him? Bear can be mean, but that doesn't sound like something he'd do."

"He made it perfectly clear."

Jake's mouth pulled to one side as if he still wasn't sure. "And that's why you didn't want to go to the hospital?"

Haley nodded. "I already have the Unsafe Work report, I can't risk getting more."

"Maybe Bear said it in jest. Accidents happen, but unless you're doing something wrong, you shouldn't be at risk of being fired."

"My only crime is being a woman."

Jake's lips pressed together. She couldn't tell if it was irritation, or maybe disbelief. "What else has been going on?" he asked.

"You mean besides turning blue and the normal insults and taunts? How about my lunch for starters. I've been eating jerky for a week because the other men keep decimating my lunch containers."

"Lunches shouldn't be messed with, but it still happens once in a while."

"For me, it's a daily occurrence. One day it was roof bolted to the ceiling, Jake. Have you ever had your lunch roof bolted to the ceiling? There should be an Olympic sport for creative lunch thieving. Someone on Bear's crew would take gold. And that's not all. I've received threatening notes, and a lump of coal was thrown through my apartment window."

Jake held a hand up to stop her. "Have you brought it up with Mr. Branch? Everything you're mentioning is against policy."

"They don't follow policy. If they did, Moose's accident report would be posted on the board, and my Unsafe Work Observation would've been kept in my private file. But no, it's just the opposite. Bear probably has my next report filled out, waiting for an accident to happen, so he can slap it up on the board and fire me."

Jake's posture stiffened. "What do you mean Moose's report isn't on the board?"

"It's not. I've checked every day for the last week."

"I know he filled it out. Bear took him into Cross's office to sign off on it."

"Well, that's why. Bear did it. He's okay with letting the guys slide, but he has to hang me out to dry."

"Let's not jump to conclusions. We can check this out easy enough. Let's go down to my office." Jake walked out.

Haley paused in the doorway. The second floor of the house was a balcony style, and she could see over the metal banister into the living room below. All of this was his personal space, and it wasn't where she planned on spending the day. The less she involved Jake, the better. Maybe she should just go down the stairs and straight out to her car and go home. Maybe. She took a deep breath and followed Jake.

CHAPTER 25

Haley walked down the stairs and stepped into the living room. Considering the Marriott bedroom she'd just been in, it wasn't surprising how nice it was. The masculine room featured a stone fireplace, leather couch, and a flat screen TV with a state-of-the-art gaming console. The space opened up into a kitchen where two sixty-four-ounce Maverick cups sat on the granite counter top along with a package of Oreos—a coal miner's breakfast of champions.

Jake disappeared into another adjacent room, but Haley lingered, still hesitant. When she stepped into the home office, Jake was already sitting at a neatly organized desk with two computer monitors. "Nice house."

"Thanks. I started building it when I was a senior."

Haley raised an eyebrow.

"It was one of those project houses the high school carpentry class does," he explained.

Haley looked past the nice molding and the paneled door and noticed a few texture bubbles on the wall that should've been sanded down. Yep, it looked like the work of high schoolers. It was nice though, and Jake had good taste. A framed artistic painting of the Batman symbol hung above his computer. It looked high-class, yet showed off his geeky side at the same time. "You still had to pay for the house, so how you do that while still in high school?"

Jake touched a finger to his monitor and swiped it to the side. The touch screen simulated a page flip and a new website appeared. "When I was seventeen, I designed a couple of gaming software apps. With some hard work, and a lot of luck, Microsoft took a liking to one and sent me a check for $70,000. It wasn't like the millionaire stories you read about, but there I was—seventeen, and I thought I was rich. I tried to be smart and invest in my future, so I got the land from a relative and paid for most of the construction on the house. But I had to take out a loan on the rest. My parents signed with me, but I was turning eighteen, had a mortgage and no job to pay for it."

"Why didn't you write more apps?"

"I tried, but no one picked them up. I made some cash on the app store, but not enough. I had bills to pay then, so my only option was to sell the house or get a job. I was trying to be an adult, so I opted for door number two."

Jake had stated it all matter-of-factly, but Haley could feel the bleak mood that fell over the room. "So you ended up in the mine?"

He didn't answer. Mining was a good thing, but it wasn't for everyone. Beyond the threats and mean pranks, Haley could actually enjoy it. But Jake was different. He seemed to tolerate it, but he didn't love it. He flipped through some more pages on his monitor then leaned back in his chair, his hand cupping his chin in a thoughtful manner.

"What is it?" she asked.

"Moose's report isn't even on the computer." Jake leaned over and grabbed an extra thick book from a nearby shelf and began thumbing through it.

Haley leaned over, trying to get a better look at the business-like manual. "Brushing up on some legal text?"

"This is the 30 CFR."

Haley made a face. "You actually have a copy of that?" She backed away. 30 CFR was an acronym for MSHA's Code of Regulations, thick enough to rival any weighty dictionary and just as appealing as a 1000-page tax audit by the IRS.

Jake ran his finger over a page. "Here it is. Part 50—Notification, Investigation, Reports and Records of Accidents of Injuries—"

"Just tell me what it says. Simple English, please."

Jake scanned several pages mumbling something about the definition of occupational injury and requirements for notification. He slapped the book shut and turned back to his computer. "It says Moose's report should've been filed."

"Maybe they haven't updated the webpage yet."

"I'm not exactly on a public web page. I'm looking at P.C.'s data, and I'm telling you, it wasn't even logged in on the mine's computer."

Haley looked over his shoulder. "I didn't know you could see that information."

"Well, technically. . ." Jake voice trailed off.

"What?" Haley gasped. "You hacked into the mine's computer system?"

"You wanted to know about the accident report, didn't you? Let me do some more digging." He leaned forward and started typing on the keyboard.

Haley glanced up and saw Mitch out the window, walking along the street curb with his head down. She hadn't noticed before, but he was wearing the clothes she had bought him. He walked a few steps then stooped to the gutter and picked something up. She wished he wouldn't do that. "I'll be back in a few minutes," she said. "I'm going outside to talk with Mitch."

"All right. If I find an explanation for all of this, I'll let you know."

Haley stepped out the front door just as Mitch lit up the used cigarette and took a drag. It was only good for one. After he exhaled the smoke, he looked at the spent nub in disappointment and dropped it on the ground. "You aren't going to throw another cup at me, are you?"

"Sorry. I'm unarmed." She looked at his leg, wondering if it still hurt.

"Good to hear." He walked along the gutter and picked up another cigarette. This one was longer and he was able to take three drags on it before he had to drop it.

"Jake said you bandaged up my head."

He grunted.

She wasn't about to let that pass as an adequate response. She wanted a conversation. She pointed to her rusted Bug in the driveway. "How did my car get here?"

"Jake's neighbor took me to the mine and I drove it back. I left your keys on the seat. I also tried to call Kim to let her know where you are, but she never picked up, and I make it a rule never to leave messages."

"She's been working on a big project, so it's kind of hit and miss with her lately. But thanks for trying."

Mitch jerked his head in her direction. "You feeling better?"

"I still have a headache." She touched the bandage on her head. "Not from my injury, but I think I had a reaction to the ibuprofen."

"That's some potent painkiller to knock you out for thirteen hours. Have you ever had a reaction like that before?"

"No."

Mitch shook his head. "It wasn't the ibuprofen then. Stomach pain, heartburn, gas—those are side effects but not blacking out. Most likely it stemmed from the concussion from when you hit your head."

"But I hit my head hours before my shift ended. It bled a lot, but I didn't have any problems until I was in the truck and took the pills. I remember getting dizzy and tired, but I can't even remember getting out of the truck."

"Did you take anything else with the medication?"

"Just the Coke. . ." Haley let her words trail off. Leech had given her the Coke bottle at the end of their lunch break. "Could someone put something in my drink to cause me to black out?" She already knew the answer.

Mitch nodded. "Haven't you heard of GHB or Ketamine? They're fairly easy to get. You think someone drugged your Coke?"

Haley went numb. That's exactly what she was thinking. "You told me things might escalate, and I think they did. Leech gave me the drink right before I was supposed to start working with him." Her stomach churned. "Maybe he wanted to knock me out while on

~ 160 ~

the job. It didn't work, so he tried running me over with the miner."

Mitch raised a brow. "Attempted murder is a serious accusation."

"Well, even if he just wanted to knock me out, I would've been caught sleeping on the job with drugs in my system. I would've been fired on the spot. Either way, he would've gotten rid of me." She let out a long breath. "I'm beginning to hate coal mines."

Mitch's face turned callous. "Say that the next time you flip on a light switch or charge your smartphone. Coal mines are what make the world go around, sweetheart, and you're burnin' that little black rock every time you surf the internet, check your email, or use the microwave, so don't act like you're disgusted with the industry that's propping up your electronically convenient life."

"I didn't mean it that way," Haley said.

"I know. Just don't blame the coal mines for a few bad lumps workin' inside them." He paused and his eyes began to scour the gutter again. "I didn't mean to lecture you. I know what you're saying. Heck, you just had a coworker drug you, and who knows what would've happened if you'd drunk that Coke earlier."

Haley hated to think about what could've happened . . . or what still might. Jake came outside and crossed to where they were. Haley wrapped her arms around herself, feeling a tremble coming on.

"What's wrong?" Jake asked. "You look pale?"

"I know why I don't remember anything." She told him her suspicions about Leech drugging the Coke. By the time she had finished, Jake's eyes were hooded over with anger. "Do you know where the Coke bottle is? If there's even a drop left, I can test it."

"I don't remember—" Haley's mouth fell open. "Wait. I think Leech took it. He grabbed it out of my hands and thumped me on the helmet with it. He walked off after that. He must have taken it with him."

Jake's expression darkened. "I think this is just the tip of the iceberg. Come inside and see what I found."

CHAPTER 26

"I looked up the recent mining accidents," Jake said as they walked into his office. He turned one of his monitors so Haley and Mitch could see the screen. "At least the ones I personally knew about, like when Scarecrow cut his thumb. He only needed two stitches, but it was a reportable accident. And the time Cockroach sprained his ankle and took a day off. He's still limping. And last week, Wing Nut went to push in a bolt and missed. It hit the roof and blew out, smashing his hand."

Haley nodded. She remembered seeing Bear bandage the injury.

"Only there's no record of any of these accidents," Jake continued.

Mitch leaned forward and looked at the computer. "So Bear or someone isn't reporting accidents."

Jake nodded. "It makes Haley stand out—like they're trying to make her look bad in comparison."

Haley's muscles tightened. It made sense. She only wished she knew why they hated her so much.

Mitch tapped the monitor. "You know what you have here isn't public record?"

Jake shrugged. "I'll ask for forgiveness later."

"But mine accidents *are* open to the public," Haley said in his defense.

"Yes, but this here," Mitch motioned to the screen, "isn't."

Jake looked at him, impressed. "You seem familiar with the data and its format. I know you were a miner, but did you have an office job too?"

Mitch shrugged. "I did more than dig coal. I was a mine owner. Once."

Kim had mentioned that to Haley, but she hadn't gotten around to asking him about it. He didn't seem like the mine owner type. "What mine?" she asked.

"I owned P.C. to be exact."

Jake twisted in his seat to look at him. "Really?"

Mitch shrugged. "That was a long time ago. Fourteen years, I think."

Haley didn't let go of his gaze. "That's where you know Bear from?"

"I'd rather not talk about it. Just be aware that diggin' into this kind of stuff is like opening a can of worms. Coal is the cheapest source of energy, and there's lots of it. That means running a mine can be like running a legal mint. I'm talking big money, and big money means power. Don't go poking your noses into things when you don't have the resources to protect yourself."

Mitch gave Haley a warning look, but she ignored it. "Can of worms or not, if accidents aren't being reported, it makes the mine unsafe. I've put up with a lot, but this is where I draw the line. Someone's already tried to kill me. I'm not going to work under these conditions when I have proof that someone is—"

"What proof do you have?" Mitch cut in. "You gonna show them how Jake hacked into the mine's computer system? That'll get you both fired."

He was right. They needed something solid, but she couldn't sit back and do nothing. "I'm probably going to lose my job anyway, so I'm not going to stand by while they hang me for minor infractions and let everyone else's accidents fly under the radar. They can't force me out just because I'm a woman."

Mitch rolled his eyes. "You still think this is about gender politics? Sorry, sweetheart, but men don't jump to attempted murder just because they don't want a woman around."

Jake rocked back in his chair and folded his arms. "You can't deny they've been trying to get Haley out of the mine. If she wants to do something about it, I can probably help her. And if she wants real proof, I can find it."

Haley met Jake's gaze and something stirred inside her, warm and confusing. She swallowed hard and rationalized the emotion away. Why was he so willing to help her?

"You guys set your own bear trap and climb into it then," Mitch said. "Whatever is going on, it's not about Haley." He leaned forward and tapped the computer screen. "Take a closer look at those dates."

"What about them?" Haley asked.

Jake examined them for a minute. "He's right. Look at the number of accidents and their corresponding dates." He traced his finger along the screen. "Whatever is going on started before you went underground. Accidents were on the rise, then suddenly dropped three months before you started. It looks like that's when they started sweeping them under the rug." He looked over at Haley. "Maybe Leech *is* a male chauvinist and wants to get rid of you, but as Mitch said, I don't think it's connected to the unreported accidents."

Haley gazed out the window as she let the information sink in. Outside an old, sun-bleached Oldsmobile slowly drove by then turned around and parked in front of the house. Mitch stepped next to her. "It looks like your other emergency contact has arrived." He nodded to the car. "You don't need me anymore, so I'll see ya later. And if you can help it—don't get in too much trouble. Take it from someone who knows."

"What does he mean my 'other emergency contact'?" Haley asked as Mitch walked out. She didn't recognize the old car, and she couldn't see the driver through its tinted windows.

"He must mean your brother Noah," Jake said.

Haley gasped. "Tell me you didn't call him." She placed her hands on the window and squinted through the glass, trying to get a better look.

"We didn't know how long you'd be unconscious, and when we couldn't get a hold of Kim, we decided to call Noah. I remembered him from school, and I found his number in your phone. What's the problem? Don't you want to see him?"

The car door opened and a tall man stepped out. Haley wanted to turn away, to run upstairs to the bedroom where she had been earlier and crawl under the covers, but she couldn't pull herself away. Noah stood next to the car. His faded jeans were not sun-bleached and threadbare to make a fashion statement. He had grown coarse and unkempt since the last time she'd seen him. He wore an old button-up shirt, the sleeves rolled up past his elbows, and he held a cigarette pinched tightly between his fingers. He leaned back against the car and dropped his head, letting his nearly shoulder-length brown hair cover his whiskered face, hiding his hollow cheekbones. It appeared he was as thrilled to be there as she was at seeing him.

Haley sensed Jake as he walked up behind her. "What's wrong?"

"I haven't seen him in a long time." She didn't want to put any emotion on it, but she was sure Jake had felt the sadness in her words.

"How long?"

"Six years."

"I'm sorry." Jake placed a hand on her shoulder. "Do you want me to talk to him first?"

"Do whatever you want. I'm not talking to him at all."

CHAPTER 27

Haley stood behind Jake's kitchen counter. It provided a good barrier between her and the front door. As soon as she saw movement, she crouched down, but Jake was the only one who walked in.

He walked over to her and leaned over the counter, dropping his head so she couldn't avoid the eye contact. "He's still outside. He had to borrow a car, and he drove three hours just to see you. You should at least talk to him."

Haley straightened up, resting her hands on the counter. "He knows I'm doing fine, isn't that good enough?"

Jake moved closer until their hands were almost touching. "I don't get it. What do you have against him?"

"Nothing."

"Come on, Haley." He leaned back, the muscles in his forearms rigid. "Why do you do this?"

"Do what?"

"Push people away."

She felt her own muscles tighten. "So what are you—my therapist? I'm sorry, but you're not an expert on my life."

A soft calm came over Jake's face as he visibly wrestled his frustration under control. "You're right. I don't know you very well—not that I wouldn't like to."

She glanced down at the package of Oreos she had been assaulting while he'd been outside with Noah. "I'm not good with relationships—not even with my own family."

"Because of your dad?"

Haley looked up. It wasn't surprising that he knew about her past. That kind of stuff didn't stay quiet, especially when it was featured in the local newspaper. But most people didn't get this personal with her. Even Liam never brought her dad up in conversation.

Jake's face softened even more. "Just because we never spent any real time together, doesn't mean I don't care, or that I don't want to help."

Haley rubbed the edge of the Captain America Shirt. Caution signals were going off inside her head. "I already went to therapy. Two years of it. And I hate talking about it now as much as I did then. And every time I tried discussing it with my peers, they jumped on the gossip wagon."

"People talked because they were concerned. I won't claim to understand what you went through, but your father is in prison now. I think you can afford to open yourself up to someone."

Someone like Jake? He wasn't exactly being subtle. She studied his face. "And why do you want to help me? Why do you care?"

He drew back slipping his hands into his pockets and shrugged. "I guess I always felt like I owed you."

"Why? I never did you any favors."

"You've done a lot for others. You've helped people. Like Charlotte on that debate trip."

Jake hadn't been in the debate class, but Haley knew exactly what he was talking about. She remembered the incident in the back of the bus where Nathan Cruise grabbed Charlotte and was trying to grope her. "How do you know about that?"

"Charlotte's my cousin," he said. "We were best friend growing up, and she was texting me during that trip, telling me what was going on, that one of the guys was harassing her. She was scared and didn't know what to do. I'd gone into the councilor's office at school to complain when she called and told me that you had taken care of it."

It hadn't been much. Haley didn't punch Nathan like she'd wanted to. She did threaten him though. And she sat by Charlotte for the rest of the trip.

"Look," Jake said. "I understand if you don't want to open up to me, but at least talk to your brother. He's waiting to see you."

Haley pulled an Oreo apart and pretended to examine the white cream inside. Jake still didn't understand her continued fear of relationships, but her anxiety wasn't just about what men were capable of, but also how damaging she herself could be in the relationship. She wasn't sure she could truly care for someone. She'd tried with Liam, she really had, but she couldn't bring herself to love him. And keeping to herself was a way to protect others from her own dysfunctional behavior.

Haley popped the cookie into her mouth and looked at Jake. There was no judgment in his expression. She almost expected it, like she wanted him to be more critical of her. She grabbed another Oreo then felt guilty for hijacking half the package. "They help me think," she explained.

"Good. Think about going out and talking to your brother."

After a long minute, Haley set the cookie on the counter and pushed it away. "He was eighteen," she said.

"Who? Noah?"

She nodded. "That was the last time I saw him. You know, it was just me and him after the accident. Kim's family took us in, but it was hard. I needed Noah. Brooke had already moved. She transferred to Texas Southern University right after it happened. Noah was the only one who understood. I needed him, and then he left me. He ran away the day he turned eighteen. Went out with some friends and never came home."

Haley reached for the cookie again, but Jake put his hand on top of hers. She recoiled and stepped away from the counter. "He left me. Brooke was gone, Dad was in prison, Mom was still in the hospital, and he left me to deal with it all."

Jake was careful not to touch her, but he leaned forward again until their eyes met. "He's here now."

When Haley walked outside, Noah was still leaning against the sun-bleached Oldsmobile sucking down the last drags of a cigarette. When he dropped it to the ground, it was so spent even Mitch would've passed it up.

"Hey, sis."

She tried to smile but failed. It would've been fake anyway. "You want to come inside?"

Noah shook his head, his stringy hair shielding his face. "I don't plan to stay long. Just wanted to see how you're doing. That guy . . . Jake said he thought you'd be okay, but since I'm here, I figured I better see for myself."

His eyes settled on the bandage sticking out from her hair. "You should sit down." He looked around like a chair might magically appear. When it didn't, he opened the door to the Oldsmobile. "We can sit in here." He hesitated then closed it again. "On second thought, it kind of stinks in there. Had to borrow it from a friend." He looked at the yellow Bug parked in the driveway. "Is that yours?"

She nodded.

"That'll work."

Haley was already in the driver's seat when Noah climbed in beside her. He promptly pulled a package of cigarettes out of his pocket, but Haley snatched them away and tossed them over her shoulder into the back of the car. "Not in here."

"Oh, right. Sorry."

There was a long awkward pause before he spoke again. "How's your head? I heard you were knocked out cold."

"It's fine now." She didn't explain that someone had drugged her Coke, so there was another awkward lull in the conversation.

Noah shifted in his seat. "How's Mom?"

"Ask her yourself. She's at the Parkdale Care Center."

"I don't think I'll have time to stop. Just tell me how she's doing."

Haley looked at him. "She had a hammer slammed into her skull multiple times, and she's still recovering, how do you think she's doing?"

"I'm sorry." He waited, but Haley didn't respond. "Come on, sis. I've apologized before. When are you going to forgive me?"

Haley's headache was coming back. She let out a long breath, trying to suppress the buried emotions that were surfacing. "Apologize to Mom. She's the one who asked you to be there that night."

Noah's face blanched but he quickly recovered, his eyes growing dull and distant. Haley couldn't tell if he was simply tuning her out or if he was in complete denial.

She gripped the stirring wheel. She had to hold on to something—anything. Her fingers tightened until they were white. "Mom asked *you* to be there that night. *You.*" Noah dropped his head, his hair hiding his expression. That bugged her. She wanted to know what he was feeling. She wanted him to take the responsibility of it. So much of that had belonged to her, pressing her down over the years, and she was tired of packing the weight of it. "Brooke was gone on that college trip, and mom was relying on you." Her voice trailed off.

"I already apologized, what more do you want?" Noah's words were barely audible.

Haley's face grew hot. "I wanted you to be there. Mom was going to ask Dad for a divorce and she needed *you* to be there because she knew how Dad was going to react. She needed someone to protect her." Haley's breath came in shallow bursts, and her heart pounded against her chest. "But no, you left. You went on that stupid Scout camp and left me alone with them, and I couldn't do anything but hide in my room and cry."

Haley balled her hand into a fist and thumped Noah hard on the chest. She expected him to grab her and shove her away, but he didn't. Finally, she sank back in her seat. She dropped her head, and tears ran down her cheeks. "Why couldn't I protect her? Why did I have to hide?"

"It wasn't your fault." Noah put a hand on her shoulder, so softly she had to look, unsure if she'd really felt it there. When he spoke again, his words sounded thick and raspy. "None of it was your fault."

Haley brushed away her tears, refusing to let any more fall. "I wished you were there. You were always the strong one. You never cried." Thoughts of her dad and his horrific punishments flooded her mind like rank oil polluting the surface of her memories. She tried to blink away the images. "You didn't even cry when he forced you to wear the jacket." She cringed. "I looked up to you for standing up to him, for always trying to protect me."

Noah dropped his head. "I wasn't the strong one. Just looking at that jacket made me cry inside."

Haley shook her head. The old thrift store coat looked like something out of a horror film. Her dad had sewn cords and washers to the arms so he could lace it up like a straitjacket. He used it when he didn't want Noah to fight back during a beating. Other times, when he wanted an added challenge, he didn't use it at all. Instead, he made Haley hold it as she watched Noah take his punishment.

"You hid it well," Haley said. "I didn't take near as many beatings as you, but I always bawled whenever he hit me. But you—you never showed it. You were brave."

"No, I wasn't." Noah swallowed several times; the lump in his throat bobbed as if he were trying to force it down. "I didn't go on a Scout campout that night."

The blood drained from Haley's face, and she suddenly felt light-headed. "What?"

Noah refused to look at her. "There was no Scout camp. I made it up. I went and stayed at a friend's house. I was scared."

It took a moment for Haley to find her words. "But you were never scared."

He glanced at her. His dark eyes seemed hollow. "He broke me, Haley. I was broken then, and I still am."

She turned away. That was the exact word Kim had used to define her—*broken*. Another tear forced its way down her cheek. "You can't be broken, Noah. I always looked up to you. I wanted you to turn out good, to be a decent guy."

"I am. Maybe I live like a bum, but I keep to myself and never put my troubles on other people."

Haley knew exactly what he was saying. He didn't create

relationships. Just like her. She looked him, his dark eyes glazed and withdrawn. This wasn't what she had wished for him. And she didn't want to end up like him either. But that's what they were doing, the pair of them. They were remaining victims of their father's abuse. She looked back at Jake's house and tried to recall what he had said about people caring for her.

"We were both scared. And I guess we can't change what happened. We can only move on from here." She placed a hand on Noah's whiskered cheek. "Now go and visit Mom. She needs to see you, and you can give her that much."

There wasn't anything left to say, at least nothing else she was willing to let surface, so she climbed out of the car. "It was good seeing you."

Noah climbed out too and nodded. "You gonna be okay, sis?"

Haley shrugged. "I'm broken too. But hopefully, it's not too late to fix things."

CHAPTER 28

Mitch's door didn't open. Haley waited, hoping. But then again, he wasn't very happy when he'd left Jake's house. She needed to amend that. It was part of her newfound plan to stop shutting people out. Jake and Mitch were the first ones on her list that she was going to reach out to. She knocked again. Finally, a crack appeared at the door jamb.

"You?" Mitch rubbed a hand across the rough stubble on his chin. "It's only been a few hours; what do you want now?"

She held up a grocery bag. "Peace offering for the cup incident."

He looked at the sack. "Do I have to do anything for it—give advice or something?"

"Nope. It's a freebie. Consider it a thank you for taking care of me." She reached up and touched the bandage. She had her hair combed over it so it was neatly hidden.

Mitch took the bag and walked into his kitchen. He didn't close the door on her, so she followed him inside. The apartment was pretty much the same, although the pile of clothes on the couch was gone. He set the sack on the counter and looked inside it. "Jake let you drive home by yourself?"

She shook her head. "No. He drove me. He's in my car waiting. Kim's not home so he's going to take me to her office. He doesn't think I should be alone."

Mitch nodded his approval. "I like Jake. He's a keeper if you get my meaning."

"He's a good guy. He took me shopping, and then even took my car in for an oil change, but don't go jumping to conclusions. We're only working in the friendship department right now." Haley picked at a chip in the Formica countertop. She was still trying to open herself up to Jake and it wasn't easy. "Anyway," she said. "While I'm here, I'll take some advice if you're willing to give it."

Mitch pulled a box of donuts out of the sack and slapped it down on the counter with a loud smack. "I knew there was a catch."

"Not really. Only if you're willing."

He grunted and pulled out a box of nicotine patches. He held it up with two fingers as if it was contaminated. "What's this?"

"You don't have to use them. I just know how much cigarettes cost, so it's just in case you want to kick the habit."

He grunted and scooted the box away then pulled out a bag of shredded cheese. "Does this mean you want me to start cooking for myself?"

"I hardly think cheese is a requirement to cook."

He opened the package, dipped into it, and then stuffed a large pinch into his mouth like a wad of tobacco. "For me, that's cooking." He went back to the grocery sack and looked inside at the remaining items. A large grin spread across his face. "Now we're talking!"

Haley wondered what had caught his attention when he pulled out a package of cigarettes and set them on the counter next to the nicotine patches. Haley stared at it in disbelief. Where had that come from? There was no way she would've let *that* slip into the shopping cart.

Mitch's eyes were still ricocheting between the cigarettes and the nicotine patches. "Here you're trying to save my soul and. . . and I have to say,. . . worst rescue mission ever."

Haley noticed the cigarette pack was open. "We didn't buy those. I think they were my brother's." She made a grab for the package, but Mitch snatched them up first. "I tossed Noah's cigarettes into the back of my Bug . . . the guys at Oil Express must have put them in the grocery sack when they were vacuuming my car."

"Bless Oil Express." Mitch held Haley off like a wide receiver fending off a tackle in the Super Bowl. She finally gave up, and Mitch patted his prize in triumph.

Haley pushed the nicotine patches across the counter. "Fine, but use these afterward."

He put the cigarettes in his breast pocket and motioned for her to sit down. "I guess these earned you something. What kind of advice do you want?"

Haley sat down on a lopsided bar stool. "I've been thinking about what Jake showed us. We know that someone—most likely Bear—isn't reporting accidents, but why were accidents on the rise in the first place?"

"Hard to say."

Haley cleared her throat. "What I really want to know is—am I working in an unsafe mine?"

Mitch shifted his weight uneasily. He seemed to know where the conversation was going, and she wasn't going to let him wriggle out of it. "Mitch, tell me what P.C.'s safety record was when you owned it."

He faked a cough but didn't say anything.

"I know it's prone to roof falls, but I mean beyond that. If it's not safe, you have to tell me."

"I'm getting to it. Keep your long johns on."

Haley folded her arms across Jake's Captain America shirt. She had her chance to change out of it, but she kind of liked it.

"You need to understand—P.C. Mine is completely different from when I owned it. It was small then. Just two work crews. Now it's big and corporate. Don Wakefield put the longwall in, and it has a new roof plan and a new ventilation plan. He's changed everything, and he knows what he's doing. He owns a lot of mines, six or seven at least, and Mr. Branch does a good job managing P.C. for him. It's a good producer for them."

"Then why did you sell it?"

He rubbed the back of his neck and pulled out a cigarette. He didn't light it up, but he stuck it in his mouth and nursed the end of it. "That doesn't really matter. The heart of your problem is why

Bear—if it's even him—isn't reporting accidents. But problems like that aren't too uncommon. Look at Crandall Canyon Mine."

Haley knew what he was referring to. In 2007 the local mine made national headlines when six miners were trapped by a collapse. Later, three rescuers were killed in the attempt to free them. There were rumors going around at the time that the mine was unsafe and that certain issues had been overlooked.

Haley was young when it happened, but she remembered how the local communities pulled together in support of the miners and their families. She could still picture the signs and posters that were hung around town. *Pray for our miners* displayed in businesses, on people's houses, and written on vehicles. She prayed. She didn't know who the men were, but every night she prayed for them like everyone else in the community. She prayed that they would be safe. She prayed for their families too. News crews came and families held vigils. People camped out near the mine, waiting for any information. Others clamored around TVs and stood by phones. The six miners were never recovered. They were declared dead and the mine was closed. Flags were flown at half-mast, and people came by in droves to funerals and memorial events to honor the lost men and those who gave their lives trying to rescue them.

Carbon County wasn't new to mine disasters, and like always, the local people picked up and moved on. But Crandall Canyon had left a permanent impression on Haley. That was the first time she'd seen coal mining as the heart of a community, and that stuck with her. She wanted to be a part of something that beat its life force through the people, something that could pull strangers together like a family. She hadn't had much luck with gaining admittance into the family of miners, but she wasn't done trying.

"You're comparing P.C. Mine to Crandall Canyon?" she asked.

Mitch shook his head. "I'm not sayin' nothin'." He walked over to the door and opened it, motioning for her to leave.

"That's all you're giving me?"

He didn't respond, so she walked out, but as she passed him, she reached into his breast pocket, snatching the cigarettes. She couldn't even get her arm out of reach before Mitch caught hold of her hand with a vice-like grip and took them back. "That's all for today, Scab. And you already know my advice."

* * *

"Bear definitely has the cleanest crew." Jake held his phone out for Haley to look at. She couldn't tell if he was on a regular web page or not. She examined the record then shook her head in disbelief and leaned back against Kim's desk. The office was neatly organized, and Haley was careful not to touch anything that looked important.

Jake scrolled through the document in front of him. "There's hardly anything from Bear's crew. Your Unsafe Work report was the last thing filed." He put the phone down and looked at the clock.

"Sorry, it's taking so long. You can go if you want." Haley really didn't want him to leave, but she offered anyway.

He shook his head. "I'm not leaving you until someone's with you. The secretary said Kim would be here soon, so I'm okay with waiting."

Just then the door opened and Kim stepped in. She looked up with surprise. "Haley! What are you doing here? And where have you been? I came home last night and you weren't there, and you were gone this morning when I got up. I tried to call you and—"

"I had an accident in the mine, but I'm fine, and Jake's been looking after me." She turned her head and pointed to the partially hidden bandage.

Kim gasped and ran over to her. "Are you all right?"

"I knew this would happen," a voice sounded from the other end of the room. Haley jerked her head in that direction and saw Liam standing in the doorway. He waved a hand toward her. "I told you to quit that job."

Kim rounded on him. "Be quiet, Liam." She looked back at Haley. "What happened?"

"It's just a little cut."

Liam walked toward her. "You need to get out of the mine, Haley. You're going to get killed."

"Why are you even here?" she asked.

Liam shrugged and looked at Kim who put a hand on Haley's arm as if trying to prepare her for bad news. If Haley were to guess, she'd have thought they had just gone on a lunch date. If anyone could handle Liam, it was Kim. Still, it'd be miserable if they were dating. Liam would be around more, and Haley could do without that.

Despite Kim's warning look, Liam approached. He glanced momentarily at Jake, and they both seemed to stiffen. "I don't understand why you're still working there—"

Jake moved closer and both men seemed to size each other up. Jake had the height advantage, but Haley couldn't picture him fighting. On the other hand, she wasn't so sure about Liam. He was more unpredictable.

"It's all right." Haley stepped between them and looked at Liam. "It's not going miles below ground surrounded by coal miners that gets to me. It's not the cold, or the heat, or the exhaustion. It's people like you."

Liam threw his hands up. "Seriously, Haley. If you stay down there, you're going to die."

Kim pulled on Liam's arm. "Can you give me a moment to talk to her alone?"

Liam didn't budge. He looked at Haley then motioned his chin toward Jake. "Are you seeing him?"

Haley's mouth went dry. She wasn't seeing Jake, and that would've been easy enough to say, but she couldn't. Maybe a part of her *did* want to be with him. She didn't let that thought linger though. Letting Jake in as a friend and dating him were two different things, and maybe he deserved better than her troubled emotions.

"It's none of your business who she's seeing," Jake cut in, sparing her from explaining.

The tendons in Liam's neck bulged, but Kim grabbed his arm and pulled him toward the door. "Come here for a minute." Her little five-foot frame strained as she dragged him into the hallway and closed the door behind them.

"Sorry about that," Haley said. She couldn't help but notice how close Jake was to her. Their arms were touching, and she could feel the warmth of his skin. She thought about moving away but didn't. She thought of Noah and her resolve to open up, but maybe this was too much too soon. She was just about to move when Jake touched her hand, lacing his fingers between hers. Surprise surged through her at his touch.

The door opened and Kim stepped inside and looked at their entwined hands. "What's going on?"

"Nothing." Haley pulled away and moved across the room. A jab of disappointment shot through her. "Nothing," she said again.

Kim looked between them. "You already said that. Which means *something*."

Haley wrapped her arms around herself and looked at the door—her only escape. Suddenly it opened and Liam stuck his head in. He directed a cold grimace at Jake. "Just a friendly warning: as soon as you do something nice, like give her flowers, she'll shove you in a dumpster." Jake looked at Haley and raised an eyebrow. She replied with a shrug.

Kim shut the door on Liam and leaned against it. "All right, tell me exactly what's going on. And I don't mean between you two. What's going on at the mine?"

"Not much," Haley said. "Other than Leech is trying to kill me, and Bear isn't reporting accidents."

"Wait." Kim's eyes widened. "One thing at a time. Not reporting accidents—that's against the law, isn't it?"

Jake nodded. "He could get fired for it, and the mine would be fined."

"What are you going to do about it?" Kim asked. "Is P.C. unionized?"

Jake shook his head. "Nope. No help there. And no Mother Jones either."

A perplexed look crossed Kim's face. "Who's Mother Jones?"

"Basic civil rights," Haley explained. "Over a hundred of years ago, coal miners worked in terrible conditions to earn four dollars a week, which could only be spent at the company store. Mother Jones dramatized working conditions and organized miners. At one time, they called her the most dangerous woman in America."

Jake must've appreciated her knowledge and graced her with a smile. It came and went within a second, but it was bright and explosive. His chin came up, his mouth parting to reveal the tip of his tongue, his eyes brilliant and framed by happy laugh lines. Earning one of Jake's smiles was something to celebrate, so as brief as this one was, Haley wanted to thank him for it. Lately, it had been a rare occurrence. She had seen hints of it, but he'd been more concerns and worries than anything.

Kim started tapping her foot. Obviously, she wasn't as moved by his smile. "So what can we do about Bear?"

"Call in a hazard complaint," Jake suggested.

"Good idea." Kim picked up the receiver from the phone on her desk and handed it to Haley. "Hazard complaints are anonymous, right?"

Haley and Jake both nodded.

Kim looked back and forth between them. "You're sure? There's no way Bear can find out that the call came from Haley?"

"No one will know who made the call," Jake said.

"Good. You can put a stop to this, Haley. You can be P.C.'s Mother Jones."

CHAPTER 29

"Are you all right?" Jake leaned on the tailgate of one of the mantrips as Haley walked out from the Lamp-house. He had the collar of his overalls turned up to block the breeze whipping down the mountainside.

She nodded and patted the phone that hung on her belt. "I'll call you if I see anything suspicious."

"Good. And don't hesitate, you don't want to risk it." He paused. "I wish I was working in your section. At the very least I could help you defend your lunch."

"I think I'm good on that front." Haley held up an old army ammo can. "I'm loaded for Bear."

A grin broke across Jake's face, completely changing his expression from concern to delight. What a way to start off the week. He was spoiling her now. Haley's lips turned up too. "I borrowed the ammo can from Mitch this morning. Think it will work?"

He shrugged. "I love how creative you are, and the fact that you're fighting back, but I'm not sure how effective that will be against professional lunch thieves. How will you keep them out without a lock on it?"

She turned the can around so he could read the paper duct-taped to the side.

Warning! Do NOT open this box.

Jake didn't seem impressed. "They roof-bolted your last lunch to the ceiling, and you think putting a warning on this one is going to make the difference?"

She patted the box. "Yep. This is definitely going to do the trick. You'll see."

"I can't wait. In the meantime, do you really plan on eating today?"

Haley's shoulders sagged. "Not today. I have some extra jerky sticks and crackers."

"That's what I thought. I packed an extra lunch for you, so come over to the belt line on your break."

"Thanks." She carefully set the ammo can in the back of the truck. "I really don't think they'll mess with it after today."

The other men were trickling out of the lamp-house. Wing Nut, Leech, and Shark piled into the back of the mantrip. Haley stared at Leech. He normally chose the cab, not the back of the truck. What was he planning? Was he going to harass her all the way down to the work face?

"Hey, Scab," Leech said. "Still stupid enough to show up?" He elbowed Wing Nut. "If she was twice as smart, she'd still be stupid."

Jake clapped his hands together in a sarcastic applaud. Haley looked toward the mine portal, wishing they could get going. The last thing she wanted was a fight. She put a hand on Jake's arm to calm him, but he pulled away and leaned over the back of the mantrip, yanking Leech forward by the front of his jacket. "You have any more bottles of Coke to hand out today?"

Leech's eyes widened for a brief moment before they grew dark and hard. He smacked Jake's hand away. "Careful what you say. I might take it as a threat."

Bennie, Stump, and some men from the longwall came out and were watching the argument. "I'm just telling you to leave her alone." Jake took a step back and looked around at the small crowd. "I'm telling all of you, leave her alone."

"Or what?" Leech let out a laugh. "What ya gonna do, Einstein? Beat us all up?"

Jake's jaw tightened, and Haley could feel the tension mounting. Her mind raced for a way to end the dispute. Jake wasn't the type of person to fight. She wasn't sure what she'd think of him if he did.

The dark recesses of her memory floated with images of her dad and how he ended every argument with his fists. But Jake wasn't violent, was he? Haley didn't realize she'd been holding her breath until he spoke.

"I don't need to fight you."

A surge of relief flowed through her, but some of the men began to jeer. If Jake showed weakness, it would only spur more cruelty, and she didn't want that either.

The corners of Leech's mouth turned up in an I-knew-it grin. "A little scared, are you, Einstein? I guess you should be because if you think you're gonna' butt in and keep all of your teeth, you have another thing coming."

Jake shook his head. "You *will* leave her alone." He tapped his finger on Leech's metal tag where the last four digits of his social security were stamped. "It won't be hard for me to get the rest of these numbers."

Leech looked puzzled for a moment then his mouth curled up in victory. "So what? Is that supposed to scare me?"

Jake shrugged. When he spoke, his words were quiet but everyone could hear him. "You've never had your identity stolen? Your personal information leaked onto the web? Social security number, credit cards, bank accounts. I'd leave Haley alone, or someone might circumvent a system and upload some malicious software that will spill your guts all over the net. It won't matter how fast you react. It won't matter if you get the cops involved. The source would be untraceable, and your information would bleed out into a nightmare you'd never recover from."

Leech pulled back, his brows pinched together.

Jake didn't have to say anything else. He walked to the other mantrip where the rest of the beltmen waited and climbed into the driver seat. Haley tried to suppress the feeling stirring in her stomach—something between admiration and just plain *wow*. She took her seat in the back of the truck and carefully held the ammo box on her lap. Leech mumbled something unintelligible and pulled his collar up to block the breeze.

"What are you all standing around for?" Bear strode toward them, his eyes settling on Haley. "This isn't tea time. Let's get to work!"

* * *

Haley didn't encounter any problems that morning, and she hadn't seen Leech since they started working. Bear kept her busy doing backbreaking odd jobs until, at last, she headed to the transformer for her lunch break. Just as she turned the corner, she ran into someone.

"Watch it!"

Haley took a step back, shocked to hear a woman's voice. Her light ran up the clean coveralls and settled next to the heart-shaped face of Layla Harper.

"Sorry." Haley moved to the side. Harper must've been doing an EO8 on the complaint she'd called in. That was good. She was a tyrant when it came to following regulations, and Bear wouldn't get away with so much as a misplaced slate bar.

Harper's light flashed across her. "Haley Carter. I heard you were down here." Her lip pulled into a snarl. "Fun, isn't it?"

Haley expected some comradery, but there was none of that. Harper was cold and distant. "I don't mind the work."

Harper snorted. "I'm sure." She looked down at her clipboard and quickly covered up a long list of what were probably citations. She seemed overly pleased, like a cat eating a canary.

Just then Roadrunner walked up to them. "Ready to go back, Miss Harper?"

She gave a curt nod and then headed toward a mantrip without a word. Roadrunner clapped a hand on Haley's shoulder and jerked his head back toward the transformer. "You better go get your lunch. I heard it's waiting for you." He grinned at her, then ran after Harper.

Haley hurried down the corridor anxious to see what had happened to her ammo can. The rest of the crew were sitting nearby and their conversation died down as she approached. The old army box still sat where she had left it. Its latches were closed, but she knew they had opened it. It was obvious by the way the men avoided looking at her.

"Having a good lunch, boys?" Wing Nut and Shark grunted a response, but Leech kept his head down, concentrating on his double-layered sandwich. Haley picked up the ammo can when Stump caught her gaze. He winked and gave her a thumbs-up. It must've worked. She smiled, patted the can, and headed off to the belt line.

A few minutes later, her light bounced off several bright reflective strips in the distance. She knew which one was Jake before she could clearly see him—at least she thought so. While all the lights had momentarily looked up, there was one that stayed on her.

"I wondered if you were coming." Jake stood up. He didn't bother brushing himself off; it wouldn't have done any good anyway. He grabbed his lunch cooler and moved further down the belt so they could have a little privacy. Once they were settled, he handed her a sandwich and a package of Oreos.

"I guess you already know what I like." She opened the Oreos and stuck a whole one in her mouth then held the package out to him.

"I know how possessive you can be of a man's Oreos, so . . ." He reached into his lunch cooler and pulled out another package. "I brought my own."

Haley tried not to laugh, but tiny bits of cookie flew out of her mouth in the attempt. "Sorry." She cupped a hand over her lips and swallowed.

"So, did it work?" Jake picked up her ammo can and started unlatching it. She gasped and carefully pulled it away from him.

"Yes, it worked perfectly. And . . . don't . . . open . . . it." She quickly re-secured the latch and set the can next to her.

"Are you going to tell me what's in it?"

Haley took a bite of sandwich and chewed as she thought how to answer. "A very effective deterrent."

"What kind are we talking about?"

"The slithering kind."

Jake's light swung from the ammo can up to her face. "You didn't."

She shifted her head out of his direct beam. "I did. A rattlesnake to be precise." Jake gave her a megawatt, ear-to-ear grin. Twice in one day. It was like winning the lottery.

"I'm impressed." Jake was still grinning, his light on the can. "Is it alive?"

"Of course."

The tunnel rang with his laughter. "I wish I had seen their faces when they opened it."

Haley bobbed her head in agreement. "Leech wouldn't even look at me when I passed him. I think he might have a fear of snakes." She couldn't help but laugh. She pictured Leech pulling the lid off and hearing the rattle just as his light illuminated the diamond back. He would've scrambled to get the lid back on.

Jake's chuckle faded. "So where did you get a rattlesnake?"

"I have a friend, Caleb. He's a very mischievous twelve-year-old." Haley nodded to the ammo can. "It's actually his friend's snake and it'll be turned loose in the desert this afternoon."

She took another bite of her sandwich. For the first time, she was actually enjoying the day. She still hurt from the exertion of shoveling black sludge from around the water pump, but it felt good. The work was hard, but the guys weren't taunting her. And then there was Jake. . . She looked to the side of him, pretending to examine the rib while studying him in her peripheral vision. She liked his easy-going nature and the mad-scientist that emerged every now and then.

"Did you see the MSHA SUV this morning?" he asked.

Haley put her sandwich down. "It's Layla Harper. I ran into her a few minutes ago. I'm sure she was doing an EO8 on the complaint."

"Are you sure you want to push this?" Jake asked. "I'll help you if you do, but I don't want to risk you getting hurt if Bear gets edgy and takes it out on you."

Bear would definitely be more moody with MSHA cracking down on him, but she could handle that. She had been in that type of situation plenty of times, and not just with Bear. It was something she had faced daily growing up, but she wasn't a scared teenager anymore, and she wasn't going to sit back and let someone else abuse her.

"I'm going to follow through with it," she said.

Haley wasn't sure what "following through" really meant until near the end of her shift. She hurried behind Stump to where the other men had gathered around the shuttle car. A pole stuck into the machine at an odd angle like a toothpick skewering a piece of meat. All lights focused on Scarecrow as two men carefully lifted him out of the driver's seat and sat him on the ground.

"I'm all right," Scarecrow said, his voice shaking. He pulled the edge of his pants down to show part of his hip. A bright red, swollen mark was starting to emerge. "Didn't even break the skin. See I told you I was all right. Pretty good for almost being run through."

Stump tipped his hat back and scratched his head. "Why'd you keep driving the car after you bent the door?"

Scarecrow shrugged. "It was almost the end of shift. I only had another half hour."

"Well, you're lucky you didn't do it when Layla Harper was here. She'd hit you so hard with her MSHA regulations, you'd be unconscious for a week."

"Not funny," Bear said. He hunched over to look at Scarecrow's bruise. "The penalties she gave us today are bad enough. Weird how she always shows up at the worst times."

Haley crossed her arms and pinched her mouth shut. What was weird was Bear allowing the work to continue when the shuttle car's door wouldn't shut properly. It was lucky the shift was over and Scarecrow was going slow in order to park the car. He must not have seen the pole which jousted its way through the opening in the bent door, turning the machine into an oversized kabob and nearly killing himself.

Haley watched Bear, waiting for him to call the surface and tell them what happened, but he didn't. Maybe he thought that since it was the end of the shift, it could wait. Still, it was a reportable injury, and she was going to make sure of it. Even if that meant she had to follow them into Cross's office herself.

Once they reached the surface, Haley walked into the lamp-house and took her time plugging her lamp into the charging station. Scarecrow followed Bear into Cross's office then came out a few minutes later. Haley walked over to the board, pretending to read it. Jake must have already gone home. He'd never said anything about waiting for her. Still, she wished he was there. She lingered by the board until everyone left. Once she was alone, she quickly crossed the room and ducked into Cross's office.

The room was empty and the computer was off. She looked on the counter where the accident report would've been filled out and left for Cross to enter later. She peeked into mail slots and fingered through stacks of paper, but couldn't see it anywhere. At last, she looked in the trash can. In the bottom were pieces of a torn, crumpled form. She darted a nervous look around, then reached in and pulled out a few pieces.

"What are you doing in here?" Bear's voice sounded from the doorway.

Haley jumped and dropped the paper in the trash can before turning around. His dark frame blocked the light from the hallway. "I wanted to talk to Cross about something."

"He ain't here."

Bear looked her up and down, his hatred intensified by the shadow of coal dust. Then he held out a paper and waited for her to take it. "It's a job offer. To go back to the warehouse. As you'll see, there's a slight pay raise from what you were previously earning there. I suggest you take it."

Haley looked at the paper. For a moment it almost seemed enticing. No more back-breaking work. No more dealing with Bear and Leech. No more chauvinistic comments. No more threats.

"Candy coated offers don't come along every day. Take it if you know what's good for you."

Haley looked at the pay increase which was only fifty cents an hour more than her original warehouse wage. It wasn't near as much as she was getting now working underground. "I'll think about it," she lied. Bear seemed to buy it and turned to leave. Behind his back, Haley dropped the offer into the trash can, but the paper made the slightest sound as it slid to the bottom.

Bear turned and looked at the can. "You'll think about it, huh?" She tried to leave, but his big burly paw caught her by the shoulder and spun her around. "That's it?" He pointed to the discarded paper. "I'm trying to do you a favor here."

"It doesn't pay enough." It was only the tip of the iceberg. It had taken some time, but some of the men were starting to come around, and she wasn't about to abandon them without figuring out what was going on.

Bear's face turned red under the coal dust. "Not enough pay? It's better than what you were earning there before. I think your die-hard feminist views are blinding you." His breath grew heavy and angry. "I shouldn't have thrown the coal through your window, I should've thrown *you* through it."

Haley visibly flinched, and her breath froze in her throat. Bear stomped away. When he reached the door, he stopped and pointed at her. "And, Scab, if you ever call in another hazard complaint, I *will* throw you through a window."

CHAPTER 30

"Maybe you *should* transfer back to the warehouse."

Haley didn't answer as she followed Jake into his study. The armchair from his living room had been placed next to his desk, suggesting he knew she'd be coming over. They both sat down, but instead of going straight to his computer, he leaned back and looked at her.

"I'm just thinking about your safety." He paused. "But you don't want to go back to the warehouse, do you?"

"Nope."

"I'm won't argue, but it worries me. There's no way Bear should've found out who called in the complaint. Maybe whoever took your call recognized your voice and told him."

"That's unlikely. The hazard complaint hotline is contracted out of the country. The guy I talked to was from India. He didn't even speak English well. They just pass the information to MSHA. Besides, I never mentioned my name."

Jake tapped a finger on his desk. "Then Bear probably just made a lucky guess."

"That's a possibility." She pointed to his computer. "Did you find anything new?"

His face lit up, his brilliant smile instantly brightening her mood. That rare Cheshire grin was coming more frequently now. Haley savored the feeling. "I did a little digging on Mitch," he said.

It wasn't what she'd expected, but she'd been curious about Mitch too. "Did he really own P.C. Mine?"

"Yes." Jake's expression dampened. "He worked at Horse Canyon Mine before it closed, then hired on at Plateau and worked his way up to a fire boss. A couple of years later, he got a few investors to back him and he opened Price Canyon Mine. Like he said, it was a small operation, but they had decent production." Jake paused and let out a long breath. "Five years into it, a roof fall killed three miners. The families accused him of neglecting safety standards. The lawsuits started, his wife divorced him, and he ended up selling the mine at a fraction of what it was worth."

Haley let her gaze drift out the window. So that was it. That was why Mitch lived in a run-down apartment, walked the gutter looking for used cigarettes, and drank himself into unconsciousness whenever he could.

Jake touched her hand, drawing her attention back to him. His fingers rested on hers. His hands were clean, but the everlasting black edge around his nails was still prevalent. She had similar marks on her own.

"I think it was good for Mitch to come help us. I think he needed it."

Haley nodded, her thoughts torn between Mitch and the fact that Jake still had his hand on hers. She liked the warmth seeping in from his touch, but at the same time, it scared her. She looked up and focused on Jake's computer. "Can we look something up?"

"Sure." He pulled his hand away and mixed feelings of relief and disappointment washed over her.

"Can you find the accident reports for P.C. Mine when Mitch owned it?"

"No problem." In a matter of seconds, he had the MSHA page up depicting the accidents during Mitch's ownership.

Haley cocked her head to the side and tried to make sense of what she was seeing. There were few accidents to start with, but there were significantly more near the end of the five-year period. "So there were *some* safety problems when Mitch owned it."

Jake nodded in agreement. "I'm not surprised that Don Wakefield bought the mine for a fraction of what it was worth. After those three miners died, it wouldn't have been hard to force Mitch to sell for pennies on the dollar."

"What if that was happening again?" Haley asked. "Kim said someone was trying to buy the mine. What if Wakefield is asking Bear to hide accidents because he wants top dollar?"

"Let's see." Jake swiped his finger on the screen and started flipping through windows quicker than Haley could read them. "According to this, the mine isn't for sale, but that doesn't mean someone hasn't made an offer for it." Jake flashed through more data, the light from the screen reflecting in his eyes. "If they wanted to sell it, they'd do a comparison with other mines in the area. Production for its size is good." Two more screens popped up, showing a split view. "Safety-wise, it still has some problems—even with the accidents going unreported. But that's only within the last few months. A year ago, it safer than some of the other mines."

Haley stared at the numbers. Jake obviously understood the data. His brows were knit together, his eyes sharp and fixed. She could almost see the synapses in his brain firing like a high-powered automatic rifle.

An eyebrow came up and he leaned forward. "Interesting."

Haley looked at the monitor. "What is it?"

"These reports, and the fines from MSHA—" Jake leaned back. "MSHA started cracking down on P.C. about the time their accidents went up, but look at this." He pointed to the screen. "Several citations are for things that the mine had passed off on during their own in-house inspections."

Jake tapped on his screen. He wasn't on a public website anymore but was looking at the restricted information on the mine's computer. "See, this rock dust was tested by the mine and checked off as good." He tapped again and MSHA's website came up. "And here it is again and P.C. suddenly gets a bad report on the same rock dust."

"Who did the testing at the mine?"

"Not Bear." Jake ran his finger along the screen "These things are being signed off by various safety guys, operators, and other bosses. Sure, Bear's done some too, but it isn't always him."

Haley slumped down in her chair. "So, Bear isn't the only one sweeping things under the rug at the mine. But why? MSHA is catching them on everything and it's costing them in fines, so why put such a collective effort into hiding stuff instead of just fixing it?"

Jake stood up and paced around the room, rubbing the back of his neck, and tapping his finger thoughtfully against his chin. Haley watched. His movements became more animated. This was the mad-scientist side of him she liked. He turned away from her, staring out the window, his hands stuffed in the back pockets of his jeans, creating a wrinkle in his t-shirt between his shoulder blades. Haley dropped her eyes. She needed to proceed with caution in the relationship department, and it was becoming harder with each passing moment.

Suddenly Jake spun around, his gestures even more expanded. He ran his hands through his hair, his teeth parting with one of his manic grins, his eyes radiating a brilliant energy, excited by an idea he'd just had.

A small thrill ran though Haley. His mussed-up hair looked far more attractive than it should have. He placed his hands on the armrests of her chair and leaned over her until he was inches from her face.

"Three months," he said, his tongue playing on the edge of his toothy grin.

Haley pressed herself into the back of the chair and hoped he couldn't hear her the wild thud of her heartbeat. "What are you talking about?"

"Three months ago. That's our key." His smile widened and he jumped back into his chair, his hands already flying across the keyboard. "That's when the numbers shifted. When they really started hiding things." He brought his finger down on the enter key with a flourish.

Click.

Haley scooted closer and leaned over his shoulder to see the screen. He turned his head slightly and looked at her. She was too close to him, her sandy-brown hair touching his shoulder. "Sorry." She leaned back to give him some distance.

He raised one brow. "I didn't mind."

"But I did." Haley concentrated on the screen. It was a posting from the local newspaper. She could still feel the excitement rolling off Jake in waves, and with her own emotions swirling, she couldn't focus enough to think straight. "What are we looking at?"

"I did a media search on the mine for that time period. Apparently, the *Sun Advocate* ran an article on them right after the last EO1 which was exactly three months ago."

Haley tried to read what was on the screen—anything to keep her mind off of Jake. It took all her willpower. He was in his element and enjoying every moment. She wanted to feel that eagerness, but she reminded herself to be cautious. She gave up and sat back in the chair. "Just tell me what it says."

He nodded, or more accurately, he kind of bounced in his seat. "It looks like this article is raking P.C. over the coals, so to speak, for their poor record. It specifically mentions several issues written up during the EO1 inspection."

"So three months ago they get some bad press. Would that be enough for them to start hiding their accidents?"

"Possibly. This was written by Tom Silver. And it looks like he's put out several anti-coal articles. In the last twelve weeks, he's written two articles on P.C. Mine . . . And he has his own blog."

Another page popped up. *No Coal for a Greener America.* Behind the title was a picture of a coal plant, its stacks spitting out black, billowing smoke while an innocent little girl sat in the foreground with an inhaler in her mouth. "He has over ten thousand followers." Jake scrolled down the page. "And it looks like he's targeted P.C. Mine in several posts."

"So you think Bear and these other guys at the mine are trying to counteract Tom Silver." Haley rubbed her temples. "This is giving me a headache."

"Come with me." Jake pulled her to her feet and led her to the kitchen. It was only ten steps, but he held her hand the whole way. A moment later, he set a glass of milk in front of her and a new package of Oreos. "I have aspirin if this doesn't work." He took an Oreo, dunked it in her glass, and popped it into his mouth.

"Hey, I thought this was my milk." She took a quick drink to hide the pink rising in her cheeks. He was so casual about sharing with her. And really, she didn't mind. She was trying to open up, but the default setting in her mind was setting off yellow caution signals.

As soon as she set her glass down, Jake dunked another Oreo. "We should have a designated Oreo night."

Haley took a cookie from the package. "And what, just get together and eat Oreos?"

He nodded. "That was my subtle way of asking you out."

Haley set the Oreo down. Part of her leaped with excitement, but the other part—the broken part—retracted, crawling back behind the caution signs where she could protect herself against feeling. "I don't know. I'll have to think about it." She wanted to say *yes*, but this was a big step, and she just wanted a friendship for now. Dating could come later. She glanced up at the clock. "It's getting late. I should go."

Jake pushed himself away from the counter, the smile on his face faded. "Are you always going to do this?"

"I'm not doing anything."

"Anytime I try to get close to you, you put up blocks. You've been doing it since high school."

A knot formed in her chest. "I'm working on it. At least I'm not like Noah." She hoped there was some truth to that statement. "I really am trying to change."

Jake shifted his weight to one side. "Yeah, I know you let Liam get close to you."

She could see the hurt in Jake's eyes. He thought she had opened her life up to Liam and couldn't understand why she wouldn't do the same with him. But it wasn't true. Her relationship with Liam had only been superficial.

"Liam's a completely different story," she said. "You don't know anything about him or what he's like, or why I broke up with him."

She stopped. If she *really* explained it, it would only prove his point, that she kept barriers between herself and other people. She turned away, trying to hide the emotion in her face. "I'm not putting up barriers." It was the lie she so desperately wanted to be true.

He reached out and took her hand. When she didn't pull away, he gently turned her around. Haley didn't want him to see the tears building in her eyes, but she looked up at him. He lowered his head as if he was about to whisper something in her ear, but he didn't. He paused for a moment then softly pressed his lips against hers.

She half expected herself to gasp or pull away, but a surge of desire shot through her. She relaxed into the kiss, her mouth moving against his. The caution signs in her mind began slipping away, leaving her so she could submerse herself in his warmth. But the default side of her wouldn't let that happen. Years of instinct and habit kicked in. Why was Jake doing this? She had never led him on or insinuated that she wanted this. She opened her eyes and shoved him away then turned and ran for the door.

Her breath came in short gasps as she climbed in her car, her hands trembling. But she had wanted friendship, not romance. Jake had weakened that resolve. For a moment, her determination had slipped away. But she was stronger than that. She threw the car into reverse, backed out of the driveway, and sped down the street.

CHAPTER 31

"I kissed him. . ." Haley dropped the words off and shook her head. "Well, that's not actually true. He kissed me." She held her breath and waited for a response.

"That's gross."

Haley looked at Caleb, who was sitting in the passenger seat of her little Bug. "It really wasn't. That's the problem."

"So you like him?"

She nodded. "Yes, I do . . . and then I shoved him."

Caleb smacked his hand against his forehead. "What are you, in fourth grade? You like a boy, so you push him?"

"It wasn't like that." Haley let out a long sigh. She shouldn't have been talking to Caleb about this. She should've been explaining it to Jake. She had regretted running out like she did. It's just that Jake's kiss confused her. With Liam, she had dodged his attempts to kiss her for weeks. But with Jake, she had willingly kissed back. And that scared her. "I thought I had my reasons for doing it. But I was wrong." She tightened her grip on the steering wheel. "I completely reacted in the wrong way."

"You apologized to him at work today, didn't you?" Caleb asked.

"I was going to. But I never saw him."

"Because you came home early?"

She nodded. She had just arrived at the mine when she received a call from the care center. A male volunteer with the same height and build as her dad had tried to help her mother to the dining room. They called Haley when they couldn't calm Mrs. Carter down. And

Haley didn't mind. Spending the day with her mother was far better than dealing with Bear, but on the other hand, she still needed to talk to Jake to apologize.

Caleb fingered the window switch and looked at her. "You can call him, you know."

"Yeah, but this is something I should tell him in person."

"That's a good idea. But don't worry. Jake shouldn't be upset because things don't get serious until the third kiss."

Haley eyed him. "What do you even know about kissing and when things get serious?"

"I kissed Kaylee Parker during recess twice. She still doesn't like me. But third time is the charm, right?"

Haley directed her car behind their apartment building and parked. "I'll talk to Jake tomorrow, and I'll be on the lookout for when we get to that third kiss." She opened her door to climb out but then paused. "Caleb, thanks for coming with me to visit my mom."

"No problem. But I really didn't have a choice. You're my ride, so I have to go wherever you go. At least until Gram gets her car fixed."

"I'm okay with that; you were good with my mom, and I know it's not very fun going to care centers and being around old people."

He shrugged. "Your mom's not as old as most of them. I guess that's what makes it sad. Anyway, it wasn't major torture. Your mom's pretty interesting. And it was cool what she said about your brother. He sounds crazy, but it was nice he came to visit her."

Haley zoned out, staring at the apartment building. "It was good of him." Noah's visit had been difficult. Cindy said that they had to calm her mother down, as they explained who the strange man in her room was. It took a while for Noah to get her to warm up to him, but once she knew who he was, she eventually she let him talk to her and even let him hold her hand.

His efforts had made a difference. Today her mother's conversation was more lucid and coherent. She hadn't called Haley by name, but she hadn't referred to her as Brooke either. She could only imagine what Noah had said to her. He always had a soft side, and she could picture him kneeling beside her and apologizing for that night—like he had done with her. It might have been enough to pull her from her illusions and back to reality.

"You coming in?" Caleb asked. "I want to steal some lunch meat. Gram hasn't gone shopping for the week yet, and I'm starving."

Haley climbed out of the car and saw Mitch walking down the alley. "I'll be right up, just give me a minute." She tossed her keys to Caleb. "Help yourself to the fridge."

Mitch veered off to the other side of the parking lot. Haley hoped he hadn't spotted a cigarette, but he stopped at Gram's car. The hood was up and a small toolbox was perched on the radiator. He leaned over the engine block and watched her as she approached.

"Nice of you to help them out like this." She gestured to the car.

"If you're thinkin' you need a mechanic too, don't get any ideas. I'm not running a business here. Caleb's a good kid and his grandma needed some help, that's all. She's too old to be walking to work."

"I'm just saying it is nice of you to help out."

He shrugged. "You still working at the mine?"

"I took the day off, but yes, I'm sticking it out." She pulled an envelope out of her pocket and flapped it against the palm of her hand. "And this is part of the reason why."

"What's that?"

"The added motivation I needed to keep going—a therapy bill I'm about to pay, and for once, there's money in the bank to do it."

Mitch nodded, then took a wrench and loosened the nut on the battery terminal. As he moved, Haley noticed a nicotine patch peeking out from under the sleeve of his shirt. She watched him for a moment then cleared her throat. "Jake found some more information."

His eyes flickered toward her momentarily.

"Bear's not the only one hiding things. Others at the mine are signing off on things that don't meet MSHA standards."

Mitch pried the terminal open with a screwdriver and wiggled it until it came off the post. "I knew that shaft was deeper than it appeared. Was there anything else?"

"We found a writer publishing anti-coal articles about P.C. Mine. His name is Tom Silver. Have you ever heard of him?"

Mitch stiffened.

"Do you know him?"

"Nope." He shook his head as if to emphasize the fact. "But it ain't the first time a coal mine has gone to war with bad media."

"What should I do? It looks like Tom Silver is trying to get P.C. shut down, which I don't want, but on the other hand, it's not safe for the miners either."

Mitch wiped his hands on a grease rag. "Environmentalists fight against the coal industry all the time. They haven't succeeded so far. They put out ads, write up reports, pour money into anti-coal campaigns, but it doesn't make much of a dent. You've seen it." He waved a hand to the south. "That billboard out by the power plant. 'Bringing you electricity . . . and as much pollution as seventeen million cars.' You really think that stops people from turning on their light switch when they get home? It does about as much good as someone throwing rocks at an armed bunker. As long as coal is the cheapest, most plentiful source of fuel, the industry is going to keep marching forward."

"Is that what you call it when P.C. hides their dirty laundry?"

Mitch didn't answer.

Haley sighed. "I just don't want anyone to get killed in the process."

Mitch threw the grease rag into the toolbox, picked up his wrench, and leaned in under the hood. "Are you sure those men at the mine are really doing what you're accusing them of? In my experience, a boss wouldn't risk the safety of his men."

"Did you?" Her voice grew thin and quiet. "Three miners died when you owned the mine—" She stopped, not sure if it was a subject she should be bringing up.

Mitch tightened his grip on the wrench until his knuckles were white. "You want to know if those men died because of something I did?" He looked up at her. "What do you want from me, Haley? You want me to help? You want me to give you advice because I

~ 200 ~

know the mine? And you think it will somehow redeem me or pull me out of the gutter? Well, I hate to break it to you, but I am every bit as bad as I seem."

He threw his wrench across the parking lot, sending it scraping across the pavement until it hit the crumbling bricks of the apartment building with a smack. "Yes, those boys died on my watch, and it was my fault. I put production over safety. Bear was there. He was one of my miners. He knows exactly what happened, and I don't think he'd make the same mistake I did."

"And what if he is?"

Mitch shook his head. "There's more to it than that. Why don't you go ask this Tom Silver what's going on?" Mitch turned back to the car and began digging through his toolbox for another wrench. "And good luck. It might be kind of hard, considering Tom Silver was one of the miners I killed while trying to make my millions."

CHAPTER 32

"You looking for Jake?"

Haley ignored Leech and sat down in the back of the mantrip, wishing the rest of the crew would hurry.

Leech reclined against the side of the truck. "That's what you're doing, ain't it, Scab?"

She tipped her helmet forward so it shielded her eyes, but it was too late. He had already noticed her watching the parking lot. Unfortunately, Jake's red truck hadn't arrived yet.

"Well, you can stop looking. Jake quit yesterday."

Haley's head came up, and Leech laughed. "Didn't know that, did ya, Scab?" He slapped a hand against the truck in enjoyment. "Now ain't no one gonna be nice to you."

He thumped her helmet with a jarring blow then climbed into the cab. Haley turned, searching the men that were filing out of the lamp-house. Quit. He couldn't have quit. A lump grew in her throat.

Men were climbing in the mantrips now. Haley looked at the belt crew. Moose wasn't there either, but that didn't bother her; it was the fact that Jake wasn't that tore at her. She still needed to apologize to him. She hoped that Leech was somehow wrong. Maybe his truck broke down. Maybe he was sick. He wouldn't just quit. He wouldn't leave her to deal with everything on her own. She recalled the crack of her hand against his cheek and another shaft of regret shot through her heart.

"Is somethin' wrong?" Stump sat down next to her.

"No," she lied. She opened her lunch box, pulled out a container, and handed it to him.

"What's this?"

"Lasagna. I made a big batch as a peace offering for someone." She glanced at the other container in her box. "But I packed one for you too."

Stump rubbed his whiskers with the back of his hand then cleared his throat. "Thanks. Since my wife passed, it ain't often I get somethin' homemade. I appreciate it."

Haley nodded and looked at the lamp-house again, praying that Jake would somehow walk out. The door opened, and her hopes rose. Bear emerged. Their eyes locked and a corner of his mouth came up—not with a smile, but a leer. She shuddered then pulled her collar up and tipped her hat over her eyes, but not before she scanned the parking lot again.

A hollow feeling spread out from her chest, inching its way down her arms and legs. She hadn't realized until now how much Jake's presence meant to her. It was far more painful than she wanted to admit, but she needed him. She almost laughed at the idea, or more likely, cried at it. She never imagined actually *needing* a man, but she needed Jake. His kindness, his understanding, even his well-intended rebukes—she needed those too. She didn't know if she could face Bear alone today.

The truck engine purred to life. It felt more like a mechanical ticking time bomb without Jake around. She glanced at the portal as they drove toward it. For the first time, she was scared to go underground. She nearly hopped out of the truck, but she steeled herself. She looked at Stump. Behind his old tired eyes, there was a sense of kindness. He probably had no idea about the deception going on. And Shark, Scarecrow, Wing Nut. Maybe none of them knew; maybe all of them did. But they didn't deserve to be caught in the middle of it. Maybe she couldn't do anything to stop it, but she wouldn't abandon them. Not like Noah had done to her on that horrific night.

The mantrip stopped just outside the portal. She wondered what the holdup was. In the cab, Bear turned and looked at her as if he were giving her one last chance to leave.

She gave the slightest shake of her head and settled down lower in her seat. It wouldn't be the first time she'd faced an abusive man. Come whatever, she was going to stick it out. The truck rumbled into the portal. Haley took one last look at the sky. If she made it through today, she'd apologize to Jake. It wouldn't make up for what she'd done, and maybe she didn't deserve him after all, but she needed to apologize.

* * *

Death stalked the underground passageways. Miners were aware of it and so was Haley.

She looked at the muddy clay-like roof and cringed. "Bad top?" she asked.

"Yep." Wing Nut's light tracked along the roof and then down to the bolting machine. "There's a stream crossing above us on the surface. We'll need to be real careful. Anytime the moisture content goes up in the roof, it's likely to fall."

Haley's mouth grew dry. Today, just when they happened to hit another patch of bad top, Bear had assigned her to bolt the roof—the most dangerous job in the mine.

Wing Nut started doing the pre-op on the bolter, telling her what needed to be checked. She followed him around, but her light kept flashing down the shaft where the uneven roof jutted out with loose rock. "Why do you choose to be roof bolter?"

"It's just how things ended up." Wing Nut walked around the machine, then paused. "Truthfully, at one time, I was going to be a dentist." Haley wasn't sure if was teasing, but there was nothing joking about his expression. "I started my schooling and hit the books, but—" He shrugged. "I couldn't pass the manual dexterity test. My dad was a miner, so here I am. It's a good job, and I like it."

"Have you ever seen anyone get hurt? I mean *really* bad?"

He gave a solemn nod. "Fingers cut off, men caught between equipment and the ribs, even saw someone get hit with a two-hundred-pound rock. He made it out, but he died a few days after. But every job has risks. Truckers and timber workers have a higher fatality rate than miners, but enough of this. No time for fear. We just gotta get the job done. You ready?"

"After that pep-talk, sure. Willing and anxious."

Wing Nut smiled. In the halo of her light, she could see he was missing one of his back teeth. "Thanks," she said. "For being nice to me."

A corner of his mouth pulled up again. "Well, that snake in your lunch box—that was the funniest thing I ever saw. You should've seen Leech. He backpedaled so fast he fell on his butt and scurried back 'til he couldn't go any further. Shark had to put the lid back on the ammo can. I thought they'd both have a heart attack before it was over." Wing Nut put his key in the machine and started it up. "All right," he called over the roar. "In Bear's words—Let's get to work!"

Haley's light went to the uneven roof, half expecting to see it dripping with water. Wing Nut must've sensed her hesitation. "Don't be scared," he called out. "Push it to the back of your mind, do the job, and hope for the best." He flashed his light on her. "Just remember, we do what we have to do to support our families." *That* she understood. He moved the machine forward. Haley inched her way along, her legs trembling.

Wing Nut showed her how the power lift held up the exposed roof while they drilled a hole and then fed a bolt into it before torquing it down. Haley concentrated on the job. It was all she could do to keep her mind from being torn between thoughts of Jake and worrying about the roof. The hours crawled by, painfully slow and filled with tension. By the time they had finished lunch and were working again, Haley was operating the drill and inserting the bolts. They still had two hours to go before the shift ended when Bear came to check on them.

A new twinge a fear crawled up Haley's spine. What did Bear have planned for her? Something to put her in the path of more danger? His dark figure towered over her, but as he opened his mouth to speak, the mountain rumbled. Haley's heart stopped as a crashing sound rolled through the tunnel. She ducked, turning her light up to the roof, but the top seemed intact. Bear ran through the check curtain while Wing Nut shut the machine down then ran out too. Haley tried to swallow her panic. She dropped the bolt she was holding and followed, her heart beating out of her chest.

When she passed through the curtain, Stump was standing there. He pointed. "Roof fall in the next intersection, in entry two."

In the distance, swirling dust expanded around a large mound of rubble which was piled nearly to the roof. It was an unnerving sight, but Haley couldn't pull her eyes away from it. Bear was on his phone, and miners were gathering. Suddenly the mountain rumbled again, and rock crumbled out of the roof from where Haley had just been. Everyone moved up the intake and watched as muddy rock came down, partially cutting off the intersection in entry three.

This couldn't be happening. Haley darted her light across the roof. Everything seemed to be closing in. A man ran down the intake to where Bear was. They put their heads together and started talking. Haley was too scared to take her eyes off the roof to get a good look at the man, but she knew it was the foreman.

Bear rubbed a hand anxiously across his beard. After another minute, the foreman hurried back up the intake, talking on his phone.

"All right!" Bear bellowed. "What are you standing around gawking at? You've all see a little cave in before." He stopped and eyed Haley. "Well, maybe the Scab hasn't, so we'll understand if she faints with fear. But for the rest of you, there's not much to look at. As far as roof falls go, this ain't a bad one and no one got hurt. We were scheduled to do an emergency walk-out drill at the end of shift today, but we're going to get to it sooner than expected. Make sure your equipment is shut down and put to bed. When you're done, meet back here." He paused, but when no one moved, he threw his hands in the air. "What are you waiting for? Get to work!"

A few minutes later, they gathered together again. Bear gave Leech a box of SCSR packs and told him to distribute them. "Just a regular drill. These are the old breathers." He held one up. "They're going out of date soon, so you get to use them for the emergency escape practice. Leech and I are staying behind to shore up the roof."

Leech held one of the SCSRs out for Haley to take, but she reached into the box and took a different one. She wasn't going to take any chances when it came to Leech giving her things. He scowled at her, and then continued handing out the rest of the packs.

Bear let his light settle on them, making sure they each had one. "You know the drill. Put your breather on and head to the secondary escape route. Stick together."

Haley opened her breather and took out the flimsy goggles and breathing apparatus which consisted of a mouthpiece and nose clips attached to a bag that would hang below her chin. She mimicked the others in putting it on, her stomach still twisting in knots.

A minute later, she followed the other men as they walked to the belt line—their secondary escape route. There they joined the other orange-hats. Haley looked at each of them, hoping Jake would somehow be among them. He wasn't. She didn't recognize the new crew boss, but he gathered them together, and they began their long walk out.

There wasn't anything complicated about the drill. They were simply required to walk out of the mine with their breathers on, but it was harder than Haley expected. The mask made it feel as though she were breathing through a straw and, with the added exertion of walking up the steep grade, it wasn't long before she was wiping sweat from her forehead.

Ahead of her, one of the miners tripped in the gob and fell to the ground. Two men walked around him and continued on. The guy pushing himself up on his hands and knees was an orange-hat. Maybe that was why they didn't stop to help. She knew exactly what that felt like, and she wasn't about to pass him by. She stopped next to him and grabbed his arm, helping him to his feet. It was Moose.

He pulled his breather out of his mouth and sucked in a lung full of air. "Thanks. Good thing this is a practice. I can't breathe with this thing on." He shook the SCSR like he was mad at it. "Did you see the roof fall?"

Haley pulled her own mouthpiece out. "Yeah. Hit too close to home." She paused then looked up at him. "I didn't see you this morning before shift started."

"I got hung up in Mr. Branch's office with Jake."

Haley put a hand on his arm, stopping him. "Jake was here at the mine? I didn't see his truck."

"He parked next to the mine office. He had me go in and tell Mr. Branch about my injury. Apparently, the report I filled out didn't get logged. Oh, and I almost forgot—" Moose pulled a piece of paper out of his pocket and handed it to her. "Jake said to give this to you if I saw you."

Her fingers trembled as she unfolded the paper. Jake's message was neatly written in pen. *It's not Bear. Talk to him. Tell him what you know.*

Haley put a hand over her mouth to control her emotions. "He's still trying to help."

Moose raised his light up from the paper. "I don't know what that's about, but Jake's a nice guy. He's always helping people, so why are you surprised?"

She didn't want to say that she had shoved Jake away the last time she'd seen him. She shook her head. "I'm just surprised he came, considering he quit yesterday."

"Jake didn't quit. He was fired."

Haley's startled as if the breath had been knocked from her. Maybe they found out about him hacking into the mine's computer system. "This is all my fault," she muttered.

"What are you talking about?"

"I'm talking about Jake. It was all me. I bumped him from Bear's crew to the belt line, then he offered his help, and I pushed him away. Now he's lost his job—and it's all because of me."

Moose frowned. "If you're worried about Jake's job, he's trying to get it back right now—him and that old guy."

~ 208 ~

"What old guy?"

He shrugged. "Some guy came in with him today. I think his name is Mitch." Haley's breath caught. Mitch was helping too? Both of them could've walked away, but they hadn't. If that wasn't a sign of true friendship, she didn't know what was. Moose put a hand on her shoulder, and his light bobbed across her face. "If you're wondering what to do—do what Jake says." He pointed to the paper.

Bear didn't do it. Talk to him. Tell him what you know.

"I can't go back to where Bear is," Haley said. "I'm supposed to be walking out."

"It's just a practice. If Jake told you to talk to Bear, then maybe you should. He's pretty smart about things."

"You think I should leave the group?"

"It's not like you're going to get lost." Moose pointed up to a small box hanging from a cable. "With the tracking system, Comspec knows where you're at, and you have your phone."

Haley looked down the belt line. Jake *was* smart, and if he thought she should tell Bear everything they found out, then she better do it. She owed Jake at least that much.

"All right." She directed her light so she could see Moose's face. "I want you to catch up to the other miners and tell the crew boss that I went back to talk to Bear. If it takes very long, then I'll call the surface and catch a ride out in one of the mantrips."

"Sure. No problem."

Haley jogged back down the belt line. When she reached the feeder, she turned and made her way to entry three. She slowed when she saw the roof fall in the intersection. A man's reflective strips flashed beyond it. She stopped, remembering that Bear wasn't the only one who had stayed behind. Leech had too. Cautiously she moved along the rib opposite of the cave in. The man was moving away, looking down the new cut where the continuous miner was parked. Haley didn't want to approach him until she knew who it was, and she couldn't tell from this distance. She scooted forward and had only gone a few feet when the man spun around, spotlighting her.

"What are you doing here?"

It was Bear, but Haley didn't feel the surge of relief she'd expected. She reached up and adjusted her hard hat. "I need to talk with you."

Bear stomped toward her, letting out a string of swear words. Haley started backing up. "Jake wanted me to talk to you."

He didn't seem to care. He broke into a run and Haley stepped back, hitting into the rib, then spun around, trying to get her feet to move in the gob. She had only taken a few steps when Bear caught her by the arm and spun her around. Behind them, the whirring noise of a motor came to life.

Bear's face contorted with anger, and a surge of fear ran through Haley as she realized it wasn't her headlamp illuminating his expression. It was the lights from a shuttle car, and it was barreling directly at them. She started to scream just as the air exploded with the loud crunching sound of metal plowing into rock, body, and bones.

CHAPTER 33

Leech turned the shuttle car and sped away, up the intake and around the pile of rubble that barricaded part of the entryway.

Haley groaned in agony. She tried to roll over and push herself up, but the movement shot pain through her arm. Without looking at it, she knew it was broken. She gritted her teeth and turned her head, shining her light through the swirling dust to where Bear had been moments ago. Fear pricked the back of her neck, scared of what she might see. He had pushed her away from him at the last second and had taken the brunt of the impact, getting crushed between the shuttle car and the rib. A deluge of guilt swept over her as her light swung back and forth searching for him. Bear had saved her. He had pushed her to safety, and she prayed it hadn't cost him his life.

Dust swirled around her and everything looked the same dirty color. Where was he? There. A flash of silver on the ground not five feet away—the reflective tape from Bear's jacket. Haley crawled toward the odd shape, her legs trembling. Bear lay motionless, his body crumpled and bent at an odd angle, his helmet off to the side, shooting its light down the empty tunnel. But he was alive. She could hear his ragged, wheezing breath.

Another explosion echoed from the intersection, and the air seemed to quake around her. She jerked her head around. In the distance, her light illuminated Leech's shuttle car as he plowed over the support timbers near the roof fall.

"No!" she tried to scream.

An ominous cracking sound filled the air as if the mine was

coming apart at the seams. Then the roof gave again. Haley hunched over, covering her head with her good arm and waiting for the entire mountain to crash down.

Dust clogged her throat, and small debris showered down from the damaged rib beside her. She kept her eyes pinched closed while an oppressive, terrible voice in her head told her that the exit was filling up with rubble. It was a long time before the terrifying sound of crashing rock fell silent. It took longer for Haley to convince herself to open her eyes, to face the dread that they had been walled into a tomb. At last, she peered through the thick, blinding dust. As the debris sunk to the ground, so did her heart. Through the earthy vapor, she could see enough to know that the low-roofed tunnel was completely sealed off.

Cradling her injured arm, Haley inched closer to Bear. His eyes were open, blinking, staring blankly up at her; a trickle of blood ran from the corner of his mouth into his beard.

"What happened?" His voice was weak.

"Leech finished knocking the roof down at the intersection. I think it's blocked entirely off." She tried to add a touch of hope to her voice, but she couldn't summon a feeling she was completely devoid of, and fear squeezed its way through her vocal cords.

Bear coughed. "Go through the cross cut into entry two and see if there's a way out."

"That's where the first cave-in happened. It was nearly blocked off then, and now—"

"You don't know," Bear cut her off. It took him a few seconds before he could talk again. "There might be an opening. You might not have much time; now get to work."

Haley staggered to her feet and forced herself to run to the other entry. She hurried, trying to summon some hope. She said a silent prayer, and strangely a feeling of comfort came over her. It wasn't to last though. As soon as she rounded the corner, her light fell upon the intersection. The bulwark of rubble was solid and daunting, obstructing the entire exit. That was it. There was no way out.

She ran back to Bear and knelt down. Her light moved over him, and she cupped her hand over her mouth. She couldn't stand seeing him broken like this, his arms and legs twisted and turned at unnatural angles. "It's blocked." There was no need for further explanation. How long would it take for rescuers to get to them? Maybe they never would.

"I'm sorry," she said.

"It's not your fault." Bear blinked. A tear broke loose from the corner of his eye and rolled down his cheek, cutting a path through the coal dust. She tried not to look at his mangled body but could only imagine the pain he was in.

"You're not going to die, Bear. You're too stubborn for that. I'm calling the surface and they'll send rescuers in. They'll get us out."

She already had her phone to her ear, anxiously waited for Comspec to pick up. The sound she heard wasn't Meg's calm voice on the other end, but a loud cracking sound above her. Haley looked up, her breath catching in her throat. The fateful sound spread like aftershocks from an earthquake. The roof and ribs around her seemed to be popping and then another rumble shook the mine. She dropped the phone and leaned over Bear to protect him from more falling debris. It seemed like several minutes passed before all was still again. She looked down at Bear.

"Sounded like another cave in," he said, his voice raspy and weak.

Haley's heart sunk further. Without a word she grabbed the phone and called Comspec. At last Meg's voice answered on the other end. "We're trapped," Haley yelled into the phone. "Me and Bear. Leech took out the roof supports and both intersections are blocked."

"We know." Meg seemed to be hyperventilating on the other end. "We've had several calls already, and we're putting together a rescue team as we speak."

"Bear's hurt." Haley lowered her voice. "It's bad. We need help. Now!"

Meg was silent for a moment and a feeling of dread filled the void. "Haley—" Meg's voice shook. "You should know. . . We got a call moments ago . . . Leech just dynamited the mains at the 9th west intersections."

Haley squeezed her eyes shut and shook her head. So that was the rumble they had just felt. The main way in and out of the mine was destroyed. What hopes she had of being rescued plummeted. How long would it take a team to get to them? Would they both be dead by then? MSHA would make sure they followed protocol. Most likely, they would set up a fresh air station in the main intake. Then they would test air quality as they moved forward and would have to shore up the roof where needed as they went. They would have to clear the dynamited section before they could even move on to deal with the roof falls. It could take days.

"It's a mess," Meg cried. "The other miners were clear of the blast, but two men are injured. They're trying to make their way out, but Leech is still somewhere in the mine. He took his tracker off so we don't know where he is. He could be hiding in the old workings, but we're doing all we can." She sounded distant. "Mr. Branch brought someone in who is familiar with the mine. He knows those old original tunnels and shafts we don't use anymore. He's here and he might—"

Her words were cut off as if she had dropped the phone. A moment later another voice came on the line.

"Haley?"

She recognized the gravelly voice. "Mitch!" she cried. "Is that you?"

"Yeah, Haley, it's me. Are you okay?"

A thick blanket of relief settled over her. It took a moment before she could choke out an answer around the lump in her throat. "My arm is broken." She let out a small laugh at the absurdity of it all. As if a broken arm was measurable in comparison to the real situation they faced. "Bear is in bad shape." The phone went silent for a long moment. "Mitch, are you there?"

"I'm here, sweetheart, just thinking."

She glanced down at Bear. Part of his mouth pulled up in an attempted smile. "Bad shape is an understatement," he muttered.

"Tell them to hurry."

She gently put her hand on his shoulder. "They're on their way, Bear. In the meantime, I'll go find the first aid kit." It gave her an excuse to move away so he couldn't overhear the conversation.

"Mitch?"

"Yeah, sweetheart, I heard him. We're hurrying as best we can. Mr. Branch has the whole safety department here and the rescue team is being put together. They'll be briefed shortly and then they'll go in. Try to be patient."

The ribs were popping again as if the weakened tunnels wouldn't hold much longer. Haley pressed the phone tighter to her ear trying to tune the awful sound out. "You know that my mom's at Parkdale Care Center. She needs someone to visit her. Brooke's too far away and my brother, Noah—I'm not sure he can do it. He needs to pull himself together, but until he does—" She let her words trail off.

"Don't talk like that."

She wiped the wetness from her cheek. "I know the situation. I know that methane emissions rise after a collapse. We aren't getting any ventilation in here. I can already feel it. It's hard to breathe."

"That could be from the dust. Use Bear's meter and check the levels. And get your breather on."

"I will when I get off the phone, but we both know what's happening here. Promise me you'll have someone visit my mom."

"Haley—"

"Tell her I love her. Me—make sure she knows it's me. And Jake. Tell Jake I'm sorry. Tell him he was right about me, and I'm sorry."

"Haley—" Mitch's voice boomed through the line. "Jake's with the rescue team. He'll be coming in with them. You can tell him yourself. He's been digging into this mess and found out that someone from the safety commission is involved."

Haley shook her head. None of that mattered anymore. "Jake will have to handle all of that. Just make sure you tell him I'm sorry. And remember my mom."

"Haley, you're not listening to me! As for your mom goes, I'm not visiting any old ladies. You can do that yourself. We're going to get you out. Do you hear me?"

She didn't answer.

"We're going to bring you out—for Jake, for your mother, for Noah. We're going to get you out because that's what we do. We bring miners home."

CHAPTER 34

Haley choked off a sob and pressed the phone to her ear. "Okay," she said. "I know you'll do what you can." She looked back to where Bear was and lowered her voice. "Mitch, you better hurry. I don't think Bear's going to last very long."

"One thing at a time, Haley. A lot of things have changed since I owned the mine, but I know where the old tunnels tie into the new ones. I think there's a way you can get out, but you'll need to work with me."

"Tell me what you want me to do."

"You're in 9th west, cross cut 15?"

Haley nodded, but it was a second before she could choke out an audible answer. "Yes, and it's open to entry two, but it's blocked off from there."

"Where's the miner at?"

"Entry two, starting into cut 16."

Mitch paused as if he were thinking. "How far until it will punch through into the entry?"

"Not far. Maybe a few feet, but what good will that do? If I broke through, it puts me in the entry where Leech dynamited the intersection. I still can't get out."

Haley heard the rustle of papers in the background. He must have been flipping through maps.

"That's where we want you. It will dump you into the return then maybe you can make your way up to cross cut 2."

"But that doesn't go anywhere. Leech and I worked in there on my first day. The roof collapsed a long time ago and they only use it for ventilation now."

"I know. But if air can get through, then there's a chance you can too."

Haley felt a flicker of hope. She envisioned the crawl space. It narrowed to the point where they couldn't fit the large jacks in, but maybe it was possible for her to squeeze through—as long as the whole section wasn't completely collapsed by now.

"If you can get through cross cut 2, it will lead you into the old works," Mitch continued. "Into the sections we dug back when I owned the mine. You'll come out into the bleeder section behind the longwall and you can get out from there."

"Okay." Haley's voice sounded more confident than she felt. "One little thing—I don't know how to run the miner."

"I'll talk you through it."

She turned and directed her light at Bear's motionless body. "I won't be able to take Bear with me. His whole body is broken. I don't think he can move."

"It's okay. We'll send the rescuers in to get him."

"He pushed me out of the way of the shuttle car. I can't just leave him."

It was silent on the other end. "That's exactly what a miner would say. I guess you're no longer a scab, are you, sweetheart? But like you said before, we both know what the situation is. You'll have roof support problems and gas build up where you're at. Get your breather on and punch through that entry. If you can do that much, we can come the rest of the way to you."

"All right. I've got to take care of Bear first. I'll call you back in a few minutes and you can give me my first lesson on how to run a miner."

Haley ended the call. A minute later she was running back to Bear, carrying a large first aid kit in one hand, her other hand cradled against her chest.

"I'm back." She knelt on the ground next to him.

Bear's bloodshot eyes turned on her. A tear rolled down his

cheek as he attempted to shake his head. "You need to go. Get to work . . . find a way out of here."

"I'm not leaving you. They've found another way to get to us, but it'll take some time."

"Look at me," Bear said. "We both know I won't be going out alive."

Haley had the first aid kit open, looking at its contents. She fumbled through bandages and wraps, her eyes glistening over. "We've got to try." She said the words, but her hope was slipping away. From the way he lay, every bone in his body was probably broken, not to mention internal injuries.

Her eyes moved up his contorted figure to his face. It didn't matter what he had done to her—how he had treated her. It all seemed trivial now as she watched him struggling to breathe. Ignoring the pain in her arm, she scooted closer to him and tried to place his head in her lap. He groaned as soon as she touched him. Her throat tightened and she fought to keep her own tears back. "What can I do?"

"Nothing," he whispered. "It's all done. We'll all have the devil to pay, but don't let them say I didn't try."

Haley wiped her eyes. "I don't understand."

He blinked and let more tears wash his cheeks of the coal dust. "It's nothing."

"Are you talking about the accidents? I know you've been hiding things. You, along with others, have been signing off on things that don't meet code."

His eyes focused hard on her. "Everything we've passed off *has* met code. It's MSHA that's been writing bogus reports."

That's what Mitch meant when he said someone from the safety commission was involved. "Like that rock dust during the last inspection? Are you saying it was good, and MSHA marked it as bad anyway?"

"I tested it myself. I swear it was good. The inspector must've snuck in a corrupted sample to make us look bad."

Haley leaned over him. "But why would they do that?"

"Don't know. If you add a poor safety record to a mine that's already plagued with bad reports, it won't take much to shut them down."

"Which MSHA inspector did it?"

"Harper was the one down here when the rock dust was tested. Everyone knows how bad she hates the mines. I've only been trying to help—minimizing the bad reports where I could by overlooking minor infractions."

"Then why did you write me up?" She felt her old repulsion rise. "Never mind. It's the same reason you threw the coal through the window and put the mine disaster book in my room."

His head wobbled to the side. "What are you talking about? I never put a book in your room. The Unsafe Work report and the coal, those I am guilty of. I wanted you out of the mine. Don't need a lady down here when someone is sabotaging the work." He paused to catch his breath. "I have girls of my own. Wouldn't want them underground, working in these conditions. It's too dangerous." He coughed, leaving a residue of blood on his lips. "Tell my girls I love them. And Mary. Tell her she's always been the love of my life." His eyes focused on Haley again. "And forgive me. I was just trying to scare you away."

Haley stared at him in disbelief. All this time she thought it was because he hated women. "You could've just warned me what was going on so I could take precautions."

He gasped, struggling to breathe. The position of his head was cutting off his airway. Gritting her teeth she used both hands to straighten his neck. He cried out in pain, but his breath came easier. After a minute, he continued, "Couldn't tell anyone what was going on. I didn't have proof. By then I was in over my head. Put my job on the line by not following protocol. Had to keep it secret."

She shook her head. "But I chose this. I appreciate you trying to keep me safe, but it's my decision to be here. And I like working underground. I see this black coal and I think about the millions of years it took to get it here. The thousands of feet of mountain above it, the layers of rock and sediment, like God's hand prepared it for us, and I get to be a part of it."

Bear blinked, his eyes bright and glossy. "Does this mean I can't talk you into going back to the warehouse until this mess with MSHA is worked out?"

"Nope. I need underground pay; I have my mom to support. Besides, I chose to be here, and I was willing to take the risk, even after I knew something was going on. It's bone-tiring work, but it's satisfying, and I like the fact that I'm expected to do what the men do, and I can do it."

"Yes, you can, Haley."

She let out a strained laugh. "What's this? You're going to stop calling me Scab now?"

"You're not a scab anymore. I guess you'll have to earn a new nickname."

Haley patted his shoulder and tried to smile.

"I can't feel anything below my chest." Bear tried to move, but only his shoulder shifted.

Haley looked down. A wet, sticky puddle was spreading out from beneath him to where she was kneeling. She took a large bandage and slid her hand under his back, trying to find the open wound.

Bear gasped, struggling to get air in his lungs. "Leech is still out there. He's gone completely crazy. I'm done for, but you'll live through this, if you're careful."

"We'll both make it out." Her throat pinched closed as she said it. Lying did that to her. She looked down at the spreading blood.

His voice was noticeably weaker when he spoke. "I can't breathe."

Haley pulled her hand out from under him, but it didn't seem to help. "Tell me what to do."

"Leave. Get to work, and find a way out."

She shook her head. "Don't ask me to *get to work*."

"I'm not asking you, I'm telling you." His words were distant now, and quiet as if each one took effort to utter.

She scooted closer to his deformed body and slipped her blood-stained fingers around his hand. "I'm not leaving you. Can you feel that? I'm holding your hand."

His breath was coming in shorter bursts. "I can't feel it, but thank you. That's what Mary would've done if she were here."

She couldn't hold the tears back any longer. She wondered about his wife, about his daughters. Had he told them he loved them before he left for work that morning? Would they be waiting for him to come home?

She closed her eyes and listened to his ragged breath. With each passing second, it grew shallower. Slowly it ebbed away with the last of the settling dust.

* * *

"He's gone." Haley choked out the words into the phone. "Bear's dead."

It was silent on the other end for a minute, then Haley continued. "Mitch, get me out of here."

CHAPTER 35

Haley squatted just inside cut 16, her breather on, her arm in a cravat sling, and the remote control box for the continuous miner perched on her knee. *Just like running an RC car*, she told herself. Noah had received one for Christmas once and had let her drive it around the house for hours. She pushed on the joystick, and the miner lunged forward. Within seconds it was chewing away at the coal with its mechanical teeth.

It was easy and complicated at the same time. She didn't have the experience to know when she was in the coal seam and when she wasn't. She also didn't have a shuttle car to carry the coal away, and once the miner was full, all that coal had to go somewhere. And on top of that, she couldn't bolt the roof as she went. At some point, she would be under unsupported top. Muddy, clay-like top, prone to falls with a stream running overhead.

She didn't need to go far—just a little farther. She kept hearing Bear's voice in her head. *Get to work. Get to work.*

The miner continued to creep forward. She had to stop and back it up every few minutes to straighten it out and get back in the seam, but at last, the wall gave way. She felt it as well as heard it. She stopped the miner and set the control box down, and then walked next to the big machine, wary of the roof but trying to get a look through the dust. A rock fell from the ceiling and hit the miner with an earsplitting crash. Haley's heart flipped in her chest, and she scrambled back, knocking her throbbing arm against the machine as she went.

She put her hand over her chest to steady her breathing and waited. A minute went by. The roof was holding, so far. She looked past the miner. As the dust settled, she saw it. She had broken through into the adjacent entryway. The phone was already in her hand, but with the toxic atmosphere, she didn't dare break the seal around her mouthpiece, so she was relegated to texting.

Made it through. Where is the rescue team? Are they close? She waited for Mitch's reply.

You need to go meet them. Don't worry, I'll walk you through it.

Haley couldn't just leave though. At least not yet. She walked back to Bear and knelt next to his body. *I broke through,* she silently told him. She couldn't talk with the breather in her mouth, so she poured her feelings out to him in thought. *I had to use the miner. I know you told me never to touch it, but I think you would've been proud of me.* She choked back the lump in her throat as she pulled his hard hat out from the rubble and gently sat it on his chest. He looked like what she imagined a tired, old coal miner would look like—one who was exhausted from his day's work and had lain down for a nap. She touched his shoulder, and then stood up and walked away, the light from his headlamp lighting her path.

* * *

Sweat dripped from Haley's forehead as she scooted forward, limping along on her knees like a three-legged dog beneath the low roof, trying to suck air through the mouthpiece of her mask. She tried to focus on the miracle that cross cut 2 hadn't collapsed completely. It was all she could do to keep her mind off the aching pain in her arm, the exhaustion that was taking over, and the fact that she had just watched Bear die and had to leave his body behind. She limped forward, trying to forget about it.

Her helmet hit against a protruding rock, jarring her neck and knocking her to the ground. She groaned and rolled onto her side and looked around. She recognized the area. This was where she and Leech had placed the last roof jack. It seemed more closed in now.

Tight and suffocating. Hopefully, it wouldn't be long before she reached the other side. Mitch assured her that it would open up into the return behind the longwall if it hadn't fully collapsed further ahead. There she could make her way to the intake and follow the lifeline out. She would get another SCSR mask from one of the stashes if this one lasted that long. She tried not to think about it.

Her phone buzzed and she looked at the incoming message. *Keep moving.* Mitch couldn't have known that she had stopped; there was no tracking system where she was. He was probably just trying to encourage her progress.

The time it took her to reply with one hand was long enough for her to catch her breath. *I'd make more progress if I didn't have to stop and read your texts. I'll let you know when I'm out on the other side.*

She pushed herself to her knees again and started her three-legged crawl. The roof sloped down, pressing against her back. It continued to narrow and before long, she was forced onto her belly. Her light shined ahead, through the narrow opening. It was like looking into a black hole. Like looking into nothingness. The terrifying passageway tapered into an impossibly small space. Maybe she wouldn't be able to get through after all. Her heart began to race. She inched along, her helmet scratching along the rock, her arm painfully pinched between her body and the ground.

A loud clang sounded in the distance, and she cocked her head and listened. There it was again. Someone pounding on something. Maybe the rescue team wasn't as far away as she thought. She had to keep going. Again, she moved forward, continuing her miserable crawl.

Haley gave a sigh of relief when the space finally widened to where she could get on her knees again. There was another pounding noise, closer this time. She kept going, and after several long minutes, she saw the opening at the end. She surged forward until the low-lying shelf above her opened up and she climbed into the entryway. She lifted her head, stretching her neck, and climbed to her feet.

She had made it. She was in the bleeder section behind the longwall. She took the multimeter from her belt and took a reading of the air. It was hot and stuffy, and the reading wasn't great, but thanks to the regulators, it was at least breathable. She pulled off her mask and sucked in the hot, stagnant air. At least it didn't feel like she as breathing through a straw.

The sound of crunching metal drew her attention and she spun around. A figure approached off to the side of her light beam. The rescue team was already here. She let out a relieved cry, but it turned into a gasp when her headlamp illuminated the man. Leech.

He stood only five feet away with a sledgehammer in his hand. A toothy white grin split his black smudged face. "Did you miss me, Scab? Apparently, I *missed* you."

Haley stumbled backward, her light drifting behind him to where a metal frame lay mangled on the ground. It took her a moment to grasp what he was doing. "You're tearing out the regulators?"

Leech glanced back at the damaged metal. "No quicker way to ruin a mine. Think about it—this place is completely dependent on airflow, and yet one man can tear out the regulators within a matter of minutes, and then what? Gasses build, one spark, and BOOM!"

Haley jumped as his voice filled the tunnel. A sickening feeling threatened to suffocate her. She knew all too well that air could go bad in a hurry. If the fans ever shut down, they had to be running again within fifteen minutes or the miners were required to evacuate. Fifteen minutes. That was the difference between good air and bad air. She stared at Leech, and then made a grab for her phone.

"Don't touch it." Leech stepped toward her, raising the sledgehammer. Haley slowly moved her hand away. "I won't miss this time." Leech's face contorted into a sadistic glare as he brought the hammer toward her.

Haley dropped to her knees, her good hand over her head. Suddenly she was a kid again, her dad standing over her, ready to punish her.

"Stop! Don't touch her!"

Another light approached. Haley held her breath then, finally, someone's face came into view. A woman's face.

"Don't touch her, Leech!" Rivers called again. "You're done here. You've earned yourself your own private jail cell."

Leech didn't move and Haley gasped in relief. She scrambled toward Rivers. It was brave of her to be the MSHA inspector leading the rescue team in. Haley grabbed onto Rivers' coveralls and climbed to her feet, hugging Rivers, and looking for the other lights to appear.

But the return remained dark and empty in the distance. No one else was coming. A feeling of dread washed over Haley as Rivers pushed her away. Leech moved next to them. He was grinning.

"It can't be." Haley directed her light on Rivers. "Bear said MSHA was faking reports. I thought it was Layla Harper—"

Rivers didn't say anything. Instead, she patted Leech on the arm. "You did well. I'll take it from here."

Haley fell back against the wall, an acid taste rising in her mouth. "It's you? All this time, it was you? You're trying to shut P.C. Mine down by faking MSHA reports?"

Rivers snorted. "It's nothing new. Each year dozens of mines are forced to close because of penalties and violations. Unfortunately, bureaucracy is too slow, so I'm helping it along. A little discrepancy in a report here and there is nothing. I'm sure Harper wouldn't mind the adjustments I've made to her paperwork. Besides, these coal companies are just as crooked, enslaving the population to dirty power, and they won't change unless they're forced to."

"But Leech—" His big form towered above them. "You can't be working with him. You said he's going to jail."

Leech laughed. "I hope I am."

"Have some compassion," Rivers said. "The man's dying."

Leech nodded. "Stage four pancreatic cancer."

Haley's expression didn't soften, and Leech noticed. "Don't judge me," he said. "I'm paying child support for two kids, and I've got a wife and one more kid at home, plus medical expenses." He jerked his head toward Rivers. "She's paying me good money. Even if I go to jail, I'll get to live out my life under the care of free doctors, and I'll be pushing up daisies before this even goes to trial."

He chuckled, a low, half-crazed sound. "The only thing that would sweeten my deal is if I died in the mine today. There hasn't been much love lost in my family, so at least I'd be remembered for something." He laughed again, louder this time. "I hope I get to blow this place—go out in a blaze of glory. But if not, jail will be like a vacation. Either way, it's a nice package deal."

Haley couldn't wrap her mind around it. There was too much destruction. Too much loss. And for what? "And can you live with the guilt?" She looked at both of them now. "Your package deal killed Bear."

Leech looked down and scuffed his boot on the ground a few times. "Never liked him much anyway. He was always harping on me, telling me to get to work."

Rivers pointed at Haley. "Progress doesn't come without cost. At least I saved you."

"You didn't save me. I was left for dead along with Bear. I clawed my way out of that section—"

"You wouldn't even be in this situation if you would've taken my hint." Rivers jabbed a finger in her chest. "I tried to tell you not to go under. And that book I gave you was a clear warning of what was going to happen."

Haley pulled back. "That was you? You left the gift bag in my room?"

"Of course. I thought you would've figured it out."

It was a slap in the face. She should've figured it out. She'd left her apartment key at Liam's house once, and Rivers could've easily made a copy of it. "I should've known. I always wondered why an environmentalist would set her brother up with a coal miner. You wanted to use me as a mole, didn't you?"

Rivers smiled. Haley's chest rose and fell with deep breaths. At least she knew why her relationship with Liam seemed forced. "That's why he was so persistent and wouldn't leave me alone. But if you wanted to use me, then why didn't you want me underground?"

"Oh, come on, Haley." Rivers folded her arms and rocked her weight onto one hip. "Liam had real feelings for you. He didn't want you underground because he knew someone would eventually get hurt, and he didn't want it to be you. We tried to warn you not to take the underground job. We could've still used you in the warehouse. And with Leech working with us underground, and Liam doing his media attacks with his blog, it was a good setup."

Haley tensed, sending pain shooting through her arm. "Liam was doing media attacks through a blog—" she stopped short. "Tom Silver." She shook her head. "He died in the mine years ago, and Liam has been writing under his name, hasn't he?"

Rivers' eyes narrowed with contempt. "Tom Silver was actually Thomas Grey—my uncle. Silver was his nickname. He died because the mine was negligent. Can't you see? We aren't just about clean energy. We're doing you a favor. This is a dangerous mine. You'll all be better off working someplace safer."

Rivers pulled a phone from her belt and began texting on it. "Who are you talking to?" Haley asked. "Liam?" She wanted to grab her own phone and call for help, but Leech gave her a warning look and tamped the head of his sledgehammer into the ground as if he were anxious to get on with tearing her apart.

"You'll find out soon enough," Rivers said.

Haley rubbed her arm. "If you wanted to save me before, then you can do it now by letting me go."

Rivers finished her text. "I probably would, if only for Liam's sake. He still kind of likes you. But it's not my choice."

Haley's brow pinched together. "Then whose choice is it?"

"Like I said, you'll find out soon. We had to get someone to expedite the process of getting this mine shut down. It's worked out great, but you know how new people in power always like to call the shots." Her phone buzzed and she looked at it. "And I've just been given my orders." She held out the phone so Haley could read the text.

I want to talk to Haley. Bring her out.

CHAPTER 36

The skin on Haley's arms prickled. "Who is it?"

Rivers didn't answer. She bounced on the balls of her feet like an excited child hiding a secret. "You'll see soon enough." She turned to Leech. "We're not paying you to stand around. Finish tearing out the regulators before the rescue team gets here."

Leech strode away and Haley stiffened. Jake was on the rescue team, and there would be other men that she knew as well. They would be walking into a trap. Leech pounded away on a regulator further up the entry. If they stayed there much longer, they would all die as the air slowly went bad.

Several minutes went by with the loud banging ringing in their ears. Then all of a sudden it was silent. Leech walked back to them. "All done." He gestured to the trail of demolished regulators. "I've got some explosives, so just say the word, and I'll light this place up."

"I'm all for that," Rivers said. "Unfortunately, our new partner won't like it." Leech swore, and Rivers patted his shoulder as if to console him. "Maybe we could blow up *part* of it."

Haley clamped her mouth shut. Her phone buzzed, but Rivers snatched it away from her. "Oh, no you don't." She took a step back and read the message. "Someone in Comspec says they haven't heard from you and they want to know if you're okay." It buzzed again. Rivers looked pleased. "Oh, and the rescue team is at 7th west."

They were close, and there was no way Haley could warn them.

"I guess you should reply." Rivers' thumbs started moving across the phone. "In the bleeder section behind the longwall, waiting for the rescue team." She hit *send* and leveled her light right into Haley's eyes. "I'll make it simple for you. We're going to be walking out with the rescue team, but for obvious reasons, I don't want you talking to them. So to keep you quiet, we're going to play a little game, okay?"

Haley hated games.

Rivers stepped next to her and took her good arm like they were best friends. "Leech is going to run off and play hide-n-seek while we walk out, and mum's the word. Got it? Hold your tongue, button your lip, shut your mouth. Whatever you want to call it, it's the silent game. I've already lost my uncle in a mine, and I'd be happy to close every coal-belching pit in the area if I could, so here's the fun part. Let's plan on Leech blowing the mine. That is unless I send him a text every ten minutes and tell him that you're being a good girl and staying quiet. If you so much as put a dust-covered boot out of line, I won't send the text. And . . . BOOM!"

Haley's mind was already racing to think of a way she could secretly communicate with Jake to let him know what was going on. Unfortunately, her sign language skills, Morse code, and ESP abilities were nonexistent.

Leech wiped the back of his gloved hand across his mouth, leaving a coal smear across his chin. "I'm up for that." He had hesitated before answering like he might be second guessing himself. But who wouldn't seem reluctant when contemplating setting off a bomb in a gas-permeated atmosphere. He was facing his own death along with those of his coworkers. Leech's eyes grew distant as if he had hardened his resolve.

"You wouldn't do it!" Haley cried. She glared at Rivers. "And you wouldn't risk blowing up the mine while you're still in it."

"I plan on walking out first. Part of the rescue team will stay behind to get Bear's body. The question is, are you willing to risk *their* lives?"

Haley shrunk back. She wasn't. She turned to Leech. "You wouldn't do it, would you? I know you said you didn't like Bear, but what about the others? What if Wing Nut or Shark is with the group? You wouldn't kill them."

"I'm already a murderer. No going back from that." He thumped the sledgehammer on the ground a few times as if he were smashing through the last of his hesitation. When he looked up, his white teeth gleamed through the coal dust—a toothy grim reaper.

"I'll be ready and waiting for those texts." He pulled a multimeter from his belt, pressed a couple buttons and held it at eye level. "Gas levels are climbing. Give it a few more minutes, and one small explosion will have flames rocketing through all the passageways."

"Let's go." Rivers grabbed Haley's arm and tried to tug her along. "I'm sure you want to get out of here before Leech expedites his own funeral."

Haley jerked her arm free. There was still one thing she could do. She glared at Rivers and sat down in the gob. "I'm not going anywhere."

"What good is that going to do? It's not going to stop anything."

"It will give the rescue team time to get out. I don't think you'd let the mine blow up while you're in it, and I won't go out until the last of the miners do. So the question is, do you want to risk *your* life?"

Leech turned his light onto Rivers, his brow crinkled in uncertainty. Haley held her breath. All she needed to do was to stall a few minutes and keep Leech there. As soon as the rescue team arrived, they'd stop him. Miners might be family, but Leech had betrayed their trust. He had killed one of their own, injured others, and was threatening their whole livelihood. As soon as the other miners saw him, they'd do whatever it took to apprehend him.

"And are *you* willing to risk your own life for this?" Rivers asked.

Haley lifted her head. "I've already faced death today. What's one more time when you're threatening the very thing I've worked so hard to be a part of?"

"It's just a dirty hole in the ground, and they're just men. You hate men."

That accusation used to bug Haley, but not anymore. She'd thought a lot about it since she'd started working underground. "That's such a generalized observation," she said. "It's more like I hate *certain* men, or more like *certain people*."

There were still things she didn't like about the miners, but she didn't hate them. In fact, Stump, Wing Nut, and the orange-hats—she actually liked all of them. And then there was Mitch. There were things she didn't care for about him, but she liked him. And with Jake—well with Jake it was complicated, but it was anything but hate. Fear maybe. She was scared of the feelings she had for him.

Rivers kicked Haley in the thigh with the end of her steel-toed boot which sent a jabbing pain clear to the bone. "You're gullible if you think this is going to save the mine." She turned her light on Leech. "You better get your breather on and get out of here before the rescue team gets here. You know the best places to hide. Make sure no one finds you and wait for my texts."

"But what about Scab here?" Leech pointed the sledgehammer at Haley.

"As soon as the rescue team gets here, they'll take us both out. The majority of the team will stay behind, and that will be enough to keep her quiet until we're out. After that, I don't care if you blow it, and it doesn't matter who's left in here."

Leech stooped over and picked up a shoulder bag. Haley hadn't noticed it sitting there before. Then again, it was filthy, covered with coal dust, and blended in perfectly with the gob. He reached inside and pulled something out. Haley's light rested on it and she shuddered. Dynamite. He turned it over in his hand, looking at it. "You text me every ten minutes."

Rivers pushed a button on her watch and it beeped. "Got it. Ten minutes."

Leech paused and scratched his head. "You know those code words you had me memorize so I'd recognize if a message was from you or not?" River's nodded. "Well, make sure you include one of those words with every text."

"Of course," she said.

Haley groaned. Any thoughts of her knocking Rivers over the head with something and taking her phone was useless now.

Leech put the dynamite back in the bag. "Don't take too long getting out of here. I'm not a patient man." He put his breather on and jogged into the nearest cross cut, leaving them alone.

"The oxygen is growing thin." Rivers sat down next to Haley and handed her a new SCSR pack. Haley hated the idea of putting another one on, but she could feel it too. A dull headache was forming behind her eyes and she was dizzy despite sitting down. She put the breather on. With the mouthpiece in, it would ensure her silence.

It wasn't long before a distant light appeared at the head of the entry, then another one, and another one. In all, there were nine total. Haley groaned. So many. And Jake would be with them. Why didn't he keep out of it? Why did he try to get his job back? He didn't care that much for mining. He should've been working for some tech company, writing code and developing software. She watched the approaching lights, wondering which one belonged to him. She dreaded seeing him, yet longed for it at the same time. Maybe she did know why he had come back—at least she hoped so.

Rivers nudged Haley's broken arm, and she recoiled in pain. She understood. It was a reminder to watch herself and behave—like a dog on a leash.

The lights were moving faster now, bouncing like fireflies. How many would stay in the mine to retrieve Bear's body? How many would be in there if Leech blew it up?"

"Haley, is that you?" A muffled voice sounded behind one of the face masks. The larger, full-face breathing apparatuses the rescue team wore allowed them to speak. Haley recognized Moose's voice and jumped to her feet. He shouldn't be here. They couldn't put the newbies on the rescue team. A moment later, she could see other orange hats amongst the white and black ones. She cringed. Not all of them.

She put her hand on her hip and glared at them. As soon as Moose was close enough, she shoved him and pointed back to where they came from. If she could've opened her mouth to speak, she would've scream at them. They couldn't be on the rescue team. They were inexperienced orange-hats.

Rivers put a hand on her shoulder and squeezed. It was another warning.

"We couldn't leave you," Moose said. He motioned to Bennie and No Name who were both nodding. "We're family, right? Us miners, we take care of each other."

Haley's throat thickened. They didn't know how dangerous it was. She shoved Moose again.

"You mean to say we're brave, don't you?" Moose asked, his voice sounding like he was talking through a tunnel.

She finally nodded. She wanted to knock each of them in the head and give them a hug at the same time. She looked at the other men. Jake stepped out from the middle of the group, and her heart ached at seeing him. It was good and painful at the same time. She forced herself to look away, to look at the others there. She knew all of them.

Boom was even there. He had a meter out taking a gas reading. He frowned and shook his head as he returned the device to his belt. "Miss Grey," He reached out and shook Rivers' hand. "I knew you were in the mine doing an inspection, but I thought you left when the crews did their walk-out drill."

Rivers pointed to her mouthpiece, indicating that she would've offered an explanation if she could. Boom nodded and then looked at Haley. "I'm glad she found you. Are you alright?" She shook her head. "Is it your arm? I see you're cradling it." There was so much more than that.

"Don't worry. We'll take care of it." Boom waved his hand. "Rabbit, Jake. Check her out, stabilize her arm, and get her out of here."

Jake moved next to her and set down a large duffle bag. He didn't say anything. He could have. Like the others, he wore the full face mask.

Maybe she was the one who needed to do the talking, but she

couldn't break the seal around her mouthpiece. *Sorry*, she thought. Her chest tightened with emotion, and she hated that she couldn't speak it at loud.

"We can put a better sling on that," Rabbit said as he pulled some supplies from the bag. Haley let him assess her arm, but she kept her eyes on Jake. He seemed to be silently pleading with her. She almost opened her mouth, but she didn't, knowing that the air might be at a fatal level now. Out of the corner of her eye, she saw Rivers checking her watch. She looked at Haley and raised a finger. One minute. She would have to text Leech within one minute.

Boom pointed at one of the damaged regulators. "Leech did this?"

Rivers answered with a quick shrug. Haley looked at Jake intently, hoping he'd somehow understand. *Yes, it was Leech*, she silently screamed, giving the slightest dip of her head.

Boom's expression saddened. "We've got to get moving. Bear's family has already been notified. The least we can do for them now is to bring him out." He leaned over and looked through the low-roofed passage where Haley had crawled through. "Mitch told us how we can get to him. Did you have any problems going through here?"

After another warning look from Rivers, Haley shook her head. The minute was nearly up, and she was counting the seconds in her mind. 39, 40, 41.

"No collapses?" Boom asked.

A tear ran down her cheek as she shook her head again. 44, 45, 46. What was Rivers doing? Why wouldn't she send the text?

"All the jacks are holding up?"

She nodded. 50, 51.

Boom took out his phone and started relaying his report to the surface just as Rivers typed a brief text on her own phone. Haley let out a long breath. They were safe, at least for another ten minutes.

"All right," Boom called out louder than needed. "An ambulance is waiting for her, get her up top." He clapped Jake on the shoulder. Apparently Jake had already volunteered for that job. "The rest of you, let's go."

Haley shook her head at Boom and pointed at the men. Surely he didn't need so many of them. Rivers tapped her watch, letting her know that the second ten-minute countdown was already going, and she didn't like Haley's body language.

Boom waved a hand and directed the men under the low roof. "You're gonna be okay, Haley. Rabbit and Jake will get you out."

Moose walked past her, but she discreetly grabbed the corner of his jacket and tipped her head down the entryway.

He shook his head. "They need us." He pulled away and followed the others crawling below the low shelf.

What could she do?

She pounded her hand against the wall as Moose's light disappeared from view. She was completely helpless. Jake took her arm, and she reluctantly let him pull her away. He met her gaze with questioning eyes, but Haley couldn't communicate anything. How many minutes were left before Rivers needed to send another text? She estimated the time, then consigned herself to Rivers' game and trudged down the entry.

CHAPTER 37

The trepidation thickened, heavy and suffocating. It was getting harder to walk. Haley counted minutes in her head, praying Rivers would send the next text. Jake and Rabbit hurried her along, probably wondering why she was going so slowly. Again, Rivers waited until the last few seconds before discretely sending the message. Haley felt the tension dissipate for only a mere second, and then another ten-minute countdown began.

Jake kept making eye contact with her, obviously wanting to talk, although it was completely impossible, and every silent word that went unspoken tore at her. She wanted to rip her breather off and tell him Rivers was the one sabotaging the mine. She wanted to tell him the other miners were in danger. And she wanted to tell him she was sorry. She hadn't meant to hurt him. Maybe it was too late for that.

At last, and far too soon, they saw the lights from the fresh air station. Curtains were hung to section it off, separating the good air from the irrespirable air. As they passed through, Haley looked around at the crew of men. It was a single backup team, ready to go in and replace Boom's crew when needed. Cross was there, along with Roadrunner, and a few other men she knew. They crowded around her, expressing their concern and their happiness for her safe return.

This is different, Haley thought. Had she finally earned admittance into their family? She looked at each of the men. Steel-toed boots and coal-smeared jackets brushed up against her own. Gloved hands patted her on the back. Their dirty hard hats turned in her direction. As never before, she was aware of the similarities she shared with each of them. It went beyond the clothes, beyond the stained fingernails. She felt it in her skin, in the beat of her heart.

Cross stepped next to her and put his hand on her shoulder. "Glad to see you're okay. We've got good air here, so go ahead and remove your breather." He gave her a reassuring smile, but she could see the worry and strain behind it, the weight of the situation still pressing on him. He moved off to the side and made a phone call to the command center outside, relaying the message about her safe arrival.

Jake already had his mask off and looked at Haley expectantly as she removed her mouthpiece. She glanced at Rivers then back to Jake. She would've told him everything. She imagined the men tackling Rivers and getting her phone, but Leech would blow the mine if he received any text without a code word. It crushed Haley, but she clamped her mouth shut and said nothing.

Jake stepped toward her. "You won't even talk to me?"

She pinched her eyes shut. As painful as it was, she couldn't risk it. Rivers put a hand on her as if to comfort her. "I think she's in shock. We better get her to the hospital."

Roadrunner directed her to the nearest place to sit down—a five-gallon bucket of flame retardant—and started examining the bandage Rabbit had put on her arm.

Jake backed away, his eyes hooded with disappointment, his lips pulled down in an overwhelming frown. The expression shot a shaft through Haley's heart. She couldn't bear it. "Wait." She reached out to touch him.

Rivers pinched her shoulder, and Haley glared at her. She wasn't about to say anything to jeopardize the people in the mine, but she had to say *something* to Jake. She couldn't leave him like this. Her mind raced to find a safe topic that wouldn't get her in trouble. "About that kiss," she blurted. Everyone looked at her.

Rivers' grip loosened, her face twisting with confusion, her eyes ricocheting between Haley and Jake. "You kissed him?"

Haley ignored her, refusing to take her eyes off of Jake. "I'm sorry for how I reacted. The thing is . . . I liked it . . . and that scared me."

A few of the men whooped and let out some catcalls. Cross shot them dirty looks as he made notes on a clipboard. Jake just stared back at her, his face blank, his eyes narrowing into an are-we-really-discussing-this expression. She returned it with the best yes-we-are look she could muster. It was awkward with all the guys around, but there was no helping that. She needed to say something.

A long moment passed. Another man knelt next to her, criticizing Rabbit's splint job and tightening the sling. Finally, Jake gave in. "You liked it, so you pushed me away and ran out?"

"I regretted it the moment I did it." Haley took a deep breath like she was mentally preparing to jump off a cliff. "Jake, I really like you. I think I have for a long time now. And the thought of getting involved with someone terrifies me."

"I get it," he said. "No one can blame you, considering . . ." He left the rest go unspoken.

Haley cradled her arm against her and tried to block out the onlookers. She hadn't intended it to go in this direction, but she needed to keep talking. She rallied her courage and continued. "I'm trying to get over that, but it's hard. Dating is hard."

Everyone was quiet like they were collectively waiting for her to go on. Cross was on the phone again and still shooting everyone dirty looks. She hated that she had an audience. It was hard enough to share the most intimate parts of her life with one person, let alone a whole crew of coal miners. But if they wanted a show, she'd give it to them. Especially if it delayed Rivers from leaving the mine.

Haley stood up. "But with you, Jake . . . Well, you saw how I reacted."

"With a shove."

"Before that." Her cheeks flushed with embarrassment, and she lowered her voice. "It felt right, and I didn't expect that."

Roadrunner took a step closer to her, pretending to examine his belt clip. Rivers moved in closer too. They were all interested. But she looked at Jake. A ghost of a smile appeared at the corners of his lips.

"Am I mistaken in thinking that I still might have a chance with you?" he asked.

Warning signs flashed in Haley's mind, a thread of uncertainty shooting through her. To Jake, this wasn't a delay tactic. He was being serious. But what exactly was he talking about? A few dates and they'll see where it goes? Maybe it'll work out, maybe it won't?

Jake sensed her hesitation and stepped next to her. "I won't push it. And I understand it's hard for you. I get that you've been hurt, but we can work through this together."

Rivers gave a huff and rolled her eyes. "No one wants to hear about your love life, Haley."

"Agreed," Cross said as he picked up his phone again.

"I do," Roadrunner cut in. "Not often we get to see a live soap opera on a rescue mission."

Jake shot him a glowering look. "She's right. This isn't the time or place."

Rivers started checking her watch again then sent another text. A fleeting moment of relief came and then vanished. Haley glanced at Jake. How could she tell him what was really going on? She darted a pointed look at Rivers while letting out a long breath. Jake noticed. He looked at Rivers as if he sensed something.

"You guys are going about this all wrong," Rabbit said. He stepped forward, smacking a glove against his leg. "Jake's not perfect, but I say, give him a chance. Walling yourself off won't keep you safe; it'll just keep you lonely."

Haley blinked at him, stunned. Since when did Rabbit become a dating coach? Several other men were nodding their approval and a few even mumbled endorsements.

"Enough of this," Cross yelled. "We're down here to get a job done." He jerked his head toward a mantrip. "Get her out of here, Einstein, so we can concentrate on other matters. We still have men out there, and they ain't working in the best conditions. We don't need this kind of distraction."

Haley felt a jab of disappointment. She'd never had such a deep conversation, had never exposed her feelings like that, but now it was over. She tried to think of another stall tactic. Anything to keep Rivers in the mine until everyone was ready to leave.

Cross pointed at mantrip again.

It was time to go. Jake reached out, briefly touched her fingers, and then slid his hand around to the small of her back so he could direct her past the other men. It was a simple movement, but it felt good. He still cared about her. It shouldn't have surprised her, but it did.

Rivers followed closely behind as they walked to the mantrip then suddenly leaned in close to Haley's ear. "I never should've introduced you to Liam. You don't deserve him." She ended the comment with a piercing glare that said she'd be happy to bury Haley in the mine if she could.

When they reached the small truck, Jake squeezed Haley's hand. "I do want another chance with you, but I want you to be sure about it. Take your time to think about it. We have other problems to deal with now anyway." His eyes flickered toward Rivers.

Jake knew something was wrong. But he didn't know about the plan to have Leech's blow up the mine, or that Rivers had someone else on the outside waiting for them.

CHAPTER 38

Rivers held a silencing finger over her lips as she climbed into the truck next to Haley. Jake got in on the driver's side and stuck the key in the ignition. Haley prayed it wouldn't start. If they left the mine, there would be no reason for Rivers to prevent the bombing.

The engine chugged and roared to life. Fear and anxiety crackled through Haley like electricity. She cursed it under her breath and darted a glance at Rivers' phone.

"Don't even think about it," Rivers whispered. "I'm the only one who knows the code words." She sat back and grinned.

The truck moved up the entry and the fresh air station disappeared into the darkness behind them. Haley shifted in her seat and glared at Rivers.

"What's going on?" Jake asked.

Rivers pointedly looked at her watch. How many minutes were left? Haley didn't know. She'd lost track. If Rivers didn't send the next text, they were close enough to the surface that they would probably survive, while those deeper in—those beyond the fresh air station—would die.

"Nothing's going on." Haley sat back with a huff doing her best to give Jake a warning look.

They rode in silence for several minutes. Jake kept glancing at her but she couldn't come up with anything cryptic to say that wouldn't be obvious to Rivers.

Finally, Jake broke the silence. "Just talk to me. Whatever's going on—" he glanced at Rivers, "You just need to tell me what you know."

Rivers gave an almost imperceptible shake of her head and tapped one finger on her watch. Was that indicating that there was only one minute left?

Jake kept one hand on the wheel, and with the other, he touched Haley's knee, drawing her attention back to him. "I need you to trust me."

Ahead, the light from the portal grew brighter as they neared the surface. Out of the corner of her eye, she saw Rivers holding her phone, but she obviously hadn't sent the text yet.

"Trust me," Jake said again. The words pulled at her.

Rivers raised her hand, her fingers lowering like a clock ticking down the seconds, indicating the mere moments that were left.

5 . . . 4 . . .

All the men in the mine facing death—

3 . . . 2 . . .

And wasn't it too late for trust?

1 . . .

CHAPTER 39

Haley held her breath but Rivers looked at the phone, unmoving.

She wasn't going to send the text. She wasn't going to send the text! Haley turned to Jake and let the words tumble out of her mouth. "It's Rivers! She and Liam are paying Leech to sabotage the mine."

Jake's eyes hardened. "It wasn't Harper?"

"No, but they have another partner. And, any second now, Leech is going to blow the mine up."

Jake's smashed his foot on the gas and the mantrip barreled toward the portal.

Rivers grabbed the door and held on. "There's no proof."

Jake grabbed his phone and hit a button just as the mantrip burst into the afternoon light. Several police cars with lights flashing were in the parking lot along with two ambulances, and a couple of fire trucks. A commotion of people mingled around a pop-up tent which must've been the command center. It was all protocol, but the cops were probably there for Leech. Perhaps Rivers had been the one to call them—part of Leech's package deal—but it was too late now.

"Do they have him?" Jake yelled into his phone. "He probably has explosives. Haley says he's going to blow the mine!"

Haley clung to his arm. "Rivers is supposed to send him coded texts to stop him. She didn't send the last one."

The truck skidded to a halt and Jake lunged across Haley, reaching for Rivers' phone, but she opened her door and jumped out, dropping the phone on the ground. Haley scrambled to get out, but just as she bent down to grab the phone, Rivers brought the heel of her boot down, smashing it.

"Oops." She looked up with a sardonic smile.

Haley cried out and lunged at Rivers, but Jake grabbed her by the waist.

"How long do we have?" he asked.

She shook her head with a sob and looked toward the mine portal, expecting to see a cloud of smoke erupt from it.

Jake turned her around to face him. "I told you to trust me, and I mean it." He still had his phone to his ear. "There's a chance that they've already caught Leech."

"It will only take a minute for him to set the dynamite." Rivers said. She took a step backward like she was going to run. "And he doesn't have a tracker on, so they'll never get to him in time."

Jake pointed at the cracked phone on the ground. "He had a mine phone on him. We can track those."

Rivers' face blanched and she turned to run, but Jake grabbed her arm. "Didn't you wonder why the inexperienced orange-hats were on the rescue team? That was our B group. The A group was sent in to apprehend Leech. We were tracking him from the time we went in."

Rivers jerked to the side, trying to get away. "That team will have to monitor air and safety conditions as they go—they'll always be a step behind him. It'll still be too late." She yanked herself free and then turned and plowed right into a police officer.

"Miss Grey." The tall officer grabbed Rivers. His face was grim, shadowed with the stress from the day, and his no-nonsense military haircut made him appear even more hardcore. "You're under arrest for falsifying MSHA reports."

Two other officers moved in as he unclipped his handcuffs from his belt, flanking him like guard dogs.

Rivers blanched, her face turning as white as the rock dust coating the mine. "What? I don't know what you're talking about." The officer turned her around and started reciting her rights to her.

"Wait." Haley reached into Rivers' pocket and pulled out her work phone that Rivers had taken from her in the mine. "This is mine."

The officer shrugged like he didn't care.

Jake still had his phone pressed against his ear. He looked at Haley and a ghost of a smile appeared on the corner of his lips. "They have Leech." He let out a long breath. "They just took him into custody."

Rivers struggled against the handcuffs, looking toward the mine as if she still expected it to blow up.

"Leech hesitated." Jake rehearsed the news as he received it. "He had the charges set, but he hesitated."

Haley put a hand over her mouth and choked back a sob of relief. For the briefest second, she almost leaned in to kiss him. But that was an impulse, and one she could control.

Jake ended the call and looked at her. "Cross is implementing a temporary ventilation plan, hanging curtains to direct the airflow so there won't be any explosive accidents."

"Looks like this is wrapping up, thanks to you." One of the police officers stepped forward and shook Jake's hand. He was younger than his military-looking counterpart, but he wore a similar expression of tired worry on his face. "We went over the discrepancies you found in Layla Harper's MSHA reports. You sent them to us just in time. We took Miss Harper into custody this morning, interviewed her, and traced the changes in her reports back to Rivers Grey."

"It doesn't matter," Rivers called out, her face contorting with anger. "I accomplished what I wanted. The mine is still going to be shut down, permanently. Bear was hiding accidents, and I didn't have anything to do with that. With the fines and red tape, and the subsequent investigation, P.C. will never open again." The stern officer directed Rivers toward a police car.

"She had someone working with her," Haley said.

The younger policeman nodded. "We have Liam."

"Someone else. I don't know who it is, but she has another partner."

The officer's solemn expression turned dark, and he rubbed the back of his neck. The black edges of a tattoo peeked out beneath the edge of his collar. "We'd like to ask you a few questions." He glanced down at her arm propped in the sling. "But that can wait until after you go to the hospital and get checked out."

"Sure, but I don't know if I can give you any more information that will help."

The officer tipped his chin to where Rivers sat in the squad car. "With luck, maybe Miss Grey will make a plea deal and give up the name."

Two paramedics walked up as if to tell her it was time to go. She had done all that she could here, the disaster had been averted, and now it was time to take care of herself.

"We have an ambulance waiting for you, ma'am." One of the paramedics pointed to the emergency vehicle. The back doors were open, ready to take her away from all of this.

Jake slipped his hand around hers. "Go ahead. I need to talk to the police officers, and I'll meet you at the hospital later." He gave her a quick embrace then walked over to join the growing crowd of officials near the command center.

Haley felt numb. Mr. Branch stood next to the tent, talking with three ladies. The oldest, a middle-aged woman, dropped her head in her hands, her shoulders heaving with sobs. The other two wrapped their arms around her in comfort. Haley's heart wrenched. It was Bear's family.

"You ready, ma'am?" The paramedic ushered her to the ambulance.

"It's just a broken arm." She cradled it against her. The sling helped, but it still ached. "It's nothing serious." She climbed in and sat on the gurney as the EMT started assessed her.

Suddenly Kim's face appeared in the doorway. "Haley, are you okay?"

Mitch must have called her. "I'm fine. It's just a broken arm."

"I'm glad it's not serious." She turned to the EMT then flipped her perfectly curled hair over one shoulder and pressed her glossy lips into a smile. "Hi, Jim. Thanks for helping Haley; we really appreciate it, but could we have a minute alone?"

"Sure." The man swiveled his seat around and stood up.

It was a little absurd how quickly he wanted to accommodate Kim. He must've been one of her friends. Once they were alone, Kim sat next to her on the gurney. "I'm glad you're okay, but I see this as a wake-up call. I know you like being underground, but P.C. is so dangerous. Why don't you get a job at another mine?"

"I don't want to." It was more than the job she liked, she'd grown to like her coworkers as well, but Kim wouldn't believe that. "I'm staying here."

"Don't be stubborn." Kim frowned. "The mine is closing; you should get your application out there before the other men do. You have a better chance of getting hired if you're ahead of the rush."

There was some probability to the statement, but there was more to it than that. Kim sounded so certain. The corners of her mouth twitched and her eyes brightened, wide and intense. Haley stared at her. "What's going on, Kim?"

A look of innocence washed over her face. "Nothing. I told you, I heard about the mine closing when I was doing research for my brochure. Besides, Liam told you this was going to happen."

"Liam was behind it," Haley cried. "He wanted to cripple the mine!" Kim stared at her, her expression flat. Haley could feel the anger crackling through her. "Why don't you seem surprised?"

Kim shrugged and lowered her voice. "Maybe because Liam came to me a couple of weeks ago and told me what was going on."

Haley gasped. "You mean he told you he and Rivers were trying to shut the mine down?"

Kim's brow wrinkled. "I didn't know the details. He said someone was sabotaging things at the mine, that it was dangerous. He came to me, thinking I could persuade you to get out."

Haley jumped up, balling her good hand into a fist. "Why didn't you tell me? We could've called the cops. We could've done something to stop it."

"I couldn't. Liam made me promise."

Haley gave a sarcastic laugh. "I don't believe that. There's no way you'd promise to keep anything a secret. Not unless he promised you something in return . . ." Her words trailed off. Kim just stood there, her expression unmovable. "What is this?" Haley threw her hand in the air. "Is this one of your business deals?"

Still no response. The air went out of Haley's lungs, and a sickening feeling lodged in her throat. "Rivers said she had a new partner."

Kim rolled her eyes. "I wouldn't describe it like that."

The skin on the back of Haley's neck pricked. "The text Rivers showed me. 'Bring Haley out. I want to talk to her.' Was that you?"

"If you let me explain, it will all make sense."

A jolt shot through her. Kim and Rivers working together? Haley turned away, unable to look at her. Kim had always been a manipulator, but this? It was too much. "You better get out of this mess, Kim, and quick."

"I can't. We have an agreement. And in a minute, you're going to thank me."

Haley's face burned hot. It didn't matter what spin Kim put on this, if she was helping Rivers in any way, it could mean jail time.

"Do you know what you're saying?" Haley started pacing in the narrow area next to the gurney. "You'll be indicted as an accomplice."

Kim stood up. "Don't worry. I'm not tied to it as much as you think. In fact, practically everything was done before I even came into the picture."

Haley shook her head. "But why are you in it at all?"

"Liam showed me some irrefutable statistics. The environmentalists have the government in their pocket, and they're bankrupting the coal industry. The EPA has set emission rates so low that virtually no coal-fired power plant will be able to meet the new standards. They're being regulated to death. Unfortunately, Rivers wanted P.C. shut down sooner than later for personal reasons. And regardless if they find her guilty of falsifying reports, the mine is still going to close. But there is a bright side. We can still do something to promote coal, and in a way, keep P.C. Mine going."

Kim opened her Louis Vuitton knockoff and reached inside. "No one's supposed to see this yet, but considering the circumstances. . ." She hesitated a moment longer and then handed her a glossy folded paper. "It's still in the preliminary stage, but this is the coal mining brochure I've been working on."

Haley looked at the glossy advertisement. It featured a picture of Price Canyon Mine—only it didn't look like the mine she knew with its yard piled with equipment and supplies. This one had a clean driveway going into the mine portal with a bright new sign above the entrance. The lamp-house was off to the side—not the boxy trailer, but a nice building with a wood facade and a grass lawn. The title in bold black lettering said: *Price Canyon Coal Mining Tours.*

It was like someone had lit a fire in Haley's stomach. She felt an explosion of heat burning her from the inside out.

"Mining tours?" She stared at the picture. "But you were working on this *before* I was even hired underground!"

"I was working on the idea and planning on using a totally different location. At the time, I didn't know anything about what Liam and Rivers were doing." She pointed to the glossy paper. "Go on. Read it."

Haley opened it and read aloud. "Price Canyon Mine offers a fun, underground trip into the life of a coal mine. An intact example of a once operating facility, we provide an authentic experience with professionally-guided underground tours conducted by former miners. Dive into history and explore the entire coal operation from mining to shipping. Admission: Adults $10.00, Children 12 and under $8.00. Group rates available for 25 or more."

She lowered the brochure. "You're crazy if you think you're going to turn the mine into a tourist attraction."

Kim waved a hand. "Don't sound so negative about it. It's an incredible idea. Pennsylvania and West Virginia have been capitalizing on this type of business for years." She pulled out her phone and held it in front of Haley, then flipped through several web pages featuring coal mine tours. "Beckley Mine and Museum,

Pioneer Tunnel, Lackawanna Coal Mine Tour—there are nearly a dozen of them. But this will be the first one in Utah."

Kim pointed at her brochure. "Visitors will be fitted with helmets and headlamps before getting into a comfortable mantrip and going on the best hour-long guided tour this state has to offer. And that's below ground. On the surface, we'll have a giant coal miner statue, a museum, hiking trails, and even a playground made from old mining equipment. Not to mention the gift shop and restaurant—well, maybe just a deli, we'll see. We're also bringing in some period coal camp buildings, and we'll host special events for holidays too. Pioneer Day, the Fourth of July, International Days. Come October we'll give haunted mine tours."

Haley shook her head. "I can't see Stump, Wing Nut, and the rest of us handing out coal shaped lollipops and giving strangers a Disneyland ride through Magic Coal Mountain in a *comfortable* mantrip." Kim's mouth dropped open, but Haley continued. "Promoting coal isn't a bad idea, but this . . . this right here—" She crushed the brochure then held the crumpled ball out to Kim. "This is wrong."

Kim wrinkled her nose at her desecrated brochure and refused to take it. Finally, Haley stuffed it in her own pocket.

"Exactly how long has this been going on, Kim? How long have you been planning on using P.C. for your tourist attraction?"

"I did consider using a mine that was already closed down, but it just wasn't feasible. P.C. Mine is perfect. It's small, close to town, and it's cost effective. We won't have to bring equipment in—it's already here. I tried to hint to you about the mine closing down—"

"How long?" Haley's words came out in a low growl.

Kim raised a sharp eyebrow. "I opened negotiations with Mr. Wakefield three months ago. I couldn't tell you; he and the board members wanted a quiet transaction. Then after Liam came to me and told me what was happening in the mine, it made sense why Mr. Wakefield was willing to sell out. With the bad MSHA reports, all the fines, and the critical media, he wanted out from under it."

"Do you know how serious this is, Kim?" Haley motioned out

the ambulance door toward the police cars. "Rivers is going to jail. Did you do anything to help sabotage the mine? Did you fund it, or contribute in any way?"

Kim gave her best outward appearance of being shocked. "Of course not."

Sometimes it was hard to tell when Kim was lying; this wasn't one of them. She was too smug.

"I don't buy it," Haley said. "Rivers referred to you as someone who was calling the shots, like you had some vested interest in what she was doing."

Kim avoided eye contact and sat back on the gurney. "If you're worried about me going to jail, don't be. There is absolutely no evidence connecting me to Rivers."

Haley rounded on her then looked at the defibrillator machine. She wanted to put the paddles on Kim and shock her back to reality. "You don't get it, do you? I just watched someone die! I knelt next to Bear and watched him take his last breath. Do you know what that's like? Do you see those people over there?" She pointed to the women standing with the officers. "That's Bear's family. And all you can think about is turning this place into a tourist attraction!"

"I didn't want anyone to get hurt. Not Bear, but especially not you. How do you think Bear found out about you calling in the hazard complaint?" Haley's breath caught in her chest, but Kim went on, "I was trying to protect you. I knew Bear would be furious if he found out you had made the complaint. And I knew he would try to get you out of the mine. It was for your own safety."

Kim put a hand on Haley's good arm, but she jerked away. "I am sorry, Haley. I tried to ensure everyone's safety. But it all went wrong today. Leech was only supposed to make the roof falls seem worse than they really were. But when Bear stayed behind . . . Leech was just supposed to hurt him, not kill him. But he'll pay for it. He'll go to jail. And I'll make sure we put up a memorial for Bear when we open for business. In fact, we can make one for all of the fallen miners in Utah."

Haley clamped her teeth together so tightly her jaw ached.

"That's your solution? Someone dies, so let's put up a memorial? Everything is just business to you."

Kim's face reddened. "Do you even know how much money this tourist project will bring in? But no, it's more than business. Don Wakefield practically stole the mine from Mitch in the first place. And turnaround is fair play."

Haley turned her back to Kim. "Do you hear yourself? I thought I knew you. I trusted you as a friend."

Kim grabbed Haley's shoulder. "There's not an option here." Her fingers gripped tighter, a clear warning that she didn't want Haley to get in the way of her project. "It's going to happen. MSHA is pulling P.C.'s roof plan today, and they'll be throwing more regulations at them which will keep them closed for months. I'm the one doing the right thing by giving the mine a chance to reincarnate itself."

"You're still a part of a plan that got Bear killed. Are you going to reincarnate him?"

Kim straightened her posture, trying to compose herself. "I'm sorry about Bear's death. I wish I could go back and change it, but it's too late. I'm on a time schedule with my investors, and things needed to move fast or I would've lost my funding. I know you don't like the idea, but the deal is already done. I signed papers with Mr. Wakefield an hour ago. I own the mine."

CHAPTER 40

Haley stepped away from Kim and nearly fell out of the ambulance. She gripped the edge of the door to steady herself. "You already signed papers?"

"I'm the new mine owner." Kim flicked a piece of dust from her blouse. "Well, me and my investors."

"That's why all of this happened *today*?" Haley made a sharp gesture toward the mine, her muscles quivering. "Making the roof fall seem worse than it really was? Did Mr. Wakefield give you a good discount since he was dealing with the mine disaster?"

A small smile peeked out from Kim's lips. "Let's just say it worked out nicely."

Haley had to restrain herself from punching her. The gleam in Kim's eye, the way her manicured brow rose, the way her fingers drummed anxiously on her leg—this was her victory dance. Haley looked around for Jake. He stood a little ways off, talking with an officer. The police already had proof of Rivers' involvement. All they had to do was connect Kim to it.

"I know you're not thrilled with the idea," Kim said. "But I'm sure you can get behind it. I'll offer you an investor's share and guarantee you a job. I'll make sure you earn enough to cover your mother's expenses." Kim looked up, her dark eyes intense and pleading, her thin figure small and unassuming next to Haley in her big mine jacket.

Haley let out a soft groan and rubbed her forehead. She and Kim had never had a great relationship, but it was something. A friendship. Haley's first. And was Haley really ready to sever it?

Kim looked at her beaded watch. "So, are you in? I'm wrapping this deal up as soon as I get back into town. Signed, sealed, and delivered."

Haley understood. By this afternoon, Kim would have every last detail finalized, and she'd get rid of any evidence connecting her and Rivers. If Haley was going to stop her, she had to do it now. She pulled her work phone out, her thumb flying across the keys. She didn't know if this would work, but she had to try. Somewhere Kim had a written contract with Rivers, a plan of some sorts, or something to track their progress—something to prove she was involved. Haley just needed to find it and turn it over to the authorities before it disappeared.

"Who are you texting?" Kim leaned over her, but Haley pulled away.

"I'm stopping you, Kim. What you're doing is wrong, and I'm not going to let you go through with it." She ended her text with *#1SignedSealed&Deivered* and sent it.

Kim just shrugged. "You can't stop what's already been done. And everything I'm connected with on paper is legal." She climbed down from the ambulance, her high heels wobbling in the gravel. "I need to go. I know you're not in the mood to make a decision now, so I'll start you on the process to becoming an investor, and the first job available will be yours."

"Wait." Haley grabbed Kim by the arm. Beyond them, Jake was looking at his incoming message. His head shot around, and he looked hard at Kim then at Haley and nodded. There wasn't much he could do without access to Kim's computer, but hopefully, the password she gave him would at least buy some time.

Kim pulled out of Haley's grip. "I already told you, you can't stop what's happening. She waved a hand toward the mine. Jake had moved away from the officers and was at the command center tent, borrowing a laptop.

Haley controlled her expression. "Have you already transferred the money?"

There was a flash of alarm and worry in Kim's eyes, but she composed herself quickly. "I've made a down payment and the rest is being taken care of shortly. Why do you ask?"

"No reason." Haley typed something else on her phone. "And you bank at Wells Fargo?" Kim pinched her lips together. Haley sent the second text and lowered her phone. "For once, I'm glad that you use the same password for everything."

"No, I don't." Kim's phone beeped. Haley recognized the sound. The three-toned chime signaled important notifications. Kim looked at the message, and her face flamed red. "My bank account?" she gasped.

A small thrill shot through Haley. Jake was fast. His fingers were still flying across the keyboard of the borrowed computer. Haley wanted him to look up at her, but he didn't.

"You did this, didn't you?" Kim glared at her. "You froze my bank account." She pushed some buttons on her phone then gave a huff. "Fix it! Fix it now!"

Haley shrugged. "Let's just build it a memorial."

Kim's phone beeped again. She had scarcely looked at it when another beep sounded. "Haley, whatever's going on, stop it!" Her eyes bulged at the screen. "My credit cards. My PayPal." The phone beeped again, and Kim squeezed it so tight, one of her fake nails popped off. "My Amazon account?"

Haley nearly laughed. That one wasn't necessary, but apparently Jake couldn't resist.

"Stop this! Do you really want to go head to head with me?" Kim shoved her, sending white, blinding pain shooting down her arm. "You might be able to freeze my accounts for a time, but it won't stop anything, and you won't find anything to incriminate me—"

"They've already traced the faked MSHA reports back to Rivers. And they'll trace things back to you too."

"Go ahead." Kim's words were low and sharp. "Talk to the cops. Have them look into it. Have them check Rivers' emails and phone records. They won't find me involved or connected to her in any way."

Haley straightened and tried to appear confident, but she didn't feel it. In her last text, she'd asked Jake to check Kim and Rivers' emails and cell phone records, but if Kim was offering them up for investigation—that was a bad sign. A small twinge of worry crept over her. Kim was a master at getting what she wanted, and by the way Jake's mouth pulled into a tight line, Haley knew he hadn't found anything.

Kim's smiled innocently. "I think we're done here. I need to go talk to my investors."

Kim was just as controlling and abusive as Haley's father. Her punches weren't physical, but they were just as damaging. Her heart sank as Kim walked away. Suddenly she was young again, crouched in the corner of her bedroom, her parents arguing in the kitchen. Then her mom was screaming. Screaming for Dad to stay away. Screaming for someone to help her. Haley could have. If she ran out, maybe her dad would've stopped. But she didn't. She couldn't move. Even her breath was frozen in her chest. Then it was too late. There was a sickening sound of metal meeting bone and then her mom's cries grew silent. The only sound was that of Haley's sobs.

It was days before she came out of her bedroom. The police told her that it had only been minutes, but it seemed like days. Dad's car had pulled out of the driveway, and that's when she finally opened her door and crept out. She saw the hammer first. Laying on the kitchen counter next to the broken drawer her dad had been working on. Then she saw her mom lying on the ground. Her faded house dress clinging to her body and pulled off one shoulder near the neckline.

She didn't remember calling 911, but the officers said that's what she did. She just remembered putting a rag on her mother's head and crying. There was so much blood. It was cowardly of her, but she wished that she hadn't been home. Noah should've been there, but not her.

Haley shook her head. She wasn't like that now. She wouldn't sit behind a closed door and listen to someone scream for help and not do anything. She watched Kim walk away, her steps confident and strong. She needed to stop her, and she needed it now. Kim would dump all her records as soon as she got back to her office.

Jake stood up and met her gaze. He shook his head. Haley understood. He could hack into websites, emails, and any networking files linked to the internet, but unless he had access to Kim's computer, he couldn't get her private files.

Kim was picking her way through the far end of the graveled parking lot. Haley ran to stop her, but Kim halted abruptly on her own, eyeing Mitch who had just walked out of the Compec trailer. "What are you doing here?"

Mitch rubbed the stubble on his chin. "I'm Haley's emergency contact person. And she was in an emergency." He looked past her and saw Haley. "And there you are. How you doing, sweetheart? I'm glad you made it out safe."

Haley stopped short. Kim hadn't come to the mine because Mitch had called her. She had already been there. She had been texting Rivers when they were underground. She might not have used her personal phone to call and text Rivers, but she *did* have a phone. A burner phone.

Haley lunged forward. There was a mixture of surprise and fear in Kim's eyes, and she stumbled backward which only made it easier for Haley to snatch the Louis Vuitton knockoff with her good hand. She turned it upside down, emptying its contents onto the ground. A perfume bottle shattered near her feet. Hand lotion, lipstick, and a powder compact went flying, along with a few feminine products. Kim was going to kill her. Haley flicked her toe through the pile. There wasn't an extra phone like she'd hoped. But there were car keys. She grabbed them, and then cradled her broken arm against her chest as she dashed toward Kim's silver Toyota at the end of the lot.

"Don't you dare!" Kim ran after her, but her high heels in the gravel were no match for Haley's steel-toed boots. She unlocked the door and jumped in long before Kim could catch up to her. A sweet vanilla smell mixed with Armor All enveloped her. The car was meticulously clean. There was nothing in the cubbies, and the only thing in the center console was a small box of Kleenex. Haley popped the glove box and rifled through it. Only a few papers and the owner's manual for the car. It would take too long to do a thorough search. Kim was getting close, hobbling along in her tight skirt and stilettos, her eyes blazing, her face turning purple. Haley popped the trunk and jumped out.

"Stop!" They reached the back of the car at the same time. Kim tried to slam the trunk shut, but Haley already had her arm inside and it caught her on the shoulder. She screamed out in pain, but she had grabbed what she wanted. Kim's computer.

Broken arm or not, she could still overpower Kim. She stepped to the side, knocking her out of the way with a swing of her hips and emerged with a throbbing arm and Kim's laptop in tow.

"Jake!" Several people had turned to watch, but Jake was already running to meet her. Kim chased after her, and Haley passed the computer off like a baton in a relay race.

"You have no right!" Kim yelled.

Jake slipped the laptop out of its case just as Kim grabbed his arm. "Help! Someone help me!" she cried.

Haley looked around to see who had noticed the commotion. Everyone had. The cops were running over to them, along with Mr. Branch, and a couple of foremen. The EMTs were coming too. The military-looking cop had his hand on the butt of his gun. It didn't go unnoticed by Jake, and he set the opened computer on the hood of a truck and held his hands up in a friendly gesture.

"They stole my laptop!" Kim yelled, tugging the wrinkles from her sleeve. "Arrest them."

Two officers moved forward, but Haley stepped in front of them. "No. You need to arrest Kim."

The younger officer with the tattoo on his neck moved to the middle of the commotion. "What's going on, Kim?"

Haley grimaced. Apparently, he was one of the many officials Kim kept in her pocket.

"She attacked me." She pointed to Haley. "And she stole my laptop."

His eyes bounced between Haley and the computer sitting on the hood of the truck. "Why did you take her laptop?"

"Why?" Haley leaned forward into the question. "Because Kim has been working with Rivers and Liam Grey in an attempt to cripple P.C. Mine."

Kim rolled her eyes. "She's been through a lot of trauma, and she suspects everyone."

The cop shook his head in disbelief. "That's a hefty accusation. Do you have proof?"

"I'm sure it's on the computer." Haley pointed at the laptop.

The officer rocked back on his heels. "Sorry, but we can't go picking through her computer without a warrant."

A triumphant smile flashed across Kim's face. It came and went so quickly, Haley was sure no one else had seen it. She had only noticed it because she'd seen the same expression on her father's face whenever she won an argument.

"Are we done here then?" Kim batted her eyes at the officer. "I'm late for a meeting, but if you want to talk to me about any of this, you can stop by my office later and I'd be happy to answer any questions." She put her hand on his arm and gave him a reassuring smile before turning away.

Haley reached out with her good arm and caught Kim by the sleeve.

"Let her go, ma'am." The young policeman tried to pry Haley's hand off of Kim.

She didn't want to be arrested for resisting an officer, but she refused to sit by and do nothing. She would never do that again—ever. She shoved her shoulder into the policeman. "I'm telling you, she's been helping Rivers to close the mine."

The officer's eyes flashed and he grabbed Haley's arm, trying to wrestle her away, but her grip only tightened around Kim's sleeve, tearing the silky fabric. It was as if someone had flipped a switch. Both officers jumped into action. Kim started yelling as Haley was jerked away, the torn sleeve her blouse still in Haley's fingers. Mitch and Jake rushed forward trying to calm the officers, and

Haley cried out as her good arm was forcefully twisted behind her back.

"The computer," she gasped. "There has to be evidence on the computer. She'll delete it as soon as she's gone." She struggled against the man, her shoulder bursting with pain as she lashed out for Kim again. She was yanked back, the officer holding her arm tightly as he pulled his handcuffs from his belt.

Haley froze with a gasp. Would he really arrest her? She didn't want to think about the fact that she might end up like her dad. That she could actually be locked away. And what would her mom do? She would worry that Haley would be in the dark again. The officer looked at her arm in the sling then at his handcuffs.

"It's not me!" she cried. "Check Kim's computer!"

The officer wasn't letting go of her, but Jake was suddenly in front of them. "She's right. You have to check the computer before everything is deleted."

The military-looking officer put a hand on Kim's shoulder as she backed away. "The only way we can do that is if there's probable cause to believe there is incriminating evidence."

Kim's face grew pale. Jake pointed to the computer screen. The window he had managed to open when the commotion started contained a single folder with a padlock icon next to it. "This appears to be the *only* secured file on her computer. Kim would've kept all the communication between her and Rivers in one location, something she could quickly dump if needed. I assume this is it. How's that for probable cause?"

The young officer shook his head, still unwilling to ease up on Haley's arm. "Lots of people keep locked files. That's not incriminating evidence."

Haley turned to the side to ease some of the pressure and staggered toward the computer, pulling the man with her. Kim tried to block her.

"Fiume!" Haley called as she leaned to the side to read the file name. "The file's name is Fiume!"

"So?" Kim spun around and grabbed her computer. Jake typed

something into his phone then quickly held it out for the officers to see. "Fiume" was in the search bar. He hit the image button and the screen filled with image after image of rivers—streams of water flowing through their channels—mountain rivers, valley rivers.

Haley twisted and met the officer's hard gaze. "Fiume is Italian for *river*."

Jake bounced on the balls of his feet, the movement accentuated his wild mad-scientist look. The young officer rubbed his chin like he still wasn't convinced, and Kim was quickly heading toward her car, her computer tucked under her arm.

"The brochure," Haley gasped. Kim hadn't taken her brochure back after Haley had wadded it up. "Let me show you." She twisted. "It's in my pocket." The officer let go of her arm and she quickly pulled out the crumpled brochure. "Kim is buying the mine with the intention of turning it into a tourist attraction." She smoothed the glossy paper out and handed it to the military-looking officer. "She started working with Rivers in order to get a better deal on the sale."

The officer's face hardened. He looked up from the glossy advertisement and locked his gaze on Kim. "All right. I'd say this is probable cause. Stop her."

Kim didn't run. She couldn't have gone far is she had. She spun around and dropped the computer, a lot more forcefully than needed.

Another officer picked it up and opened it. "Screen's cracked. But it looks like it still works. "What's the encryption key to unlock it?"

Kim shot him a deadly look. "You may search my computer, but I don't have to help you. I don't have to give you any passwords until I get a court order from a judge."

"You have to open the file now," Haley said. "What if she deletes or alters it through the cloud from another computer?"

The military-looking officer grunted. "Not much we can do. I'm not a computer expert."

Haley nodded toward Jake. "But he is."

The man raised his brows. "You think you can open it?"

Kim ran forward, trying to grab the computer. "You can't do this.

I'm going to take your badge numbers and file a complaint."

Mitch put a hand on her shoulder. "Don't get anxious, Kim. If you're innocent, there won't be a problem."

Jake started typing and Haley silently prayed his limited hacking skills would work. "It's protected with a steganographic code." Jake frowned. "They're complicated. You have to have the correct font type, letter size, and even customized spacing. She probably copies and pastes the passcode from somewhere."

He started typing again. "Luckily, the computer logs the times when this file is accessed. And if I correspond it with her internet history. . ." He hit a button with a flourish.

Everyone leaned in, examining the page that popped up.

"*No Coal for a Greener America*," Haley read aloud. "That's Liam's blog! He's been working with Rivers to shut down the mine." She looked at Jake and they both eyed the title at the top of the web page.

Jake's face lit up, his tongue peeking out from behind his toothy grin. Haley could feel his excitement as he copied the title and pasted it into the field requiring the access code.

Kim let out a growl-like sound and tried to push her way forward. At one time, she might have had some sway with the cops, but not anymore. The young officer held her back as Jake hit the *enter* button. A list of file folders appeared on the screen.

Everything was there. Documented conversations, plans, progress reports. Goosebumps rose on Haley's arm as Jake opened the folders in various windows.

The tall officer crowded in next to her, his brow raising in surprise as the examined the document Jake had paused on. "This looks like an official contract between you and Rivers." The young officer immediately pulled Kim's hands behind her back and slapped handcuffs on her wrists.

Haley slipped her fingers around Jake's, feeling the pulse of his energy. It rushed through her, wrapping her in his excitement. Without thinking, she leaned in and pressed her lips firmly against his. She felt his surprise and his quick intake of air before she realized what she was doing. Jake relaxed into the kiss, drawing her closer against his chest, but Haley leaned away.

"Sorry." She brushed her hand across her lips. "I . . . um . . . I don't know what happened. I didn't mean to do that." She stumbled over her words.

Jake's mad scientist side had melted away into something else— something more tame but with a yearning that was hard to resist. But she wasn't committing to anything, yet. The kiss was just. . . Haley wasn't sure what it was. Maybe it was an apology. Maybe it was her way of saying that she *did* like him. But maybe she was still broken, and he deserved more.

Jake seemed to be trying to figure it out too. He stared at her, pressing his lips together. Not in a disappointed way, but it seemed as if he were savoring something. She tried to look somewhere else. At his hands, strong and etched with signs of coal work. They reached out and gently pulled her closer.

"Haley," he whispered, "that kind of caught me off guard. Can we try it again?"

"Excuse me, I don't mean to interrupt." Mitch cleared his throat. "But your other emergency contact person is here." He pointed to the parking lot.

Haley spun around. "Noah can't be here." She looked for the old Oldsmobile.

"Not Noah," Mitch said. "But they did notify your next of kin about the incident."

There was only one car moving through the crowded parking lot. It passed by several open spots and made its way up front. At last, it stopped. Both front doors opened. Haley put a hand on her chest to steady her breath. Her mother slowly stood up from the passenger side, clinging to the door as Nurse Cindy and Miss Frackle got out to help her.

"Did they get her out of the dark?" she asked, shielding her eyes from the late afternoon sun. "Where is she? Where's my Haley?"

CHAPTER 41

Haley stood next to the car, talking to her mom and soothing her worries. Mrs. Carter didn't talk much. She nodded in response, asked a few questions, and wrung her hands. Mainly she was content to know that Haley wasn't trapped in the dark anymore.

By the time they said goodbye and Haley went back to the ambulance, Kim had been placed in the back of a police car, and Leech had been brought out of the mine already in handcuffs.

"Are you ready to go to the hospital?" The paramedic asked her as he helped her into the back of the medical unit.

Before she could answer, Jake rapped his knuckles on the open door and stepped in. "Can I have a minute with Haley?"

The paramedic rubbed his hand across his balding head with a sigh. "Why not? Apparently, no one's in a hurry." He walked over to the command tent, leaving them alone.

Jake moved next to Haley. She thought about sitting down, but she didn't. Maybe she was nervous about being alone with him. Nervous of what feelings might surface.

"Your mom didn't stay long." Jake paused and gazed out at the parking lot. "But it seems like she's doing a little better."

Haley nodded. "It's been years since she's called me by my name. Her therapist, Mrs. Frackle, said that seeing the all of the emergency vehicles stirred up some of her old buried memories. It's painful for her, but ultimately it's a good thing."

Jake stepped closer. So close they were almost touching. She knew it would be a mistake to look at him, so she dropped her eyes to where their steel-toed boots met. He cleared his throat. "That kiss you gave me back there—"

She tried to brace her emotions. "I didn't mean to—"

"Yes, you did." He touched her shoulder then slid his fingers up her neck, drawing her gaze up to him. "I know you better than that. There's no way you'd *accidently* kiss someone. What I don't know is what you meant by it."

She thought about stepping away from him, but she didn't. His touch wasn't invasive. It was comfortable. Haley shrugged. "I'm still broken." It wasn't what she intended to say, but it summed everything up. It wasn't fair to have him deal with the issues that came with her.

"Most people are broken in some way or another," he said. "No one's perfect. I know that your trust has been compromised too many times in your life. I know you struggle with things, but I promise you, we'll work at it. Together."

"Together? As in . . ." She let the words trail off and looked up at him.

"As in I'll put my whole heart in this. I love you. I always have."

Jake's fingers intertwined in her hair as he gently pulled her against his chest. He lowered his head. Her heart pounded with expectation, but he stopped when his face was just inches from hers. He was letting her choose whether to close the distance or not. Letting her choose whether or not she wanted to step into a relationship with him.

She let out a long, deep breath. Third kiss. She smiled as she thought of Caleb's philosophy. The point where things got serious. It had always been easier to rely on herself than someone else. But she wanted more, and to get that, she'd have to have to start trusting. And wasn't it simply a choice? If that's what it was, then she would choose hope. She would choose to trust. She would choose Jake. She went up on her toes and pressed her lips firmly against his.

She trembled with nervous worry and almost pulled away. But she didn't. Slowly a surge of warmth pulsed through her. His kiss deepened and she responded to it. She clung to him a moment longer until he stepped away. He looked at her, eyebrows raised as if to ask if she was okay with it.

She was. In fact, it was good. It would be nice to have someone to lean on, and she would need Jake's support as she waded through the emotions of everything that had happened. Dealing with Kim was going to be painful, and that wasn't the only thing that weighed heavy on her heart.

"The mine is still going to shut down," she said quietly.

Jake nodded. "For a while. Until they straighten out this mess."

"I wish it wouldn't. I was just getting used to the idea of packing a normal lunch box to work."

"You still can if you want to. I hear Lila Canyon is hiring."

It was hard to think about going under again after what had happened, but eventually, she would. She could still feel the draw of mining pulling at her. "And what about you?"

Jake shrugged. "I think I'm going to try something else for a while."

She wasn't surprised. He was meant for something different than coal mining, but it was sad to hear him say it out loud.

Jake's brow wrinkled. "Are you okay? I'll still mine if that's what you really want."

She shook her head. "I'd love to work with you, but you should be doing something *you* like. Isn't that part of this relationship thing? You trust, and love, and stand behind each other's decisions? Whatever you choose to do, I'll support you."

His face lit up with his bright smile. "So, this is really happening? We're officially dating?"

Haley leaned forward, pressing her head against his chest. He held her for a long time and didn't move until she tipped her head up to meet his lips. It was a brief kiss, but it pleased her when Jake let out a soft moan. She pulled away to steady her breath. "I still need to take things slow."

He nodded. "I think we're going to get along just fine. As long as I don't give you flowers."

"You can give me tools," she said with a laugh.

"I think I found my soulmate." Jake allowed her the luxury of another smile then slipped his fingers slipped around hers. Haley tightened her grip around the sensation, her stomach twisting with nerves and excitement. Love would be a new adventure—her walk of faith into the unknown. It was like going into the mine that first day. Back then, her headlamp illuminated the path so she could make her way through the darkness. But Jake would be her guide now.

She gave his hand a soft squeeze. "I think I can handle anything. Even flowers . . . once in a while."

* * *

(Eight months later)

Haley walked out of P.C.'s lamp-house, her antique metal lunch box in one hand and her white hard hat in the other. It was dirty, scuffed, and clad in stickers; the most prominent one—a coiled rattlesnake. Mitch stood next to the mantrips. Since Mr. Wakefield offered him the management position at the mine, he'd walked out to the parking lot almost every day, visiting with the crews before they went under.

He waved to her as she approached. "Jake invited me over tonight for some BBQ. You gonna be there?"

She stuck her lunch box in the back of the truck. "I might show up later, but I have a family thing after work."

"Noah? I've noticed he visits more."

"It's not just Noah. Brooke is coming into town."

Mitch's eyes widened. "That'll be interesting, but I'm sure it helps now that your mom's been doing a little better."

"She almost always calls me Haley now."

"I'm glad." He paused, a small smile appearing behind his stubble. "Glad things are working out, and you won't be asking me to visit any more old ladies."

Haley snickered. She could tease him right back if she wanted to. She'd seen him spending time with Caleb's grandma. But it was best not to mention it; she didn't want to jinx anything. There were just some things you didn't talk about. For Haley, it was Kim.

She didn't like to talk about Kim with anyone. Well, except for occasionally with Jake. He had a way of getting her to open up. And slowly she was dealing with what happened. She had talked to Kim once since she'd been arrested. She was apologetic, but it seemed she was more disappointed in being caught, still believing that ultimately she'd been in the right. That was painful. How could shutting all of this down be good? Haley looked around. She loved this place.

Stump walked past and patted her on the shoulder. "You ready to go to work, Baby Bear?"

She was still adjusting to the new nickname. For a while, they had called her Baby Doll, and thankfully that one hadn't stuck, but *Baby Bear*—that was doable. "I'm ready anytime you are."

He held out the key to the mantrip. "You're driving." She stared at him. Crew bosses usually didn't pass along that privilege so easily. Stump nodded his head over his shoulder. "We can wait a few minutes. I thought you might want to talk with our special visitor."

Haley looked past him. Jake was walking toward her, dressed in a gray Oxford shirt with the Clean Coal Solutions logo embroidered over the pocket. The mine hadn't pressed charges against him for hacking into their computer system in exchange for him helping to boost their security. After that, he had started working for Clean Coal Solutions, helping to develop better clean coal technology.

"Good to see you, Einstein." Stump reached out and shook Jake's hand. "How's it coming over at the power plant?"

"Great!" A wide grin spread across his face, his whole body animated with excitement. "We're working on increasing the efficiency of the furnace to capture pollutants during combustion and using lime which will soak up ninety percent of the sulfur."

Mitch waved a hand like he was swatting a fly. "Don't get him started. Next thing you know, he'll be talking your ear off about sulfur dioxide removal machines or how static electricity can be used to capture dust."

Jake's eyes brightened more. "We're doing amazing things. And that's why I'm here—to discuss conveying systems that will prevent dust while transporting and storing the coal."

Moose came over to join them. "It's good to see you. We're taking care of Baby Bear." He clapped Haley on the back, "But we miss you. It was hard to see you leave."

"I really didn't go anywhere." Jake slid his arm around Haley's shoulder. "Once a coal miner, always a coal miner, right? It leaves a permanent mark on your soul."

Haley nodded. She understood. She felt it in her bones and coursing through her blood. She wished she could put a monument to coal miners in every town across America. But no, they would continue their work day after day with little recognition. But she knew what they did. Everyone else might distance themselves from the working class, but not her. She was finally a part of that elite group that silently and invisibly powered the country. There were those people who had walked on the moon, and then there were those who walked miles beneath the earth's surface. It was an experience only other miners understood, and it didn't matter how long she did the work, it would always be a part of her.

Haley pressed her thumb to the corner of her eye like she was trying to wipe away a piece of dust. "Once a coal miner, always a coal miner." She gave Jake a hug then turned to the men. "All right, boys—" She called them boys, but they were her friends, her family. She nodded her head, gesturing toward the mine portal. "Let's get to work."

<<<◇>>>

Dear Reader,
Your time is precious. You do me a great honor by picking up this book. A lot of research, hard work, and many hours went into creating this story. I hope you enjoyed your read. If you liked the book, would you please consider leaving a review on Amazon.com? It helps get the word out.
Thanks again!

ABOUT THE AUTHOR

Jennifer K. Clark has spent twenty-five years in the heart of coal country. Carbon County is a rural community in central Utah where mining runs in the blood of its residents. Jennifer quickly embraced the Carbon way of life and discovered that the topic of coal mining was everywhere—cropping up at family get-togethers, community events, and even in Sunday school analogies. After years of collecting interesting facts and stories from local residents and family members, many ambiguous details of the coal mining world made their way into these pages.

Jennifer loves to hear from her readers. You can contact her through her website: jenniferkclark.com or email her at jennkclark@gmail.com.

ACKNOWLEDGMENTS

First and foremost, I need to offer a huge thanks to all of the coal miners who helped me understand their unique world of mining. Many of them endured countless hours answering my relentless questions. And to those who wished to remain anonymous—your name might not be mentioned, but you have my deepest gratitude for the help you gave me.

Below is a list of some of the people who contributed in making this book what it is.

My husband, Jack Clark, who worked in Skyline Mine's warehouse and freely gave advice and details about the coal industry. Thanks for being patient while I spent longer than normal in the writing process in order to get the details right.

Jerry Clark, my brother-in-law (30 years at various coal mines), and Muggs Clark, my father-in-law (27 years at the coal mines.) Thanks for letting me turn our Sunday dinners into question and answer sessions. Both of you were so enthusiastic to share your knowledge about coal mining with me, and I appreciated it.

Ace, for giving me such a thorough tour around the surface of a working mine, for showing me the buildings, equipment, introducing me to people, and answering so many questions.

Jose Hernandez, for making me a mock-up map of a coal mine, and the hours you spent at our house discussing the mining process. The information you gave was invaluable.

Shirley Haycock (the first woman to work in a Utah coal mine, and who inspired a sit-down strike from the miners the first day she went underground), you gave me Haley's perspective on what it's like to be the only female miner working in a man's domain.

The Mine Safety and Health Association (MSHA) inspector (you know who you are). Thanks for all the discussions we had and for letting me borrow your books, magazines, and newspapers on mining. You gave great advice, and this book is better because of your suggestions.

Josh Patterson, for your perspective on being an orange-hat, and for giving me the details about all the jobs you had to do.

Mike Durrant, for sharing your passion for coal mining. The industry has benefited from your hard work.

My sisters-in-law who added to my information—Lisa Clark, a coal miner's wife, and Jo Varner, who worked on the surface at a mine.

George Anderson, for sharing your experiences on the belt line and accepting my spontaneous phone calls when I needed things answered right away.

My critique group, beta readers, and editor—Maria Hoagland, Michelle Jefferies, Sara Price, Shirley Haycock (mentioned above), Rebecca H. Jamison, Tiffany Farrell Odekirk, Don Kilgrow, and Linda Kilgrow. Thanks for reading, editing, and brainstorming with me.

Becky Hill, who has experienced first-hand being the only woman working underground at West Ridge and then again at Lila Canyon. Thanks for letting me use your namesake in the story, and for being courageous enough to go underground in a man's world.